W9-AQG-076

GERRI HILL
THE LOCKET

BELLA
BOOKS
2018

Copyright © 2018 by Gerri Hill

Bella Books, Inc.
P.O. Box 10543
Tallahassee, FL 32302

All rights reserved. No part of this book may be reproduced or transmitted in any form or by any means, electronic or mechanical, including photocopying, without permission in writing from the publisher.

This is a work of fiction. Names, characters, businesses, places, events and incidents are either the products of the author's imagination or used in a fictitious manner. Any resemblance to actual persons, living or dead, or actual events is purely coincidental. The publisher does not have any control over and does not assume any responsibility for author or third-party websites or their content.

Printed in the United States of America on acid-free paper.

First Bella Books Edition 2018

Editor: Medora MacDougall
Cover Designer: Micheala Lynn

ISBN: 978-1-59493-586-2

PUBLISHER'S NOTE

The scanning, uploading, and distribution of this book via the Internet or via any other means without the permission of the publisher is illegal and punishable by law. Please purchase only authorized electronic editions, and do not participate in or encourage electronic piracy of copyrighted materials. Your support of the author's rights is appreciated.

Other Bella Books by Gerri Hill

Angel Fire
Artist's Dream
At Seventeen
Behind the Pine Curtain
Chasing a Brighter Blue
The Cottage
Coyote Sky
Dawn of Change
Devil's Rock
Gulf Breeze
Hell's Highway
Hunter's Way
In the Name of the Father
Keepers of the Cave
The Killing Room
Love Waits
The Midnight Moon
No Strings
One Summer Night
Paradox Valley
Partners
Pelican's Landing
The Rainbow Cedar
The Roundabout
The Secret Pond
Sawmill Springs
The Scorpion
Sierra City
Snow Falls
Storms
The Target
Weeping Walls

About the Author

Gerri Hill has thirty-three published works, including the 2017 GCLS winner *Paradox Valley*, 2014 GCLS winner *The Midnight Moon*, 2011, 2012 and 2013 winners *Devil's Rock, Hell's Highway* and *Snow Falls*, and the 2009 GCLS winner *Partners*, the last book in the popular Hunter Series, as well as the 2013 Lambda finalist *At Seventeen*.

Gerri lives in south-central Texas, only a few hours from the Gulf Coast, a place that has inspired many of her books. With her partner, Diane, they share their life with two Australian shepherds—Casey and Cooper—and a couple of furry felines.

For more, visit her website at gerrihill.com.

CHAPTER ONE

"Detectives…Jeremiah, Springer, I need to see you."

Harper and Reid exchanged glances. "What did you do now?" he asked with a grin.

She stood and pushed her chair from her desk. "Yeah…it's usually me, but this time it's probably you. He found out you've been dating that hooker."

He held his hand up. "One date! And I didn't know she was a hooker!"

"Yeah, yeah." She shook her head. "Can't believe you slept with her." She tapped the lieutenant's door. "Sir?"

"Come in, Harper." Lieutenant Mize looked past her to Reid and shook his head. "A hooker, Springer? Really?"

Harper laughed as Reid's face turned bright red. "I swear, Lieutenant…I didn't know."

Lieutenant Mize turned his attention to her. "And what's got you so jovial?"

"I'm always jovial."

"Yeah…in what universe?"

She shrugged. No, she wasn't normally jovial, especially with Lieutenant Mize. The man rarely cracked a smile. "Well, you know, I'm trying to chill out."

"So the anger management class has helped, huh? Good. Keep that in mind when I give you your new assignment."

"New assignment? We've got a serial rapist. Springer and I—"

"Springer's got a serial rapist. *You've* got an actress."

She frowned. "An actress?"

He tossed a file on his desk. "Orders from the top, Detective. Danielle Stevens is going to shadow you for a week or so."

Reid's eyes widened. "Danielle Stevens? Oh, my God! She's going to be here? In our squad?"

"Looks like it."

Harper narrowed her eyes. "Who…is Danielle Stevens?"

They both looked at her as if she'd grown a second head. "Come on, Harper," Reid said. "*The Cruise? The Manhattan Dance?*"

"Blond…sea-green eyes," the lieutenant added wistfully, his mouth almost lifting in a smile. "Beautiful. She's like a combination of Jennifer Aniston, Meg Ryan, and Sandra Bullock. Beautiful, smart, sexy, lovable."

"No offense, Lieutenant, but you're showing your age with those comparisons."

She stared at both of them and shook her head. "No. I'm not doing it. Find someone else."

"I'll do it! I'll do it!" Reid said quickly, raising his hand and practically dancing in front of Lieutenant Mize.

"Sit down, both of you," he said. "Detective Jeremiah, you've been selected. You don't have a choice."

"What do you mean I don't have a choice?"

"It means exactly what I said." He motioned to the chair. "Sit down. Apparently they're going to shoot a movie here. We'll get some exposure, some of our officers will get to be extras—whatever the hell that is—and it'll give us a chance for a little community outreach and some positive PR for once."

She leaned forward in her chair. "So you're saying that catching a serial rapist, one who's been terrorizing our citizens for six months now, is taking a backseat to some goddamn Hollywood actress? Yeah…that's good for our community outreach. What idiot decided that?"

He stared at her, that same cool expression on his face that she'd seen for the last year. "Calm down, Detective. Most people would jump at this chance."

"I'm not most people. This is a goddamn waste of my time."

He took his glasses off and tossed them on his desk. "I swear, Harper…every day you remind me more and more of Tori Hunter. It's uncanny, really." He picked up his glasses again. "And that's not really a compliment."

"So you keep saying."

"Hunter? From Homicide?" Reid shook his head. "No, I don't see it. Harper's too nice. About the only thing they have in common is their track record with partners. They say Hunter went through like ten of them or something. Most of them got killed too. Pushed one of them out of a two-story window, I hear."

She glared at him. "Well, you're still alive. For now."

He laughed. "It's only because I'm such a good guy that I put up with your shit, Harper. I do believe since you've been in Assault, I'm like your fifth partner, right?"

"They're all still alive," she said dryly. "I think."

She'd never met Tori Hunter, but this was the third time Lieutenant Mize had mentioned her. The first time was after she'd thrown a suspect out of a window when he spit on her.

"Seven days or so, Harper. Again, it's not a choice."

"Why me?"

"She'll probably be asking herself that question after she meets you."

"What does that mean?"

"That means she selected you from all of the files that were sent over. If it's any consolation, I think Detective O'Connor in Homicide was a close second." He shoved the file closer to her. "That's her. And a briefing of what she hopes to accomplish while shadowing you."

Harper picked up the file and she literally stopped breathing when she saw the photo.

"Wow," she whispered.

"Uh-huh," Reid said as he peered over her shoulder. "Wow is right."

Jesus...no wonder he wanted this assignment. Long, blond hair, parted just off-center, dark eyebrows and...sea-green eyes? No, more deep ocean blue. The lips were turned up in a smile revealing perfect white teeth. The smile was a...a hauntingly beautiful smile, one she didn't want to look away from. The eyes, however, weren't quite smiling. They were guarded, shadowed. As striking as Danielle Stevens was, the somewhat pensive look in her eyes made her even more so, in Harper's opinion. What were those eyes hiding? she wondered. She finally moved the photo out of the way and looked at the one-page directive instead.

"A car chase? She wants a car chase?" She shook her head. "And a murder scene?" She closed the file and tossed it back down. "She does know that we're not Homicide, right? Maybe you should give Detective O'Connor a call."

CHAPTER TWO

"Why are you driving all the way to Dallas? That's crazy. What if there's a storm or something?"

Danielle impatiently closed the trunk of the car she'd rented. February in Dallas was practically spring, she'd been told. She turned to Shelly, her assistant. The fact that she *wanted* to drive didn't seem to be a good enough answer. "We've gone over this twice already."

"So you hate airports."

She sighed. "I told you, I don't like people staring at me." And demanding autographs and pictures, she added silently.

"Dani, you're an actress. You're hot. You're *it* right now. Take advantage of it while it lasts. Once you hit thirty, it's all downhill from there. How many times have you heard that?"

So in less than two years she should be home free, she thought wryly. She stared at the modest house she was renting. "You'll get the locks changed while I'm gone?"

"Yes, I told you I would. And I'll look for something else for you."

"Something small, quiet. Gated community would be good."

"I know, I know." Shelly shook her head. "But why rent? Why don't you just buy something? You're on the verge of superstar status, Dani. I don't know why you refuse to act like it."

Danielle blew out her breath. Superstar status? No, she wouldn't go that far. And it would do no good to tell Shelly that she didn't want to *be* a superstar. That would be blasphemy.

The truth was, she didn't want to be an actress at all. She wanted to be anything *but* an actress. Yet here she was, about to head to Dallas to prepare for a new role…and her fifth movie. She hadn't told Shelly. She hadn't told anyone—not even her agent—but it would be her fifth and *final* movie. She simply couldn't continue to live like this.

She'd had no aspirations of stardom. No aspirations of living a public life. She had always been a very private person, even when she was a child. She always guarded her feelings, her emotions, her thoughts. Private. Yet there was nothing private about her life now. In fact, she had no life. The friends she'd had before all of this were gone for the most part. She rarely saw or even spoke to her parents. Even with her sister, she remained distant. Because the world she lived in now…it wasn't real. She wasn't real.

No. She was this caricature created by the movies, by the parts she played. She wasn't Rachel from *The Cruise*. She wasn't Brianna from *Manhattan Dance*. She wasn't Clair from *Shores of St. Clair*. She wasn't even Danielle Stevens.

"Are you okay? Has this stalker thing really gotten to you that much?"

Dani gave her a half smile. "I thought you didn't believe me."

"The police don't believe you. I do. I've seen the dolls."

"Yes, the stalker thing has gotten to me," she admitted. Which was one reason she was heading out early for Dallas. She would take three days to drive there. Three days to clear her head. Then she would have a week or so with Detective Jeremiah—she absolutely loved that name—and hopefully her stalker will have moved on to someone else by the time she got back.

"They say you haven't really made it big until you have a stalker."

"Well, according to the police, I don't have one."

Yet, she did. At first, she thought she was imagining things— or losing her mind. A picture was moved. Books out of order. Dishes rearranged. But she couldn't explain fresh flowers waiting for her on the dining room table. Or the box of chocolates that were sitting by her coffeepot one morning. Or the love letters that started appearing. The police thought she was a diva wanting attention. There was no evidence of a break-in. No fingerprints. Nothing taken. She'd had the locks changed three times. She had a security camera installed. A security camera that mysteriously stopped working at the most inopportune times...like when a dozen roses were left in her kitchen during the night. Black roses this time. Or when the doll was left just inside her front door...the doll whose hair had been chopped off and its belly ripped open, revealing benign cotton stuffing inside, stuffing that had been spray painted red. The police took notice after that, but she suspected the detective assigned to the case thought she might be doing it all herself, like stopping the camera long enough to plant the flowers...the doll.

She got a gun after that incident. That didn't help her fall asleep though. Especially not after reading the latest love letter that was left for her. She couldn't tell who he was in love with or who he was mad at. At first, she thought it must have been Brianna. Brianna had been fun and flirty...and sexy. But after reading the last letter, she thought maybe it was Clair. Clair had been engaged. Clair met someone new...her fiancé's best friend. Clair fell in love...and broke a heart in the process.

Her stalker had a broken heart, he said. Her stalker, while saying he loved her, was mad at her. Her stalker thought she needed to be punished.

She thought she needed to get away. And fast.

CHAPTER THREE

"I can't believe you've never heard of Danielle Stevens. She's like the hottest thing out there right now."

"I don't go to movies," she said as she dodged two officers bringing in a guy in cuffs.

"Standing in a grocery store checkout, surely you've seen her picture on magazines," Reid said as he struggled to catch up with her.

"Look, I get it. She's a big star. All the guys love her, blah blah blah." She shrugged. "Means nothing to me. My only concern is I've got to babysit her while freakin' Hernandez works our case with you."

"It's not like it's going anywhere, Harper. The last three victims can't even agree if he's black or white."

She stopped and ran a hand through her hair. "You'll keep me in the loop, right?"

"I will. We should get the lab results back this afternoon." He looked at his watch. "So when's she meeting you?"

She smiled at him as she started walking again. "Come on, Reid. Mize already laid down the rules. No harassing her, remember."

"Yeah…but you're going to introduce me, right? I mean, Danielle Stevens. I get a chubby just thinking about her walking into the squad room." He nudged her. "Don't you?" he teased.

"Yeah, right. She is *so* my type, isn't she?" she asked sarcastically.

"Sadly, you don't have a type, Harper."

An image of Jan flashed before her eyes. Her light brown hair a shaggy mess, as usual, her mouth lifted at the corners in a smile, her dark eyes twinkling as they looked into hers. Yeah… she had a type. Once.

"And I don't know why," Reid continued. "You're cute. You're too cute, really. You know…for a tomboy and all."

"Shut up, Reid."

"Hey, that was a compliment. Your attitude could use a little adjustment though, that's all I'm saying."

She stopped and stared at him. "What's wrong with my attitude?"

"Well, you know. You're a little…abrupt sometimes. You're all business. You could stand to lighten up some and smile more. I mean, you've got a really pretty smile. You should use it."

"What's to smile about in our line of work?"

"That's your problem. You never get away. You work 24/7. I keep telling you, you need to get a personal life. You need to get laid."

"Like you? And the hooker?"

He laughed. "Not going to let that one go, are you?"

"No way." She stopped again. "Why do you think Mize dislikes me?"

"He already told you that he wasn't the one who gave you this assignment."

"It's not just that. He's been my boss for nearly a year and he still keeps me at a distance. He doesn't do that with you."

Reid looked around them, then pulled her off to the side. "You want to know what I heard? His wife left him…for a woman. A cop."

"Great. And he takes it out on the only lesbian in his squad."
She shook her head. "So who's this Tori Hunter that he keeps
mentioning?"

"Bad ass," he said with a grin. "In her younger days, anyway.
She's mellowed, they tell me. She left Homicide and went to the
FBI for a few years, but she's back. And man, you should see her
wife." He whistled. "Now *that* would be your type. Samantha
Kennedy…she's over at CIU."

"How do you know all this?"

"I worked Homicide before I came here. Jesus, don't you
listen to anything I say?"

"Yeah, that's right. You tried to impress me with all of your
skills." She smiled at him and patted his cheek. "And I believed
you. Right up until the time we came across the man whose wife
cut off his penis." She laughed. "Your second week on the job, if
I recall. First partner I ever had who—"

"—threw up, yeah, yeah," he said. He gave an exaggerated
shudder. "*God*…that was awful. I had nightmares after that."

"Hell, *I* had nightmares."

"You…you think they salvaged that thing? It was pretty
mangled."

"I try not to think about it."

"You probably don't want to tell that story to Danielle."

"A whole damn week," she groaned. "What the hell are we
going to talk about for seven days?"

"I'm still trying to figure out why she picked you in the first
place."

"Well, obviously, she wanted the best."

He laughed. "Yeah, now there's that cocky attitude that I
love so much."

CHAPTER FOUR

Dani took a deep breath before opening the door. She was told she wouldn't be flooded with requests for autographs and pictures. She was told it would be very professional. She was also told that Detective Jeremiah wasn't thrilled with the assignment and that she shouldn't take it personally if the detective was short or rude to her. In fact, they'd offered to assign her to someone else if, after they met, she wasn't happy with her choice. They were being extremely accommodating. The fact that Detective Jeremiah didn't want her to shadow her made her more confident that she'd made the right choice.

She took a moment to look at her attire. A black T-shirt. Her favorite pair of jeans. A black leather belt. Dark gray Saucony running shoes. A black jacket. And a Dallas Cowboys cap that she'd picked up just that morning. It wasn't enough to hide who she was, but with her hair pulled back in a ponytail, she hoped she looked less like a celebrity and more like an everyday person.

She finally pushed open the door and walked inside the squad room. Activity and conversation ceased immediately as all eyes turned her way. She put on her famous façade, she smiled brightly—a smile that no one but her would know was forced—and faced them all. As promised though, no one rushed forward.

"Hello, everyone," she said cheerfully. "Lieutenant Mize? I'm supposed to meet with him."

They all seemed to look at each other, no one speaking. She raised both eyebrows questioningly.

"Down...down there," someone finally said, pointing. "Second door."

"Thank you." She headed in that direction, then turned back around. She gave another smile. "Relax, everyone."

Nervous laughter followed and she mentally rolled her eyes. *Men.*

Lieutenant Mize's door was ajar, and she knocked twice on the glass before pushing it open. Two men turned to look at her. One older, sixtyish she would guess, the other younger, a handsome man with sandy blond hair, perhaps in his early- to mid-thirties. They both stared openly, neither speaking. She turned to a woman who was seated. Dark, thick hair, parted on the side and swept across her forehead—Detective Jeremiah. The scowl on her face was only slightly less than the one in her photo. The eyes, however, were the same...the dark brown eyes that had drawn her in the first place.

"Judging by the idiotic looks on their faces, I'm assuming you're Danielle Stevens."

Dani nodded. "Yes. And you're Detective Jeremiah." She held a hand out. "Pleased to meet you."

"Yeah." The woman hesitated before standing and shaking her hand. She was taller in person than she'd appeared in the photo.

"Yes, I heard you weren't thrilled when you accepted this assignment."

"Yeah...that's not exactly how it went down. You know, accepting it and all."

Dani nodded. "I know. Your people told my people."

"Oh? We have people?"

Dani smiled, so wishing she *didn't* have people. "We do. And I'm sorry if this is an inconvenience."

"An inconvenience? Yeah, I'm sure for my five rape victims, it's an inconvenience that I'm being pulled off the case...you know, to babysit you for seven damn days."

Dani was surprised by the hostility in her voice, and it must have pulled Lieutenant Mize from his trance. He came around his desk and held his hand out.

"Pleasure to meet you, Ms. Stevens. I'm Lieutenant Mize. This is Detective Springer," he said, motioning to the other man, who still hadn't found his voice. "And I assure you, Detective Jeremiah," he said, casting a glare in her direction, "meant nothing by that. We have her workload covered while you're here."

Dani shook his hand firmly. "That's good to know, thank you." She turned to Detective Springer and held out her hand to him. "Detective, nice to meet you."

He shook her hand, holding it a second or three too long. "I must be in a dream," he muttered as if to himself. "Danielle Stevens. Oh, wow. You're...you're—"

"Take a deep breath, Reid," Detective Jeremiah said. "It's okay, buddy."

The man blushed and took a step back. "I'm sorry. It's just..."

"I understand." She turned her attention back to Detective Jeremiah. "So? How does this work? Do we hang out here and wait for a call or do we hit the streets?"

"Oh, yeah. You wanted a car chase and a murder scene," she said dryly.

"Well, that's what they told me to request. I'm really more interested in getting a feel for how you react in different situations, things like that."

"*Her* reaction? I don't think you should model your character after Harper here," Detective Springer said with a laugh. "She's like...so not you."

"Shut up, Reid. You're acting like an idiot." Detective Jeremiah headed for the door. "Come on, Ms. Stevens. Let's get out of here. Maybe we'll get lucky and stumble upon an assault or something."

Dani hurried after her, then remembered her manners. She turned back, giving both men a smile. "Nice to meet you. Thank you for lending her to me."

"Don't thank me yet," Lieutenant Mize said. "You may be begging for someone else by the end of the day."

"I'm fairly certain I can handle her."

"You coming or what?"

Dani caught up with her before she reached the outer door. "Sorry, Detective."

Harper Jeremiah held the door open for her. "In case you couldn't tell, I am the envy of every man in here."

"Yes. And you're probably the only one in here who would have said no to this assignment, if given the choice."

"You're right about that." She paused. "Is that why you picked me?"

"Being female was the main criteria, obviously. But no, I picked you because of your eyes," she said honestly.

"My eyes?"

"The profile picture they sent me," she explained. "In that photo, you looked like you wanted to be anywhere other than sitting there for a picture. Your eyes...it was like you had better things—more important things—that you should be doing." Plus, she was really, really cute, she added silently.

Detective Jeremiah gave her a smirk. "Yeah. Like now, for instance."

"Ah. Your rape case. Five victims?" she asked as she followed her outside the building. "Same guy?"

"That's the assumption. Same MO. Wears a mask, gloves. No evidence left behind. Not even a pubic hair." She pointed to a drab green Ford Taurus. "This one."

"So, are you and Detective Springer partners normally?"

"Yeah. He's not usually such an idiot."

"I've seen worse."

"You mean when people meet you?"

"Men...yes."

"I imagine so." She pulled out onto the street, merging with traffic. "So, Ms. Stevens, you want to pick my brain or you just want to drive around or what?"

"How about let's not use Ms. Stevens? Danielle—or better yet, call me Dani. I'm kinda tired of being Danielle Stevens. I wouldn't mind leaving her behind for a week."

"Okay. You can call me Harper."

"Is that your real name? Harper Jeremiah?"

"Why wouldn't it be?"

"I was just curious. I love your last name. And Harper? After Harper Lee?"

She nodded. "My grandmother was so taken by the book that she named my mother Harper Lee Monroe. Everyone calls her Lee though. Technically, I guess I was named after my mother and not the author." Harper glanced at her. "My grandmother wanted to name me Scout."

Dani laughed. "That would have been precious." She tilted her head. "I was told you were hard to get along with. In fact, your lieutenant said that I might be begging for a change after today."

"Yeah. And?"

She shrugged. "I don't see it."

Harper looked at her quickly. "Well, you just met me. I guess I need to try harder, huh?"

A car pulled up so close to them that Dani could have reached out and touched it had her window been down. She turned, looking at the driver. She gasped when all she saw was a clown face...an evil, creepy clown face that stared back at her. She screamed as something was thrown at her window, splashing it with a red, gooey substance, then the car sped off, turning down a side street and disappearing into traffic.

"What the hell was that?" Harper demanded as she pulled over to the curb and stopped.

Dani was shaking when she turned to look at her. "I...I guess I should have told you. I kinda have a...well...a stalker. That might have been him."

CHAPTER FIVE

Harper stood with her hands on her hips, staring at the mess on the side of her unmarked police car. She then turned to Danielle Stevens who was standing beside her, staring at the red goo as well.

"A stalker?"

Dani nodded without looking at her.

"Are you kidding me?"

Dani turned to her then. "I wish I was."

Harper ran a hand through her hair. "Jesus," she muttered. She stared at her with a shake of her head. "What kind of a stalker?"

"What kind? The creepy kind." Dani held her hands up. "What other kind is there?"

A horn honked three times. "Hey, beautiful…you look just like Danielle Stevens!"

"Jesus Christ. Get back in the car," Harper said quickly.

She slammed the door, trying to decide what to do. She tapped the steering wheel with her thumbs. A stalker. A goddamn stalker. She turned to Danielle Stevens.

"So…who has a stalker?"

"What?"

"I mean…who…really…has a stalker?"

Dani stared at her. "You don't know who I am, do you?"

Harper shrugged. "You're an actress. And according to Reid, the hottest thing out there." She wasn't sure what reaction she was expecting, but a laugh wasn't it.

"Oh, my God. You really don't know, do you?"

"Okay, look. In my defense, I don't do movies. Never have. So…no."

Dani leaned her head back. "Do you have any idea how this makes me feel?"

Oh, great. Now I've insulted the actress. She sighed. "Look, I'm sorry. You're a big star, I guess. That's what they tell me. But—"

Another laugh. "No, no. I'm saying, this is so refreshing. You don't know who I am. You don't *care* who I am." Dani met her eyes and Harper was taken aback by their blueness. "Somehow, I knew that, I think. When I picked you…I think I knew that."

Harper wasn't quite sure how to respond to that, so she said nothing. She started the engine and pulled out onto the street, trying to decide what to do. Should she head back to the station and report the incident? Should she brush it off and ignore it?

"You don't believe me, do you? About the stalker."

Harper glanced at her. "Forgive me if I'm not experienced in stalker protocol for celebrities."

"They didn't believe me either."

"Who?"

"The police. I think they thought I was making it up… looking for attention or something. Publicity."

"Okay, so you've reported it?"

"Of course I have. The police have been to my house several times."

Harper turned to the right, going down a side street and she pulled into the first parking spot she found. She cut the engine and turned in her seat to face Danielle Stevens.

"Okay…let's start over. You have a stalker."

Dani nodded. "Yes." She took off her seat belt, turning to face her too. "It started months ago. Five or six, maybe."

"And you think this guy...in a clown face...was the one?"

"Yes. What else would it be?"

Harper rubbed her eyes. "And the police there said what?"

"Look...I know it sounds crazy. I know that. The police that came...yeah, they said I was crazy. But I'm not." She reached out and grabbed Harper's arm. "At first, it was little things. Pictures moved around. Dishes in different places. Just enough stuff to make me think I'm losing my mind." Her fingers tightened on her arm. "Then...during the night, while I'm sleeping...stuff started appearing. Flowers. Chocolates. Love letters." Her hand slipped away and she wrapped it around herself. "Then suddenly the tone changed. Black roses. Dolls. Dolls that had been...well, violated."

"Okay...and the police did what?"

"Nothing. Like I said, they thought I was making it up or something. For publicity. There was no evidence of a break-in. No evidence of anyone being inside my house."

"That makes no sense."

"I know. I had the locks changed three times. I installed a security camera. Nothing helped. He still got in. The security camera conveniently malfunctions at the time he's there."

"So you're saying some guy came into your house at night, while you were sleeping?"

"Yes. He comes during the day while I'm gone and he comes at night, while I'm sleeping."

"And the police didn't believe you?"

"After the first doll...the detective who was assigned the case, he was sympathetic—I was practically hysterical—but I'm not sure he believed me and he said there was nothing he could do. Without the security camera, without any evidence of forced entry...well, there wasn't anything. They increased patrols there, that was all. He suggested I hire a bodyguard or a security detail to park at the house."

"And that didn't work either?"

Dani shook her head. "I didn't do it. I can't live like that. I *won't* live like that."

"Okay. So? Then what?"

"I came here. I hoped maybe my being away would make him stop."

She sighed. "I don't think stalkers just stop, Dani. My experiences with something like this are ex-boyfriends harassing the old girlfriend or the new boyfriend. I've seen far too many of them end badly."

"I'm sorry. It didn't occur to me that he would follow me here."

Harper frowned. "How did he even know you would be here? Has it been publicized?"

Dani shook her head. "No, not at all. Not unless your department put out a statement or something, which we asked them not to."

"But you've got people? You know, your people talked to my people."

Dani nodded. "Yes, of course there are some who knew of my plans. But I guard my privacy. They know that. They would never advertise it without my consent."

Harper started the car again and pulled out into traffic. "Well, if the clown guy is really your stalker, he knew you were here somehow. Not only that, he apparently followed us from the station."

"Where are we going?"

"I need to let Lieutenant Mize know. I'm responsible for your safety."

"I don't think he wants to hurt me, really. I mean, he's had ample opportunities already. He wants me scared, I think. He wants me punished."

Harper looked at her questioningly.

"The letters," Dani explained. "Each one gets a little more… well, detailed."

"Do you have them?"

Dani shook her head. "No. I mean, yes, I have them, but not with me."

"You've shown them to the police?"

"Not the last few. I really didn't see the point since the detective there thought I was making it all up anyway."

"Okay. Give me an example of the letters. What do they say?"

"The early ones were just love letters...infatuation. But now, he's mad at me. He's in love with me, but he's mad at me. I deserve to be punished. That sort of thing."

"What do you take that to mean?"

"I don't know. The only thing that comes to mind would be my character Clair in *Shores of St. Clair.*"

Harper raised her eyebrows.

"Oh, yeah. You haven't seen it." Dani smiled. "I find that fascinating, by the way."

"That I don't do movies or that I don't know who you are?"

"Both. Anyway, Clair was engaged to be married...she meets the best friend, they fall in love, Derik's heart gets broken—he was the fiancé—and the wedding at the end was for Clair and Brian...not Derik."

"And the clown-faced guy equates himself to Derik?"

"That's just my guess," Dani said. "I don't know what else it could be."

"Well, I don't know how much shadowing you're going to be doing if I've got to keep an eye out for a damn clown stalking you."

CHAPTER SIX

"A clown? A clown threw red goo on your car?"

Harper nodded. "Yeah."

Lieutenant Mize looked over at her. "A stalker?"

Dani nodded. "Yes. Like I told Harper—Detective Jeremiah—I had no idea he would follow me here. I don't see how he could possibly even know that I was here in the first place."

He tapped his fingers together a few times, then folded his hands, resting his elbows on the desk. "I'll need to run this by the upper brass, but our main concern here, Ms. Stevens, is your safety. Having you riding along with Harper makes you a little vulnerable, I think. We may need to rethink this operation."

"Vulnerable? Quite the opposite, Lieutenant Mize. What could be safer than me riding with a police detective?"

"From Harper's account of the incident, if this guy had had a gun, you'd be dead. He was that close to you."

"As I told Harper earlier, I don't think he wants me dead."

"Stalkers stalk. It's a mental thing at first. But eventually that's not enough. They want physical contact as well. If your guy followed you here, if he got that close to you where he could actually touch you if he wanted…then I think he's at that point."

"The guy was in my house while I was sleeping. If he wanted to physically touch me, he could have."

"Maybe he wasn't at that point yet."

"So what do you suggest? I go back home and deal with it there?"

Lieutenant Mize looked at Harper as if for confirmation. Dani was surprised that he appeared to be leaving it up to Harper to decide.

"The police there, they don't really have a handle on it, Lieutenant. Maybe they see too many cases of celebrity stalking, but they don't appear to be taking this one too seriously."

"And you think we should?"

"I had already resigned myself to having her ride with me for a week anyway. Might as well stick to the plan. Maybe we can catch the bastard."

"I'm not sure we want to risk her safety, Harper. Can you imagine the black eye the department would take if something happened to her?"

Harper looked at her. "I think that would be up to Ms. Stevens to accept the risk, not us."

Dani nodded quickly. "And I do." She had known Harper Jeremiah all of a few hours but she knew without a doubt that she could trust her. Going back home, knowing this guy was following her, was not an option. Her only protection there would be to do as the police had suggested—get a bodyguard around the clock. That wasn't something she was willing to do. Not yet anyway.

Lieutenant Mize watched her for a few seconds, then turned his gaze to Harper. "Okay. I'll run it by the captain, but it may need to go higher. I am surprised, though, that you're willing to do this…considering."

Dani wasn't sure what he meant by that. Considering what? But Harper only gave him a slight shrug and said nothing.

CHAPTER SEVEN

"Thank you. I know you could have suggested we cancel the whole deal and your lieutenant would have gone along with you."

Harper nodded. Yeah, that's probably what she should have done. Send Danielle Stevens back to where she came from. It was the look in her eyes, the fear—panic—she saw there that made her hesitate. She pointed to a chair beside her desk, then pulled out her own. Reid was out with Hernandez, chasing a lead on their case. And she was here, willingly babysitting a Hollywood actress with a stalker, of all things.

She looked over at Danielle Stevens, an attractive young woman, a celebrity, a star...a woman who had told her to call her "Dani." She drew her brows together.

"Why are you tired of being Danielle Stevens?"

Dani raised her eyebrows. "Excuse me?"

"Earlier in the car, you said I should call you Dani, that you were tired of being Danielle Stevens."

"Oh." Dani glanced around them, and Harper did the same, finding a few pairs of curious eyes on them.

Harper lowered her voice. "Not something you want to share out here in the open?"

"No."

Harper nodded. "Well, my guess is that the captain will allow your presence here to continue as we'd planned although he may have you sign off on something, just to cover our ass."

"I signed a consent form already."

"Yeah, they'll probably tweak it a bit to add your clown friend and all."

"What did Lieutenant Mize mean when he said he was surprised you'd agree to stick with the plan…considering?"

Harper smiled quickly, then it left her face. "Well, I wasn't exactly thrilled with the assignment, as you already know. In fact, I refused to do it."

"But?"

"But I was told I didn't have a choice. So now, I had a choice. I could have said that it was in your best interest and our best interest that you leave here and take your stalker back with you."

Dani shook her head. "But it's not in my best interest."

"No, it's probably not. Besides, it might be kinda fun to try to catch a stalker."

"I'm with a police detective. Do you think he'd be so bold as to try something again?"

"I think stalkers live for the chase. I don't think they consider the consequences, really."

"Couldn't that be said of all criminals? They surely *know* the consequences of their actions, they just don't consider them."

"Yes, a murderer, a thief, sure, they know the consequences. They do it anyway because they don't think they'll get caught. A stalker, in their mind, they don't think they're doing anything wrong. My experience is mostly with jilted lovers. They think they are still a part of this other person's life, so they feel like they belong there. In your case, whatever this guy is thinking—whether he's in love with you or what—in his mind, what he's doing is perfectly acceptable." She paused. "He's not somebody you know, right? Old boyfriend or something?"

Dani held her gaze for a moment. "No. No, I don't know him, and no, there is no old boyfriend."

Harper nodded. "Do you live alone? Or…"

"I live alone, yes." She smiled. "Are you fishing for gossip you can sell to a trashy magazine?"

"I thought they made up all that crap anyway."

"They do. They've had me dating actors that I've never even met before. Then we mysteriously break up and I'm linked to someone else. It's crazy. I'm waiting for the one that says I'm pregnant or dying from some mysterious disease."

"Must be hard not having a private life."

"You have no idea."

Harper shrugged. "Price you pay, I guess, for fame and fortune."

"Well, sometimes things just fall in your lap, whether you wanted them or not."

Harper wasn't sure what she meant by that statement, but she didn't get a chance to ask. Lieutenant Mize motioned them back into his office. Judging by the look on his face, Danielle Stevens was being given a reprieve on her dismissal, as Harper had expected. She wasn't sure how she felt about it, really. She had been so adamantly opposed to this assignment at first, she was shocked that she didn't jump at the chance to get out of it. But she'd already gone into protection mode. She'd only caught a glimpse of the clown face, but she could still hear the frightened gasp that Dani had uttered, the scream when he'd thrown the red goo at them. She was a cop and Dani was a woman—not a celebrity—who needed her help. It was as simple as that. The assignment to have an actress shadow her as she prepared for a movie had morphed into a protection detail in a matter of minutes.

CHAPTER EIGHT

"You sure you don't mind?" Dani asked. "I know it's been a long day."

"I don't mind."

"Thank you. I really appreciate it."

The thought of going up to her hotel room, alone, was too intimidating to even consider doing. She had already resigned herself to begging if Harper had said no. But she hadn't. Harper would go up with her, make sure everything was in order, then wait until the door was locked before leaving. Harper would then pick her up in the morning so she wouldn't have to make the drive herself. They'd left her rental car at the station.

"What about dinner? Will you feel safe ordering room service?"

"I hadn't even thought about dinner. I suppose room service will be fine." She stared at her. "Don't you?"

"I imagine so."

Her shoulders sagged. "Maybe I shouldn't have come. Maybe I should have done what the police suggested—hire a bodyguard and a security detail."

"Yeah, that might keep him at a safer distance. Might even be enough to make him move on to someone else."

"You don't really believe that, do you?"

"No. If he's fixated on you, obsessed with you…then no, I don't believe he'll just quit, bodyguard or not."

"I hate living like this—in fear."

"How did you manage? I mean, knowing that he could get into your house at will. How did you sleep?"

"I got a gun. I don't know if that made me feel safer or not. Half the time I was afraid I'd roll over and shoot myself."

Harper glanced at her as she pulled into the hotel parking lot. "You slept with it?"

"Yes. Although slept is relative. I'm not sure I've had a good night's sleep in months."

Her room was on the fourteenth floor and they rode up alone in the elevator. She felt Harper's eyes on her and she looked at her questioningly.

"Nice cap. Are you a fan?"

Dani smiled and touched the bill of the Dallas Cowboys cap. "Not really, no."

Harper nodded. "I'll bring you a police department one tomorrow. You'll blend in a little better riding with me."

Dani took her cap off now and removed the band that was holding her ponytail in place. She straightened her hair out with her fingers, longing for the day she could cut it again. Longing for the day when she could get her life back. Longing for the day when she could go back to being just Dani Strauss and not have to live the life of Danielle Stevens.

The elevator came to a stop and she followed Harper out.

"This way," she said, motioning to their left when Harper hesitated.

Harper took her keycard from her and paused to listen at the door, tilting her head slightly before inserting it. The familiar click sounded and the green light appeared. Harper pushed the door open slowly, and Dani peered over her shoulder into the shadowy room. She followed Harper inside, her gaze drawn to the bed. She gasped when she saw the doll. Harper put a steadying hand on her arm.

"Stay here."

The doll was propped up against the pillows, the soulless eyes staring out into nothingness. It appeared to be larger than the ones he'd left before, although this one, instead of having the hair cut off, was topped with a red wig. She watched as Harper picked up the note that was beside the doll. Harper read it silently first, then looked at her.

You broke my heart when I saw you in the red wig. You lied. You'll be punished.

Jesus. She closed her eyes. He *saw* her? How could she explain this?

"Dani? Does that mean anything to you?"

She stared at Harper for a moment, trying to decide what to do. She finally shook her head. "No," she said, hoping Harper believed her. She looked around; looking for anything else that was disturbed. "How did he get in?"

"I don't know."

She tucked strands of hair behind both ears. "He had to have been following me. When I got into town, I came straight here. He had to have followed me. But how did he know my room number?" She walked closer to Harper. "I...I can't stay here tonight. I need a new hotel. I need—"

"No. You're my responsibility. Pack your things, but don't touch anything else. Let me call Lieutenant Mize."

"What are you going to do?"

"Get somebody up here to dust for prints, collect the doll for evidence. The doll and the note."

She swallowed down her panic. "The...the note too?"

Harper raised an eyebrow. "What is it you're not telling me?"

"Nothing," she said quickly. Too quickly.

"Uh-huh." Their gazes held and Dani didn't dare look away. Harper finally conceded, giving her a quick nod. "Okay, then. Pack your things. I'm going down to see if I can pull their security footage."

"Wait. *Now?* You're going to leave me here alone?"

"Lock the door behind me. Don't let anyone in. I'll be right back."

"Harper, no. I'm…I'm scared."

Harper walked closer to her. "I won't let anything happen to you. I promise. The door locks from the inside. Don't let anyone in but me."

Dani let out a shaky breath. "Okay."

Before leaving, Harper looked under the bed, then opened up the wardrobe. Then she stepped into the bathroom. "All clear." She came back out. "Pack your stuff. I'll be back as soon as I can."

Dani nodded, then followed Harper to the door, locking it behind her. She turned and leaned against it, her eyes closed. How in the world was she going to tell Harper about the wig… about the bar? God, she *knew* she shouldn't have gone that night. She knew it. And now she was going to have to explain it to someone. Explain it to a cop who was investigating her stalker. There would be a police file. The doll would be evidence. So would the note. And her confession? Would that be evidence too?

"Had to go to the damn bar," she murmured.

CHAPTER NINE

"So he had a keycard?"

"Yes. He was dressed as if he worked there. Walked up to the door with a serving tray. I imagine that's where the doll was hidden."

"But he doesn't work there?"

"He knew where the cameras were," Harper said as she turned the corner. "There wasn't a clean shot of his face, but they don't think he works there."

"He knew what room I was in. He had a keycard." She raised her hands up. "How could he know?"

"When's the last time he left something for you?"

Dani leaned back in the seat, trying to remember. Three days ago? Four? "He didn't come inside. It was left at the door." She glanced at Harper. "A doll. A little smaller than this one, with the hair cut off. It was three or four days ago. The day before I left."

"Why does he cut the hair?"

"I'm not sure."

Harper stopped as the traffic light changed from yellow to red. "So when are you going to tell me about the note?"

Dani looked over at her. "I…I can't."

"Can't or won't?"

Dani swallowed. "Both."

Harper studied her and she wondered what she saw. Could she see through the lie?

"If you want me to help you, you're going to have to trust me."

As their eyes held, Dani realized that yes, she could trust Harper. That was the reason she'd picked her in the first place. Her eyes. But damn…

She finally blew out her breath. "Okay."

Harper simply nodded, then pulled through the intersection when the light turned green.

Dani turned and stared out the window, oblivious to the traffic around them. Was she really going to trust Harper with this? Even though she'd tried not to think about it, a part of her worried that her stalker might follow her here. And he had. And he was now threatening her. She had to trust Harper. There was no one else. She turned back, watching Harper as she drove. "I'm sorry I'm being such a bother."

"No bother."

"Is there someone…well, that you share your house with? Someone who will mind that I'm there?"

"No," Harper said quickly. "There's no one."

Dani was surprised by the dark shadow that crossed Harper's face, but she didn't comment it on. "I appreciate you letting me stay with you." She smiled. "Well, insisting I stay with you."

"It's no problem. Until we find out how this guy is following you, I'd feel better if you were close by."

Dani laughed. "*You'd* feel better? I'd feel better if you never let me out of your sight."

Harper smiled at her. "That's probably what's going to happen. You'll be sick of me."

"No. To be honest with you, for the first time in months, I actually feel safe."

Harper nodded. "And I plan to keep you safe. But we need to talk. You've got to be honest with me. We need to figure out why this guy is stalking you and how the hell he knows where you are."

"Yes, I know. We'll talk."

* * *

Dani took the glass that Harper handed her, feeling a bit nostalgic as she watched Harper slide the bottle away. "Growing up in Tennessee, Jack Daniels was the only whiskey my friends drank." She took a sip, savoring the flavor that she remembered.

"Tennessee? No way. You don't have an accent."

Dani smiled. "Get me back home around my family and I can Southern twang with the best of them," she said with an exaggerated accent.

Harper laughed. "Yeah. Okay. I believe you." She sipped from her glass as well. "Do you get home much?"

The smile left her face. "No. Not in a while." She leaned back in the chair. "What about you? I don't detect a Texas accent."

Harper shook her head. "No. Tucson. Born and raised."

"How long have you been in Dallas?" Harper paused so long, Dani wasn't sure she was going to answer her. She finally let out a quiet breath.

"Three years."

"Were you a police officer there too? A detective?"

Harper nodded. "Yes. I was in Homicide, though, not Assault." She cleared her throat. "But back to you."

Dani sighed. "Back to me." No amount of small talk would get her out of it, she supposed. She just wasn't sure how she was going to tell Harper Jeremiah, a perfect stranger, her secret.

"The note? The red wig?" Harper prompted.

Dani took a deep breath, letting it out slowly. "This is very hard to...to say."

"If you're worried about the tabloids or gossip or something like that...you can trust me."

Dani nodded. "Yes, I think I can." She took another swallow from her glass—for courage, perhaps. "I was out. One night. I was, well, I just wanted to be a normal person. At a bar."

"So you wore a red wig?"

"Yes. Not bright red, not like the doll's wig, no." She met Harper's curious gaze. "I didn't want to be recognized because I was at a…a gay bar."

"Okay. So…doing research for a part or something?"

Dani swallowed. "No."

Harper frowned slightly. "So…like a dance club? Going for the music?"

Dani shook her head. "No."

Harper raised an eyebrow. "So…like…"

"Like I'm gay."

Harper nearly dropped her glass. "*What*?"

"I know, I don't look like a…a lesbian. Whatever we're supposed to look like," she murmured.

"No. *I* look like a lesbian. You look like…well, like a beautiful Hollywood actress."

Did Harper look like a lesbian? Yes, Dani had assumed Harper was gay. Not that the photo she'd had screamed gay, but there was something that drew her. Her hair was a little longer now than it'd been in the photo. She was taller than she'd imagined—tall and lean. Early thirties, perhaps.

Harper leaned closer now. "Seriously? You're gay?"

"Seriously."

"And…nobody knows?"

Dani shook her head. "Well, someone knows, yes," she said with a half-smile. "But no one in the business, no. Not even my assistant."

"How old are you?"

"Why? Is that relevant?"

"Mid-twenties?"

"Twenty-eight, nearly twenty-nine."

"So who knows? People from college? Your family?"

"God, no. My family…they're conservative. Church-going. Older. I could never tell them."

Harper scratched her forehead, her eyebrows drawn together in a frown. "Okay...so you're a big star. News like this would be what? A bombshell?"

"Yes. Quite the bombshell."

"So how is it that no one has spilled the beans?"

Dani wrapped both hands around her glass. "In college, I had a...a relationship. Discreet relationship," she added.

"Discreet? Meaning both of you were in the closet?"

"Yes."

Harper stood up, pacing slowly around the table. "Okay. None of this is really any of my business. But the stalker?" She stopped pacing and stared at her. "What do you think?"

"I think it makes more sense now," she said. "He's mad. I've disappointed him."

"Because he's in love with you and he finds out you're gay?" Harper shook her head. "Just because you went to a gay bar doesn't mean you're gay. What was he doing there? Or was it a mixed bar?"

"No. I would assume he followed me."

"Okay. I thought the stalking started after the bar. No?"

"No. I went to the bar...I don't know, it was well over a month ago. But that's when the notes that he left started to change tone. That's when the fresh flowers that he'd leave changed to black roses. That's when the dolls started showing up."

Harper sat down again. "So he's infatuated with you. He's spying on you. Leaving you things. He's in love."

"Yes."

"You go to a gay bar wearing a red wig, in disguise. He follows you. He's...appalled by it. You've shattered his view of you."

"Yes. He's mad. He wants to punish me."

"So...again...how did he know you were going to be in Dallas?" Harper tapped her finger on the table. "Maybe he's got your house bugged. You flew here?"

"No. I drove."

"You *drove*?"

"I needed some alone time. And I hate airports."

"You hate airports or you hate the people at airports?"

She was surprised at how astute Harper was at reading her. "I don't make a very good celebrity, do I?"

Harper tilted her head, studying her. "If you don't like all the trimmings that go with it, why are you in the business?"

Dani's smile was brief as she remembered that fateful day. "It just sort of happened. By accident. Literally." She slid her empty glass over to Harper and nodded at her unasked question. Harper added a splash to the glass and slid it back to her. "After college, I really had no idea what I wanted to do. I'd worked for a real estate company while I was in school and...well, I got a license because...well, men had a hard time saying no to me. It was fairly easy to sell houses."

"And what? With your looks you got discovered?"

"No. A friend of mine was an aspiring actress. She needed a lift one day. She was auditioning for a part." She remembered that day with vivid clarity. It was the day her world changed. She looked up at Harper. "It was a rare rainy day. Instead of waiting in the car or going somewhere to kill time, I went in with her. There were maybe twenty or twenty-five women in there. Kate went over to join them and I went to get coffee for us." She shook her head. "I tripped and fell. Tossed two cups of hot coffee on, like, six of them." She laughed quietly. "It was a little chaotic there for a minute. The next thing I know, I'm being pulled into a back room to read from a script."

Harper smiled. "*That's* how you got discovered? Really?"

"Really. Kate hasn't spoken to me since." She took a sip of the whiskey. "I hate it. I hate all of it." Then she gave a quick laugh. "Well, not the money. I don't hate that part of it." Her smile faded. "I hate that I have no life to speak of. It's not something I ever aspired to do. Growing up, I was rather shy. And when I discovered I was gay, I fiercely guarded my privacy. So for me to have zero privacy now...I can't continue to live this way. This movie will be my last." She looked quickly at Harper. "And you're the very first person I've told. I'm going to do this movie, which will be very different from the others that I've done. It's darker, grittier. I don't play a dumb blond in some far-fetched love story for once. I'm going to honor my obligations, then I'm done."

"Hoping to change your image?"

"At the time I signed on for it, yes, that was the plan. Now? Now it's just a means to an end."

"So you're going to walk away from fame and fortune just like that?"

"I'm going to run, not walk."

"And do what?"

"I don't know. Dye my hair dark. Chop it off. Go back to my real name."

"Real name?"

"Danielle Stevens. No, that's not me." She smiled. "Dani Strauss. That's my real name."

"Why Stevens?"

She shrugged. "I was told Strauss didn't fit me. Besides, I wanted to protect my family and their privacy." She leaned back and brushed the hair away from her face. "Which brings us back to my stalker."

"Yes. You hate airports so you drove."

"I rented a car. Could he have found out from them where I was heading?"

"He had to have known what you planned to do here, not just that you were heading to Dallas. How would he find you in the city?" Harper stood up again, pacing. "You locked your house at night, yet he still got in. Did he go into your bedroom?"

"I don't think so. After the first time when I knew he'd been in the house, I started locking my bedroom door and I'd put a chair under the doorknob. And I hung a bell. And of course, I got a gun."

"A bell to alert you? That was smart. But do you think you could have shot him?"

Dani stared at her. "I don't know," she said honestly.

"Let's hope you don't have to find out." Harper leaned on the chair. "I don't think it's as simple as him following you though. Across four states? What are the chances? I think—"

Harper's phone interrupted her and she pulled it out of her pocket. "Yeah, Reid…what did you find?"

Dani could tell by her expression that Detective Springer found absolutely nothing. She wasn't surprised. They'd never been able to find anything at her house either.

"Okay. Thanks." Harper paused. "Yeah, she's here with me." Then she smiled and met Dani's gaze. "I'll try to control myself." She pocketed her phone and shrugged. "He's extremely jealous that you're staying with me."

Dani nodded. "And I'm extremely happy that it's you and not him." She grinned. "You're much cuter than he is." She was surprised that Harper blushed. "So…back to my stalker."

"Yeah." Harper sat down again. "The doll was clean. No prints. They're going to try to trace the doll. Find out what kind it is, what brand, and see if they can trace it back to where it was purchased." Harper shook her head. "Very long shot and probably a waste of time."

"Am I getting special treatment? I mean, a doll was found in a hotel room. If that had happened to anyone else…"

"Yes."

"And being here with you? If it was anyone else, you wouldn't have offered your home to me."

Harper shrugged. "Depends. I may not know who you are, but I can be charmed just as well."

Dani laughed. "Charmed? Am I charming you?" Again, Harper blushed.

"So back to this. I don't think he's following you. I think he's tracking you."

"Meaning?"

"A tracking device. He may have bugged your home. Maybe that's how he knew when you weren't there so he could pop in and leave you gifts. A listening device would have allowed him to hear your conversations on the phone, know what your plans were, that sort of thing."

"But a tracking device? On my own car, maybe. But I rented one to come here."

"Did you pick it up ahead of time? Did you leave it at your place overnight?"

Dani sighed. "Yes. Damn. It was delivered the day before I left."

"It's just a thought. The car's in our lot, right?"

"Right."

"I'll have someone do a sweep on it."

"Okay. And not to be a bother or a rude guest, but I didn't have lunch and I'm starving."

"Yeah, me too. We can order pizza, you know, if Hollywood stars eat that sort of thing."

She knew Harper was teasing, but it hit home. She *was* a Hollywood star. She no longer had the luxury of having pizza delivered to her door. She no longer could go out to eat at her favorite Italian restaurant, a little mom-and-pop place that served the best traditional lasagna she'd ever had. It was a once-a-week stop back in the old days, back before she was "discovered." Back when she was just Dani Strauss. The last time she'd tried to go there, it had caused such a commotion, the owners had ushered her out through the kitchen with her food boxed to go.

"What is it?" Harper asked gently.

"Feeling sorry for myself," she said. "Privacy is something most people take for granted. I never wanted to be a celebrity. I wasn't prepared for it."

"Well, you must be a good actress. You obviously have the looks. Talented too."

Dani laughed. "Talented? First of all, you've not seen any of my movies. Secondly, I don't know that there's much talent involved. I'm pretty much just playing myself. All four of the characters I've played have been almost identical."

"So what? Romantic comedies? Drama?"

"Three fall under romantic comedies. *Shores of St. Clair* was more drama."

"Right…the jilted lover and all."

Dani laughed again. "I'm going to guess you'd hate all four of them."

"But now you're going to play a cop."

"Yes. And I think this will be the movie that I'm exposed in. Like I said, I think my so-called talent is limited. That's one reason I wanted to shadow somebody. Watch the way you carried yourself, how you reacted, how you talked to people."

"I think Reid already told you not to model your character after me."

"Yes. Why is that?"

"I'm not very likeable."

Dani frowned. "No?"

Harper stood up. "No. So pizza? Or something else?"

Dani wondered at her sudden abruptness. Was Harper trying to remind herself that she was unlikable? Was it true or was it something she chose to portray? At Harper's questioning gaze, she realized she hadn't answered her.

"Yes. Pizza would be great, although pepperoni is not my favorite."

"Italian sausage is my usual go-to. What about veggies? Anything you don't like?"

"Not a big fan of olives."

"Consider them cut."

CHAPTER TEN

Harper handed Dani the remote. "I don't watch TV, but I think it still works."

"You don't watch TV. You don't go to movies." Dani raised her eyebrows. "What *do* you do?"

"I work." And sit alone and think and remember and…and sometimes cry. She sighed quietly, wishing the pizza would come already.

She moved away from Dani, choosing to sit in the lumpy chair instead of sharing the sofa. The chair was picked up at a thrift shop, as was most everything else in the house. When she moved to Dallas, she'd brought nothing with her but her clothes and her laptop. She'd rented an apartment at first, but noisy neighbors soon had her regretting that decision. This house—a rental—belonged to Sergeant Helms's sister. Because of that, she was getting a break on the rent, which she appreciated. The house was in a decent neighborhood so she had no complaints there.

She stared absently at the TV as Dani flipped through channels. She then turned her attention to the woman sharing her space. Not just any woman. Danielle Stevens. A damn actress, for God's sake. An actress with a doll-loving stalker chasing her. Dani Strauss. A woman relying on her to keep her safe. The last time that had happened…well, no. She didn't want to go there. She needed to be alone if she was going to let those memories in. Because those memories always brought tears.

The doorbell sounded. Finally. She got up, opening the door without looking. Not that she was on first-name basis with all the delivery folks, but she smiled at Jamil, who delivered to her most often.

"Hey there, Miss Harper. Large pizza? That's a change. You got company?"

"Got a guest tonight, yeah." She took the receipt he handed her and added a tip before signing it. "Thanks, Jamil."

"Thank you. See you next time," he said as he hurried back to his car.

She was about to turn away when she saw the porch light reflect off of something by her tire. She walked closer, putting the pizza on the hood as she squatted down to inspect it.

"Son of a bitch," she murmured.

A knife was sticking out of the front driver's side tire. A quick glance to the back told her that all of the tires had been slashed.

"Harper?"

"Yeah. Over here."

Dani walked down the porch steps. "What's wrong?"

She stood up and pointed at the knife. "The bastard is really starting to piss me off."

Dani's eyes went from the knife back to her. "How did he find us?"

"I don't know. I made sure we weren't followed." She handed the pizza box to Dani. "Go back inside. I need to call Reid."

* * *

"Damn, Harper. Maybe I'm glad I didn't get this assignment after all." He closed the door, then held up the note. "He must be pretty slick if he can get inside your car without setting off the alarm."

"I'm more concerned with how the hell he found us. I was overly cautious. I took a different route home. I went out of the way. I got into traffic. I would swear there was no one following us."

"Then you know what that means."

"Yeah. She's got a tracking device somewhere."

"Luggage? You said he'd been in her house."

"Could be."

"What about phone?"

Harper shook her head. "She's very private. From what I gather, not many people have her number to begin with. Just her inner circle."

"We both know there are ways to find cell phone numbers. This guy seems very careful. Professional, almost."

"A professional stalker?"

"You know what I mean." He shined his flashlight on the note. "Okay, let's see what we got." He smiled. "He pegged you for a dyke cop. Wonder when he figured that out?"

"Just read what's on the note, Reid," she said a bit impatiently.

"It says 'Danielle Stevens belongs to me, dyke cop. I'm not afraid to take you out.'" Reid glanced at her. "Kinda lame. Like a bad TV show." He slipped the note into an evidence bag. "I'll take this and the knife and see if there's something on it."

"Thanks."

"Yeah, yeah. I know you're busy, what with trying to keep Danielle Stevens safe and all. Tough job you got there, Harper."

She lifted up the corner of her mouth in a grin. "Well, someone has to do it." She let her smile slip away. "You let Mize know about my tires?"

"No. I didn't even tell Hernandez. I just told him to pick me up here because you wanted the squad car first thing in the morning." He paused. "You going to let Mize know?"

"Yeah, I'll get with him in the morning. What about the sweep on her rental car?"

"They'll do it tomorrow. What about her luggage?"

"I'll have her bring it with us."

He leaned closer and nudged her elbow. "Need me to stay here with you? Help protect her?"

"You know what, buddy? I think I can handle it."

"So…what's she like? Is she nice like she appears in the movies? Or stuck up like a big-shot celebrity?"

"She's nice." She glanced toward the house. "You want to come inside? I got a pizza," she offered.

"Oh, yeah," he said eagerly. "Will she mind?"

"I don't think so."

She found Dani in the kitchen, pacing. Her eyes flew first to Harper, then to Reid.

"You remember Detective Springer," she said, jerking a thumb at Reid. "He's waiting for a ride. If you don't mind, I thought we'd share our pizza with him."

"I don't mind at all."

"There's beer," she said to Reid as she brought the pizza box to the table.

"Better not. I'm going to drop the knife off before I go home."

Harper smiled when she opened the lid and found one slice missing. She glanced over at Dani, who smiled a bit sheepishly.

"Sorry. I was starving."

"Yeah, me too." Harper took out a slice before sliding the box toward Reid. "Found a note in the car."

"Oh? He got inside? Was it locked?"

"Yeah. Talented little bastard." She glanced at Reid. "Tell her what it said."

"Are you sure?"

"You said yourself it was pretty lame."

He nodded, then glanced at Dani. "It was a warning, Ms. Stevens. For Harper. He said that you…well, that you belong to him."

"Show her the note," she said around a mouthful. "Make sure it's the same handwriting."

Reid took the evidence bag from his inner jacket pocket and handed it to Dani. Harper watched her as she read it, her expression changing only subtly. Harper reached for another piece of pizza, waiting for her reaction.

"So he's threatening *you* now." Dani met her gaze. "I'm sorry. I—"

"It's the same handwriting?"

"Yes." Then she smiled. "'Dyke cop,' huh?"

Harper shrugged and returned her smile. "What can I say?"

Dani handed the evidence bag back to Reid. "I understand my rental car will be checked for a tracking device," she said.

"Yes, tomorrow." Reid took another piece too. "And something else. We think maybe...your luggage too."

"My luggage?"

"He found my place somehow," Harper said. "I wasn't followed. I'm sure of it."

Dani sat down at the table with them. "You think there's a tracking device in my luggage too?"

"Possibility, yes," she said.

"This is crazy. Who does stuff like this?"

"An obsessed fan, I guess," she said. "Probably some guy like Reid who thinks—what did you say? 'She's the hottest thing out there'?"

Reid nearly choked on his pizza and his face turned bright red with embarrassment.

He kicked her leg under the table. "Must you?"

Harper laughed. "Sorry."

Dani gave his arm a friendly pat. "Thank you for the compliment, but I can name several actresses who are hotter than I am. And younger," she added.

The question was on Reid's lips, but before he could ask it, a horn honked outside. There was a look of relief on his face at the sound.

"That's my ride," he said as he got up, taking his slice of pizza with him.

"Thanks for coming out," she said. "We'll hook up tomorrow."

"Right." He turned to Dani. "Good night, Ms. Stevens."

"Good night, Detective."

Harper walked him to the front door. "She's twenty-eight," she said quietly. "Too young for you."

He grinned. "I'm only thirty-five. Certainly not too young."

"She's closer to my age," she said, baiting him.

He laughed. "Come on, Harper. Danielle Stevens? You wouldn't stand a chance with that woman in there." He lowered his voice. "Did you see the way she looked at me? Did you see her touch my arm?"

"Yeah, but who is she sleeping with tonight?"

"Oh, in your dreams, Harper!" Hernandez honked again and Reid jogged away. "See you tomorrow," he called before shoving the pizza into his mouth.

She was smiling as she walked back inside. Dani was still at the kitchen table, but her glass now had a splash of amber liquid in it. Dani looked at her questioningly and Harper nodded. Dani added a bit to her glass too.

"I'm sorry I got you into all this," Dani said as she slid the glass over to her. "I should have stayed home. I should have canceled my plans here."

"Stayed home and done what? Dealt with it yourself?"

Dani sighed. "Continued to call the police there, I suppose. Hired a bodyguard."

"You already said you didn't want to live like that. And stop apologizing. It's my job."

"This certainly isn't your job," Dani said, motioning to the pizza, the whiskey. "You could have dumped me off at another hotel."

"I could have. But I didn't."

Dani held the glass loosely in her hands, then ran her thumbs across the surface, back and forth. "The note...is it legit? For real? Or just an idle threat."

"You mean the part about taking me out?"

Dani looked at her. "Yes."

Harper shrugged. "We have to take it at face value, I suppose. But don't worry. I can take care of myself. It's you we're trying to protect here, not me."

"You think it'll be okay tonight? You think he'll try to break in here like he does at my house?"

Harper shook her head. "He knows I'm a cop. Surely he's not that crazy."

Later, however, as she was lying in bed, listening to every slight noise, Harper wasn't so sure. This was a man bold enough to go into Dani's house at night, while she slept. He was bold enough to come to her own house and slash the tires on her car...while she was at home. Would he try to come inside tonight?

She tossed the covers off for the third time and crept silently into the hallway. All was quiet. She went to the spare room, the door ajar as it had been earlier. She pushed it open, listening to Dani's even breathing. As Dani had told her when they'd gone to bed...her problem was that she slept like a log and rarely woke during the night. Harper had looked in on her three times now and she appeared to be in the same position—on her side, the extra pillow pulled to her as if she were holding a lover.

She had a sudden sense of loneliness and she turned from the sight, closing the door a bit as she went back to her own room.

CHAPTER ELEVEN

Dani leaned against the counter, then stifled a yawn, watching as Harper did the same. "Did you sleep?"

"Not much."

"On guard?" she guessed.

Harper nodded as she poured coffee into a travel mug.

"You know, we should have just shared your bed. That way you wouldn't have had to look in on me during the night and I wouldn't have worried so much."

Harper smiled. "I don't know that worrying kept you up. You were sleeping like a baby. But how did you know I checked on you?"

Dani shrugged. "It seemed like something you would do. Did you?"

Harper nodded. "I may have looked in on you a time or two. Couldn't sleep."

"So you were more worried than you let on, huh? Thanks for hiding it from me."

Harper closed the lid on her mug. "I don't normally do breakfast, but we can pick something up if you'd like."

"I'm okay as long as we don't skip lunch again." She drank the last of her coffee, then set the cup in the sink and rinsed it with water. "Do we have a plan for today?"

"I've got to let Lieutenant Mize know what happened last night. I really don't want to go out until your rental has been checked and your luggage too."

"Do you think your lieutenant will change his mind about me riding with you?"

"Afraid we're going to send you away?"

"Yes, actually."

Harper shook her head. "Don't worry about that. He'll most likely leave it up to me as to how we play this."

"And if that's the case, what would be your course of action?" she asked.

"I want to catch the bastard," Harper said bluntly. "But it's a fine line. It's you he's after, not me. How exposed should we leave you?"

Dani frowned. "What are you saying? Use me as bait?"

"Something like that, yeah."

Dani chewed on her lower lip. Bait? For her stalker? The creepy clown? She met Harper's gaze. "I'm not sure how I feel about that. You want to let him get close to me?"

"Close. But not too close." Harper shoved away from the counter. "Come on. We're going to hit traffic if we don't get going."

* * *

"Are you out of your mind? Use her as *bait*?" Lieutenant Mize took off his glasses and tossed them on his desk. "No way, Detective. If something happened to her," he said, pointing at Dani, "can you imagine the negative publicity this department would have?" He shook his head. "Absolutely not. Find another way."

"I didn't mean to use her exactly, Lieutenant," Harper said. "The tracking device they found on her rental has already been disabled, so he now knows we found it. But the device that was found on her bag, I told them not to disable it." She stood up, walking behind the visitor's chair that Dani was sitting in. "We'll get someone to drive the rental—with her bag that has the tracking device on it—and go somewhere that we've already staked out. All we have to do is wait for him to show."

"And she's out of the picture?"

"We'll leave her someplace safe, yes. She can sit at my desk until it's over."

He put his glasses back on. "Okay, Harper. That sounds almost too easy, but it might work. Unless he's got eyes on the rental and knows it's not her driving it."

"I'll drive it. I'll wear a blond wig."

Harper was surprised by the quick laugh he gave. "Oh, now this I've got to see."

"If you're planning to go to someplace that's already staked out, why not just let me drive the car?" Dani asked.

"No," she said with a shake of her head. "I don't want to take a chance of him intercepting you en route or something."

"Even if you wear a wig, if he gets close enough, he'll know it's not me."

"We'll go after dark. It should be fine." She turned to Mize. "Can we find an abandoned house or building or something where we can lead him to?"

"Yeah, I'll find something. Take Springer and Hernandez," he said. "I'll let Sergeant Helms know you'll need backup. Let's do it right at dusk."

She nodded. "I'll fill them in." She turned to Dani. "Probably best if you stay here until it's over with. You can sit at my desk. Watch the comings and goings." She smiled. "You know, a little background for your movie."

Dani nodded. "Okay. I guess I can't be any safer than here, can I?"

Harper noticed her hesitation and when they walked out of Mize's office, she nudged Dani's arm. "What's wrong?" she asked quietly.

"I don't know. On the surface, it sounds like it might work."

"But?"

"Like your lieutenant said, it seems too easy. The stalker seems…I don't know, too smart. Where do you even get tracking devices?"

"You can buy GPS tracking devices anywhere. These are pretty simple ones." She shrugged slightly. "If all he's doing is following the device, it might work." In fact, it seemed so simple, she felt like it *had* to work. "Worth a try, right?"

Dani gave a half smile. "Worth a try."

Harper could tell she wasn't convinced and she wished she knew what Dani's reservations were. Maybe intuition told her it wasn't going to work. There was a look of concern in her eyes and Harper thought maybe it was the fact that she'd be left here in the squad room alone.

"If you're worried about the guys bothering you while I'm not here, I'll pass around a word of warning to them," she offered. "Although Lieutenant Mize and the captain have both told everyone to leave you alone."

"I'd rather be with you, but I suppose I'll be fine here. I'll entertain myself by people watching, as you suggested."

Dani wasn't very convincing, but Harper didn't have time to reassure her. "I need to get with Springer and Hernandez," she said apologetically. "Fill them in, get our plan down." She glanced at the clock on the wall. "I see we're well past lunch already. Sorry."

"I'll get some chips or something from the vending machine."

"Give me an hour or so, then we'll go grab something to eat. Late lunch, early dinner."

Dani smiled. "You make a terrible date, you know."

Harper nodded. "So I've been told."

Yeah, by all of two women who she'd been out with in the last three years. The first one—Harper couldn't remember her name—barely made it through dinner. The second one—Missy something or other—lasted for two whole dates. Tears had ended the second date. Harper's tears, not Missy's. Harper had given up on dating after that.

Dani was looking at her questioningly, and Harper gave her a quick smile. "Be right back."

CHAPTER TWELVE

Dani stared out of the third-floor window, watching the light rain splatter against the glass, blurring the headlights of the cars on the street down below. She pulled her jacket a little tighter around her, subconsciously feeling the chill from outside on this early February evening. So much for the spring weather she'd been expecting.

She didn't know why she was feeling apprehensive, but she was. It was similar to the feelings she would have at home, in the mornings, when she knew—even before stepping foot outside her bedroom door—that he'd been there. She just hadn't known how to explain it to Harper.

She moved her jacket aside on her wrist, looking at her watch. It had been nearly an hour since Harper had donned the blond wig—to much laughter from the guys in the squad room—and headed out in her rental car. With luck, Harper had said, they'd have her stalker in custody tonight.

Dani had a sneaking suspicion that luck would not be on their side.

She turned away from the window and resumed her seat at Harper's desk, a desk that was impeccably neat, nothing personal on it at all. There were four other detectives still there. Two were on the phone and one had his nose stuck in his computer. The other was leaning back in his chair, twirling a pencil between his fingers. He'd glanced at her a few times, offered a smile or two, but had left her alone. In fact, no one had approached her at all. If not for a few curious glances her way, she could almost forget she was Danielle Stevens.

She folded her arms across her waist, letting her thoughts drift to Detective Jeremiah. She was a hard one to read. One minute...friendly, open. The next...abrupt, guarded. Harper did seem more protective of her personal life, though. If she had to venture a guess, she'd say that Harper had no personal life. That was a shame. While she deemed herself unlikeable—and at times tried very hard to be that person—Dani would never describe her that way. And judging by her interactions with Detective Springer and the others, they didn't view her that way either. She wondered why Harper had given herself that label.

* * *

"So we've been here over an hour, Harper. How long do we wait? Maybe he drove by and could tell it was an abandoned house and kept going."

"Yeah...maybe this plan wasn't all that great."

"It's a great plan, provided he plays along," Reid said. "Since we found the tracking device on the car, maybe he's decided to lay low for a night or two and didn't follow at all."

"His intent is to terrorize, cause fear," she said. "From what Dani says, it's escalating, if anything."

Reid raised his eyebrows. "Dani?"

Harper shrugged. "That's what she told me to call her."

"Damn, I'm so jealous you got this assignment. She's so pretty. Pretty beyond words."

"You think?"

"God, don't you?"

Harper smiled. "Yeah…she's pretty damn cute."

Reid elbowed her. "So…does she have a boyfriend? Is she seeing some cute actor? Has she name-dropped and stuff?"

"She's a very private person. She hasn't shared anything with me," she lied. "It's strictly business."

Reid leaned back in the seat and stretched his legs out. "How come you and me never talk about personal stuff?"

"We talk about personal stuff all the time. I know every woman you've slept with."

"What I meant was, how come I don't know anything about you?"

"Nothing to know."

"Come on, Harper. We've been partners for almost a year. I know you came from Tucson—homicide detective—and you've been here three years or so. That's about all I know."

She stared straight ahead at the rental car that was parked in front of the vacant house. Was that really all she'd told him? She turned her head and looked at him, then turned back to the rental car.

"There's not much else to tell. If you're looking for juicy personal details, there aren't any. Work…this is it."

"That right there will drive you to an early grave. You know what they say about all work and no play."

"Haven't been in the mood to play," she said honestly.

"Why'd you leave Tucson? You got family here in Dallas or something?"

She took a deep breath. Yeah, Harper…why did you leave Tucson? She could see Jan's face clearly…the laughing dark eyes, the teasing smile, the tiny scar on her chin from taking a tumble on her bike when she was a kid. She stared at the rental car, no longer seeing it, instead seeing the tangled mass of light brown hair, made sticky from the blood…the mangled hands from fingers that had been smashed. And she saw the crushed skull, the lifeless eyes. She saw the sheet they'd covered her with, the sheet that was soaked in blood. She saw their sympathetic gazes, heard their hushed words, felt their comforting touch as they led her from the bedroom.

It took two days before it hit her. Two days before she shed a tear. Two days before reality set in...and changed her life forever. She looked over at Reid, seeing him watching her. She gave him a halfhearted smile.

"Or something," she said quietly.

"In other words, none of my business."

"I needed to get out of Tucson. I just happened to land here, that's all."

"Okay, Harper. None of my business."

She should tell him, she supposed. Reid was the closest thing she had to a friend. She'd left all of those behind in Tucson too. But she wasn't ready. She'd kept it locked away in a nice, safe, secret place. She took the memory out from time to time, but only for a little while. That was all she could handle. She kept thinking every day that passed, every month, every year, that it would get better—easier. But no. She still felt hollow inside, empty. She knew Jan wasn't coming back, knew that part of her life was over with for good. Jan would tell her to get over it already. Jan would tell her to get on with her life.

She would if she could. Oh, if only she could.

*　*　*

Dani stared in disbelief as a man walked into the squad room carrying a handful of balloons on a string. He spotted her and walked her way. She would have panicked if not for the friendly smile on his face.

"Danielle Stevens, right? I recognize you from the movies," he said as he handed her the strings. "Some guy outside, dressed as a clown of all things, said he had a delivery for you. I didn't let him come up, of course, but I told him I'd see that they were delivered." He pulled a note out of his pocket. "Here. There's a card or something."

She stared at the paper in his hand, then looked back at him. "He was here? In the building?"

"Yeah. Downstairs."

She saw that her hand was trembling as she took the note from him. "Thank you," she murmured.

"Sure."

There were five balloons, all different colors, all with smiley faces on them. Her first inclination was to pop them all, but in a room full of cops with guns, she didn't think that was a good idea. Instead, she tied them to Detective Springer's desk chair before sitting back down at Harper's desk.

They were from him, of course. Who else? The note, however, was different. The paper was thick, expensive stationery, not like his normal notes. She was almost afraid to open it and she realized she was holding her breath as she revealed the words written there.

Are you hiding from me, Danielle? No need to try. I can always find you. You will be mine...now and forever...until death. Your lady cop can't help you. No one can.

"Jesus," she murmured, her heart hammering in her chest. She fumbled with her phone, so thankful Harper had given her cell number that morning. Three rings...four before Harper answered. "He was here," she blurted out.

"*What?* Where?"

"Here. Downstairs. Some guy—a cop, I guess—came up and brought me balloons. He said a guy dressed as a clown wanted to come up and give them to me," she said in a nervous rush.

"Son of a bitch. No wonder he didn't show here." A slight pause. "Are you okay?"

"There was a note. Can you come back here?" she asked, her voice shaking with panic. "I'm afraid he might get in, come up here and find me."

"Yeah, we're abandoning this," Harper said. "But Dani...it's a building full of cops. You're safe there."

Dani jumped as the outer door opened and two men walked in, neither paying her any attention. "Can you hurry? Please?"

"Be right there. Just stay at my desk. I'm coming."

Dani squeezed the phone tightly in her hands before putting it in the pocket of her jacket. She wrapped the jacket tighter around her, her eyes glued to the door.

Please hurry.

CHAPTER THIRTEEN

Harper made Reid bring the rental back while she drove the squad car, lights flashing. Yeah, it was a bit of overkill, but the panic in Dani's voice had...well, it had tugged at her conscience. Dani was scared. Dani was alone. And yes, she felt responsible for her.

And the son of a bitch hadn't taken the bait, he hadn't followed the tracking device. Had he known it was a setup? Or was he watching the rental all along and knew it wasn't Dani who had gotten behind the wheel?

Regardless, leaving Dani there alone probably wasn't the wisest thing she'd ever done. Numerous scenarios crossed her mind—the stalker posing as a cop, for one—for the bastard getting into the building unimpeded. She had assumed Dani would be fine there. But what if the guy had gotten up to the third floor? Then what?

He was dressed as a freakin' clown, she reminded herself. No way he got past the front desk. Again...what if he wasn't? What if he wasn't dressed as a clown, but a cop? Well, until they had this crazy clown bastard, she'd take more precautions.

A few minutes later, when she stepped into the squad room, Dani jumped to her feet, an obvious look of relief on her face. For a second there, she thought that Dani was about to fly into her arms.

"Thank you," she mouthed as Harper walked in.

"You okay?"

"No." Dani handed her a piece of paper. "I think he's...well, I no longer think that he doesn't intend to harm me."

Harper read the note, her jaw clenched. She read it again, trying to read between the lines. There really wasn't much between the lines though.

You'll be mine...now and forever...until death.

Yeah, there wasn't much between the lines. It was all right out in the open. But as Reid might say, his notes were kinda lame. "I'm sorry I left you here," she said. "I was so sure he'd follow the tracking device."

"I don't know how to explain it, but I think I knew that he wouldn't." Dani pressed closer to her. "Is he watching me? Did he know it was you in the car and not me?"

"That seems the most logical explanation."

"So now what?"

Harper pulled the small plastic tube out of her pocket, the one they'd put the tracking device into. "We leave this here, for one thing." She put it into her desk drawer. "He knows where I live so I don't know if that's safe tonight."

"Hotel?"

"Might be too public. Do we want to chance someone recognizing you?"

"Where else?"

The double doors burst open and Reid hurried in. He nodded at Dani, then pulled her to the side.

"Got a call. Rape victim," he said quietly.

"Our guy again? Where? This makes number six."

"No, no," he said with a shake of his head. "Not our guy." He pulled her a few more feet away from Dani. "There was a doll left at the scene. A doll with chopped-off hair and a red wig."

"Jesus," she murmured, glancing quickly at Dani. "Do you want me to go with you?"

"No, me and Hernandez got it. I just wanted to give you the heads-up."

"Okay. Let me know what you get after you interview her." She ran a hand through her hair. "Hell, Reid...you need a female detective with you. Sometimes, they won't talk to you, you know."

"I know. I've got someone on standby."

She nodded. "Good. And I need a favor."

"Name it."

"Can we crash at your place tonight?"

He grinned. "Danielle Stevens at my place? Wow."

"Don't get too excited. I imagine I'll get to share a bed with her, not you."

"And that's a damn waste, Harper," he said as he handed her his keys. "The square one," he said. "There's probably nothing to eat there."

"We'll pick up something. Call me after you interview her."

"Yeah. Hopefully I'll get home at a decent hour. We can talk then."

She watched him leave, then she turned back to Dani, who was sitting at her desk. She offered a quick smile and held up his keys.

"Reid offered his place."

"Is it safe?"

"Apartment. Gated entry, for what that's worth." She looked at the three bags of luggage beside her desk. "Is there any way you could combine that into one bag?"

Dani nodded. "Easily. A couple of pairs of jeans and I'm good."

CHAPTER FOURTEEN

Dani actually moaned when she bit into the burger. "I haven't had a decent hamburger since I don't know when."

"Yeah. Whataburger…they tell me it's a Texas classic."

Dani wiped her mouth with the napkin, then used the straw to take a sip of her Coke. "Why haven't you asked me any questions?"

Harper put her burger down and grabbed three fries from her plate. "What do you mean?"

"I mean, I tell you my secret—the secret I've been keeping from everyone—and you haven't asked me a ton of questions."

"Oh. You being gay and all."

"Yes."

Harper shrugged. "Other than it's what triggered your stalker to get a little testy with you, it's not really any of my business."

Dani stared at her. "That's it?"

"What? Should I be shocked?" She shrugged again. "I don't know you. I haven't seen your movies. Maybe if I had, then, yeah, I might be surprised."

"Surprised?"

Harper held her hands out. "What do you want me to say? No, you don't look like a lesbian. You hide that very well, if that's your concern."

Dani wasn't sure what she expected Harper to say; she only expected more of a reaction than what she'd gotten. "Have you ever been in the closet?"

Harper smiled. "God, no. What you see is what you get. I knew I was gay from the start, so...I didn't try to hide it."

"And your family? Did they treat you differently?"

"No. I have two older brothers and growing up, I always tagged along with them on their adventures. Classic tomboy," Harper said. "I think they would have been more shocked had I been straight."

"Did anyone ever call you Scout?" she asked as she picked up her hamburger again.

Harper laughed. "You mean other than my grandmother? Yeah, when they felt like picking on me, they'd call me Scout." Harper reached over and stole a french fry from her plate. "So you? Growing up? Did you know you were gay?"

Dani nodded. "Yes. Only I fought it. Constantly. Steady boyfriend in high school. Well, once my father allowed me to date, that is."

"You sleep with him?"

"Yes."

"Let me guess...quarterback of the football team?"

Dani felt a blush cross her face. "Am I that predictable?"

"Head cheerleader?"

Dani sighed. "Yes."

Harper laughed lightly. "Well, you have the look of a head cheerleader. Isn't it some rule that the head cheerleader and the quarterback date?"

"I don't know that I had the look of a cheerleader back then," she said as she tucked her hair behind her ears. "I always kept my hair fairly short." She looked at Harper's hair. "Not as short as yours, but certainly not what I have now."

"They make you grow it out for the movies or what?"

"Yes. Well, they didn't *make* me, but it was suggested. The first movie, I had extensions put in to make my hair longer."

Harper nodded. "What about college? Did you still date guys?"

"Of course."

"And the gay thing?"

"I ignored it." She met her gaze. "Until I couldn't."

"The discreet affair?"

"Yes," she said. "Traci."

"What happened?"

"She was dating this guy named Jason. I was dating Brock." She shook her head. "He was a jerk. Anyway, Traci and I...well, we ended up...in bed one night." She leaned back, remembering that night well. They'd been out on a double date and the guys had gotten plastered on cheap bourbon. Neither she nor Traci had been in the mood to deal with them and had ended the night early. She still didn't know which of them initiated the first kiss. She looked up at Harper. "Traci called it experimenting."

"She wasn't gay?"

"Oh, she was. But her family was even more conservative than mine. Her father was a Baptist minister and she was frankly terrified of him. So she called it experimenting."

"How long did that last?"

"The rest of that year. Neither of us went to summer school so we both moved back home between semesters. I got an email from her. She and Jason were getting married—she was pregnant—and she wouldn't be coming back to school."

"Wow."

"Yeah. I never saw her again. Anyway, that's when I moved to California. I worked for a year to establish my residency—real estate—then went back to college."

"But you were still in the closet?"

"Yes. Very."

"Why? I mean, especially there."

"I'm not sure, really. I was hanging on to my small-town fears, I guess."

"But you had another relationship?"

"Yes. An older woman. She was fifteen years older than I was." She swallowed. "She was married."

"You sure can pick them."

"I know. Crazy."

"How long did that last?"

"Over a year. She...she committed suicide."

"Oh, Dani...I'm sorry."

She shoved the rest of her hamburger away. "I should have seen it coming, I suppose. She was so miserable in her life."

"Why didn't she just divorce her husband?"

"Three kids. The thought of them finding out...she couldn't deal with it. And on top of it all, he was a really good guy. She was living with such guilt—because of me—that it just ate at her and ate at her until she couldn't take it anymore."

"How did you handle that?"

"I handled it much like I handled the first one. I pushed it all aside and acted like it never happened." She rested her chin on her palm. "I wasn't in love with her. There wasn't an emotional involvement. But she satisfied a need I had."

"To be with a woman?"

Dani nodded. "I felt...disconnected, I think. Her family didn't know I existed, so it wasn't like I could share their grief. Her name was Tara. She worked for the real estate company I worked for." She shook her head. "And no one knew."

"And that's it? That's been your life?"

"Well-meaning friends would set me up on dates with handsome guys. Work friends always included me in their outings. I was very sociable. Yet very lonely. I've learned to live with it."

"And the bar that night?"

Dani blew out her breath. "It wasn't the first time I'd been. Even before the movies, I always wore a disguise when I went."

"Damn, you really were in the closet."

"Yes. I never went home with anyone. Never took anyone to my place. I went just to be around people...like me. I made a few friends. It was enough."

"Yet you weren't able to be you. Did you give your real name?"

"God, no. Ironically, I used Traci's name."

Harper stood up and took their plates to the sink. "You're twenty-eight years old," she said. "And not that I have any business giving you advice, but don't you think that's plenty old enough to come crawling out of the closet? Times have changed. Honestly, I don't think I know a single person who's still in the closet. Gay marriage is legal. Is it that big of a deal really, if you came out?"

"Most celebrities who are gay but not out, there are at least rumors swirling around about them. So if—when—they do come out, it's not such a total shock. Me? The only rumors swirling around about me is which guy I'm currently sleeping with."

"So which one *are* you sleeping with?"

Harper was smiling, most likely teasing her with the question, but Dani didn't return the smile.

"It's a hard game to play, Harper. It wears on you."

Harper's smile faded too. "Then quit playing it."

"Like you said, I'm twenty-eight years old, nearly twenty-nine. I've played it for a long time. I'm good at it. I'm used to it."

Harper sat down again. "So is this the sole reason you want out of the business? So you don't have to play the game anymore?"

"I make a terrible celebrity," she said. "I've been told that by nearly everyone."

"So why did you keep doing it?"

"At first, I was still in shock, I think, that someone wanted me in a movie. In the blink of an eye, I had an agent and an assistant and all these people 'managing' me," she said, making quotations in the air. "The first movie was such a success, before I knew what was happening, I had contracts for two others and the whole thing just kinda got out of control. I was so far in over my head, I had no choice but to trust these people."

"Did they take advantage?"

"Of my naiveté? Sure. Plus the fact that I didn't want all of this attention made me rely on them that much more. I may have been inexperienced, but I knew the more popular

I became, the more money I made…the more they made. I know they pretend to have my best interest at heart, but it's all a business."

"So you're going to walk away. Then what?"

She took a deep breath. "I don't know. I want to go back to being Dani Strauss. I just don't know if I can. I mean, I don't want to have to wear a wig the rest of my life," she said with a shaky laugh. "I'll cut my hair, maybe dye it brown." She smiled at Harper. "You think anyone will know?"

"Maybe if you start using that Tennessee twang." Harper stared into her eyes for such a long time Dani was wondering what she was looking for. "You have such striking eyes," Harper said, almost to herself. "A mix between green and blue. To me, that's what stood out the most when I looked at your photo. I don't think a disguise with your hair would change that."

Dani frowned. "What photo?"

"Oh, they had a file on you."

"A file?"

Harper shook her head dismissively. "Just your photo and the particulars of your visit, that's all." She smiled apologetically. "When I didn't know who you were, Lieutenant Mize offered your photo to me."

"Oh." Dani leaned her elbows on the table. "What about Detective Springer? When he came in, the two of you were being very secretive. Did he find something?"

"Not exactly."

"What does that mean?" When Harper looked away, Dani noticed her hesitation. "What is it?"

"A rape." Harper met her gaze. "There was a doll left at the scene. A doll with a red wig."

Dani's eyes widened. "Oh, my God," she whispered. "A rape? This is all my fault."

"It's not your fault, Dani. You don't control his actions."

"But I came here. I brought him here. Now some poor woman—"

"It's my fault, if anything," Harper said. "I tried to draw him out. He knew it. I think this is his way of letting us know."

"But...someone was *raped*."

"Dani...it's not your fault."

She stood up. "Then whose is it? And don't try to pacify me by saying it's yours."

Harper stood up too. "You're overreacting."

"A woman was *raped*, for God's sake! By my goddamn stalker!"

Harper held her hands out in defeat. "Okay. Take the blame. It doesn't change anything. He's still out there."

Dani let her shoulders sag. "How do you take this? Assault... rape. How do you deal with it?" Dani saw the shadow that crossed Harper's face when she looked away.

"You disconnect," Harper said quietly. "If you didn't, you'd go insane."

CHAPTER FIFTEEN

Harper sat in the chair facing the door, her phone held in her hand. She'd expected Reid to call by now. Surely they'd already interviewed the woman. She glanced over at the sofa, smiling a little as she watched Dani sleep. She was curled into a ball, tucked into one corner, her hands folded under her cheek. She'd told Dani to go on to bed, but she wouldn't hear of it.

Harper had found the spare bedroom to be cluttered and the bed unmade, but at least there was a bed. She'd found sheets and a blanket, and Dani had helped as they got the bed ready. There'd been no discussion as to who would sleep where. She knew Dani assumed they would share and she did too, even though she would offer to take the sofa once they did call it a night.

They'd both showered and changed clothes, but she was restless as Dani tried to find something on TV to occupy their time until Reid got home. Dani had left it on a cooking show as she'd settled into the corner of the sofa. It wasn't ten minutes later that she'd fallen asleep.

The similarities between this case and Tucson were eerily familiar, but Harper had no illusions that it was the same guy. In Tucson, the guy left a Raggedy Ann doll at each scene—the Raggedy Ann Killer, as the paper called him. As far as she knew, he'd never stalked anyone, although they assumed he watched his intended victims for several weeks, if not longer. For two years they'd hunted him, to no avail. They'd found a partial print one time, but that had gone nowhere. They'd called in expert after expert, even resorting to a mathematician whiz who wrote an algorithm hoping to find a pattern. Unfortunately, the pattern was—there was no pattern. Eight women—over the course of two years—raped and murdered. And the bastard slithered away into the night each time. Even that last time. No, the clown couldn't possibly be the same guy. Could he?

A jiggle of the doorknob brought her attention back to the present, and she got up, pulling her gun from its holster.

A quick tap. "Harper…it's me."

She holstered her weapon and unlocked the door quietly, bringing a finger to her lips indicating to Reid he should be quiet. She pointed to the sofa where Dani remained asleep.

"She claims she can sleep through anything, but if we're going to talk, I'd rather it be in private."

Reid's gaze landed on her sleeping form. "God, she's adorable," he whispered back.

Harper motioned to the back. "Let's go into your bedroom."

Reid grinned. "If only it was Danielle Stevens saying that instead of you."

If you only knew, she thought with a shake of her head. She left his bedroom door ajar, peeking out once to make sure Dani hadn't woken up.

"You're a slob, by the way," she said.

"Oh, yeah. I forgot the spare room is kinda messy."

"I found sheets." She walked farther into the room. "What's going on? I thought you were going to call."

He shook his head. "After we left the hospital, we went back to the scene. Then had to meet with Mize," he said.

"This late?"

"Yeah. It's the same doll, same wig," he said. "But get this… the dude was in clown makeup when he raped her. Not only that, he's calling her Danielle the whole time he's doing it."

"Jesus," she whispered. "Was the woman cooperative?"

"Oh, yeah. She did great, considering." He pulled out a notepad from his coat pocket and flipped it open. "She got home around eight thirty. He was already inside. Grabbed her in her bedroom as she was changing out of her work clothes. He was there maybe thirty minutes. Left her on the bed, put the doll beside her, and walked out."

"Evidence? Sperm?"

"Yeah, they did a workup, but she said the guy wore a condom. Disposed of it in the toilet."

"Well, that was nice of him," she said dryly.

"He had duct tape over her mouth, tied her to the bed. Before he left, he untied one hand so she could get free. That's kinda unusual, isn't it?"

"In this case, no. He wanted her free so she could report it. So we'd know what he did." She paused. "So Dani would know what he did."

"So he's playing with us? That makes no sense. I thought he was just a stalker."

"What is 'just a stalker'?" she asked.

"Yeah, I know." He put his notepad back, then shoved his hands in his pockets. "Mize wants to meet with us in the morning. But from what I gather, he's going to let it be your call."

"My call on what?"

"On what to do with Danielle Stevens."

"My call? What? Is he afraid to make a decision?" She shook her head. "There's not much of a decision anyway. Her stalker has turned into a rapist. He's here now. It's not like we can cut her loose and let her fend for herself."

"If this was anybody else, we probably would," he said. "We don't make a habit of doing protective custody, you know."

"You complaining?"

"Well, like you said, it won't be my bed she's sharing tonight."

"You're a pig, Springer."

"Nah…just teasing. By the looks of it, she'll be sleeping on the sofa tonight anyway. But what about tomorrow? And the day after? How long do you keep this up? As we both know, catching a rapist ain't the easiest thing to do."

"Is he a rapist? Or is he a stalker just doing the rape to get our attention? It's still Danielle Stevens he's after."

"Yeah, well, our attempt at luring him didn't work. And you know Mize won't let you put her out on display somewhere as bait. She was only supposed to be here for a week," he said. "We both know we're not going to catch him in a damn week."

"I know. Let's worry about it when the time comes." She rubbed her eyes. "It's been a long day, and I didn't sleep for shit last night."

"You turning in? I got some Crown I've been saving for a special occasion."

"And this is special?"

"You've been to my place like, what? Twice?"

"How about we save it for when we're celebrating something?"

"I guess. You going to wake her or let her sleep out there?"

"I think wake her. Out in the living room like that, she's kinda exposed."

"Unless the guy can be in two places at once, I doubt he followed you here."

"After what's been going on, I don't want to leave anything to chance."

* * *

Dani felt a hand on her shoulder, nudging her. She was about to panic. *Had he found her?* But a soothing voice made her relax again.

"It's me. Time for bed."

She opened her eyes, finding Harper squatting down beside the sofa. She blinked several times, then sat up. "What time is it?"

"Going on midnight."

"So my nap turned into a couple of hours," she said around a yawn. "Did Detective Springer get back?"

"Yes."

Dani could tell by the tone of her voice that she didn't want to talk about it. So, she simply nodded and stood up.

"Are there water bottles in the fridge?"

"I doubt it. How about a glass of water with ice?"

"Thanks." She turned, finding Reid Springer watching her. She smiled at him. "Thank you for offering your apartment to us, Detective."

"No problem, Ms. Stevens."

She was about to correct him, tell him to call her Dani, but... well...she wasn't sure she wanted to be that friendly with him. Experience told her that men had a hard time differentiating between "friendly" and "something more." She pointed down the short hallway where Harper had disappeared with her water.

"I guess then...I'll head on to bed. Good night."

He nodded. "Good night. And don't worry about a thing. I'm a very light sleeper. Not that, of course, we expect him to know where you are or anything."

"Of course. Thank you."

She wasn't really worried. Not with Harper sleeping next to her. She stopped off at the bathroom, then went into the spare room. Harper was sitting on the bed, waiting for her. Dani paused at the door.

"Should I close it?"

"What would make you feel safer?"

Dani smiled. "Closed, locked, and barricaded."

Harper stood up. "How about we just close it? It'll drive Reid nuts."

"What?"

"That I'm in the same bed as you are, behind closed doors."

Harper put the lamp on and Dani turned out the overhead light. "Are you two close?"

"What do you mean?"

"Partners. Do you mix your personal lives as well?"

"I don't have a personal life and Reid has too much of one."
Harper laughed quietly. "The last one was a hooker."

"A hooker?"

"He met her at a bar. Asked her out on a date." She laughed
again. "A real live date. And she was a hooker! He had no idea.
He just thought she was really coming on to him."

"What happened?"

"Hell, he slept with her. Cost him two hundred bucks."

"Damn. She must have been good."

"Blow job was extra."

Dani wrinkled up her nose. "Gross."

"Yeah…tell me."

When Harper looked at her thoughtfully, Dani held up her
hand. "I know what you're going to ask…and no. I've never."
Then she tilted her head. "Have you?"

"God, no! The closest I've been to a penis was pulling a tick
off it with tweezers," she said. "I was in high school. One of my
brother's friends." She laughed. "God, I haven't thought about
that in years."

"He let you near his penis with tweezers?"

"It was either me or Michael," Harper said as she pulled
back the sheet on the bed.

"Your brother?"

"Yeah. You have siblings?"

Dani nodded. "An older sister. Sixteen years older. I was sort
of an accident."

"Does it matter which side of the bed you sleep on?"

"No."

Harper took off her jeans and tossed them on the floor. Dani
did the same.

"Are you close to her?"

Dani got under the covers. "My sister? We used to be." She
paused. "I think."

"You think?"

"Sixteen years older, so as close as you can be with that age
difference. When I knew that I was gay…well, I withdrew. From
her. From my parents. We never discussed anything personal,

anyway. At all. That's how things were in our family. We didn't talk about things. Ever. And when this all happened," she said, referring to her acting career, "our divide got even deeper." She rolled over to her side, facing Harper. "It was mostly my fault. I never knew it would morph into all of this. I thought—after the first movie—that my acting would be so bad, it would be a short-lived career. My family, they didn't understand any of it. I think they assumed I was sleeping my way to the top." She tried to smile, but it never materialized. "I don't have any friends," she said sadly. "I didn't know who to trust anymore."

"What about from your work? The real estate place?"

"It's a cutthroat business. The women were jealous of me and the men...well, the men just wanted to sleep with me," she said bluntly.

"So you not only withdrew from your family, but from everyone," Harper stated.

"Yes."

"Hell of a way to live," she murmured, almost to herself.

Dani nodded. "Like I said, I don't make a very good celebrity."

"So why even do this last movie? Why not walk away now?"

"I wish I could. But I don't like to back out of things I've committed to." She rolled back over and stared at the ceiling. "This role is not glamourous. Frankly, I'm surprised they wanted me for it. It's hardcore drama, nothing I've done before. When I read for it, I didn't think it went particularly well, but they wanted me." She turned her head toward Harper. "I play a stressed-out cop who drinks too much. She's having an affair with a defense attorney—married guy—who ends up defending a guy she arrested for murder. Her partner's in love with her. She's in love with her bottle of bourbon." She sighed. "And it has a tragic ending."

"The cop dies?"

"Yes."

"And you're hoping Danielle Stevens dies as well."

Dani nodded and closed her eyes with a sigh. She felt Harper move, heard the click, sensed the room darkening from the lamp being turned off. She kept her eyes closed. She was safe. Harper Jeremiah, a cop she'd met only yesterday, was keeping her safe.

Harper settled back down again, and Dani knew, if she moved a foot or more, she'd be touching her. In the darkness, her lips turned up in a smile. She knew Harper would be like this. From the moment she saw her photo—looked into the dark eyes as they stared back at her—she knew Harper Jeremiah was the one who would protect her.

"Are you going to tell me about the rape? About what Detective Springer found?" she murmured quietly, her eyes still closed. She could tell Harper was hesitating, could almost see the indecision in her eyes…then a quiet sigh and the rustling of covers.

"We'll talk tomorrow. Okay?"

"But it was him? For sure?"

"Yeah…it was him."

Of course it was. "Okay. We'll talk tomorrow." She finally opened her eyes, turning toward Harper. "Good night," she whispered.

"Good night, Dani."

CHAPTER SIXTEEN

Harper stared in disbelief at the doll…the dull, drab eyes seeming to stare right back at her. How in the hell had he found them? She looked past the doll, out to the parking lot, expecting to see their tires slashed, but the patrol car she driven looked intact as did Reid's Toyota.

"Harper? What is it?"

She turned, finding Dani coming to the door. She stepped aside, pointing down to the mat.

"Oh, Jesus…not again." Dani looked at her. "How did he find us?"

"I don't know." She closed the door on the doll, forgetting what she was going out for in the first place. "Is Reid up yet?"

"I'm in here," he called from the kitchen. "What's up?"

"A goddamn doll is sitting on your mat outside."

Reid paused in mid-drink. "One of *those* dolls? You're kidding."

"So not kidding."

He put his cup down. "How could he find her *here*?"

Harper shook her head. "He didn't follow us. I made sure."

"You think he followed me? Maybe he was watching the scene, followed me back."

"How would he have known Dani was staying here at your apartment?"

"Mize knew." He gave a quick, embarrassed laugh. "And I may have told a few of the guys."

"But how would *he* have known?" Dani asked.

Harper ran her fingers through her hair—above her ear—several times, trying to make sense of it. How *could* he find her here?

"Unless he was watching me, not Dani," she said, looking first at Dani, then Reid. "He knows that I'm assigned to her, judging by the notes he's left. Maybe he was watching me, saw what car I was driving, put a tracking device on it."

"Well, that would be pretty arrogant of the son of a bitch to walk up to the police station to place a tracking device."

"I would say, yeah, he is arrogant, considering everything he's done." She turned to Dani. "Get your things. I don't trust it here. He knows where you are, what apartment you're in."

"Where will we go?"

"Obviously trying to hide from him is not working. We need a plan."

"We're supposed to meet with Mize this morning," Reid reminded her. "About...last night."

Harper nodded. The rape victim. She looked over at Dani, who was watching her. Dani had questions in her eye. She knew last night that she'd been full of them, but she hadn't pressed. She imagined she wouldn't be spared them this morning.

"You follow us in," she said to Reid. "Right on our tail. No cars get in between."

"You got it."

* * *

"I feel like a sitting duck," Dani admitted as Harper pulled out onto the street. It was just barely seven, but the morning traffic was already thick.

"The direct route will take only about fifteen minutes."

"Last night was twice that."

"At least. I took the long route, in case we were being followed."

Dani looked around them in all directions, obviously looking for someone suspicious—like a clown—following them. It was still dark outside and headlights obscured her view. "Maybe I've seen too many movies, but do you think someone in the department could have tipped him off?"

"Not likely. He followed you here to Dallas. I doubt he's got any contacts in the city, much less the police department." Harper glanced at her quickly. Had Dani guessed that Harper was thinking that very thing? That there was a leak somewhere?

Dani took a deep breath. "Tell me about last night."

Harper didn't pretend to not know what she meant by the request. She was gripping the steering wheel a little too tightly and she made herself relax.

"The guy who raped her...he was calling her Danielle during the...the assault." She glanced at her quickly. "His face was...well, he was in clown makeup."

"Oh, God," Dani whispered. "Why? Why is he doing this? Why go after somebody else?"

"Maybe just to let us know that he can. He wanted to make sure that we knew it was him. Before he left, he untied her so she could get free. So she could call the police."

"So that I would know."

Harper was amazed at her astuteness. "Yes."

Harper stopped at the red light, looking into her rearview mirror. Reid was right behind them. She looked over at Dani, seeing her fingering the gold necklace that she wore around her neck.

"He wants me to know that that's what he's going to do to me," Dani continued.

Harper should have said no, that it meant no such thing, but Dani was looking into her eyes, seeing the truth there.

"I won't let anything happen to you."

Dani reached over and squeezed her arm. "I'm so happy I picked you." Then she smiled. "And I bet you are doubly excited to have been picked by me."

Harper laughed. "Glad you still have a sense of humor about it all."

The smile left Dani's face. "Seriously, Harper. What if I'd picked someone else?"

"They'd be doing the same thing I am."

"Would they?"

Harper drove on when the light turned green. Would they? She'd like to think that they would. But yeah, it was a bit unorthodox letting Danielle Stevens spend 24/7 with her. But after yesterday, there's no way she'd let Dani out of her sight. She glanced over and gave her a quick smile. "They would have probably fed you better than I have. We seem to have missed more meals than we've had."

* * *

"Did the victim connect being called 'Danielle' to Ms. Stevens?" Mize asked.

"I don't think so," Reid said.

Mize turned to her. "How's Stevens holding up?"

Harper looked through the window in his office, seeing Dani at her desk. She was sitting with her legs crossed and appeared to be calm, but Harper saw the unconscious movement of her index finger as it tapped against her thigh nervously.

"She's okay. Concerned, obviously. She feels responsible for the rape yesterday."

Mize leaned back in his chair and folded his hands together. "As she should," he said callously. "So we've got a stalker in clown makeup. He's been tracking Ms. Stevens. Follows her to Dallas. We find the tracking device and try to lure him into a trap. Somehow he knows this. So instead—perhaps in retaliation—he picks a victim at random, in her own apartment, and rapes her. And leaves his calling card—a doll."

"And for good measure," Reid added, "he leaves a damn doll at my apartment."

"To let us know that he knows where she is." Mize shook his head. "So how's he still tracking her?"

"The bulk of her luggage, we left here last night," Harper said. "The one bag she did take with us, they're checking it again now."

"What about a purse? A wallet or something?"

"Yes, that too."

"Harper thought—since he knows she's the one assigned to Ms. Stevens—that he may have put a tracking device on her car last night. While it was here."

Mize looked at her and she nodded. "They're checking it too." She shrugged. "It was just a thought."

"And you're sure you weren't followed?"

"I'm sure. We got swallowed up in traffic. I ran red lights. No one followed us."

"Maybe Reid is right then. Maybe our guy was watching the scene and followed Reid. If he's watching everything, he knows that Reid is involved. Reid went to the hotel after the doll was found. Reid came to your place after your tires were slashed."

"I think that's a long shot," she said. "If he's tracking Danielle, then why would he hang out at the hotel after we left? For what purpose?"

"He didn't have to follow her," Mize reminded her. "He still had a tracking device on her luggage."

"Still…why would he stay at the hotel?"

"Why does he wear clown makeup? Why does he do anything he does? I'm just suggesting that it's a possibility that he took a chance that Reid is involved in this case and when he no longer had the tracking device, he followed Reid, hoping he would lead him to Ms. Stevens."

"So he leaves a doll at the door on the off chance that she's in his apartment?"

"He could have seen your car in my lot and assumed she was there," Reid said. "Maybe he was watching us this morning when we left, just to verify that she was there."

"To what end?" she asked. "He's bound to know we're not going to leave her alone now."

Reid shrugged. "Maybe he's just fucking with us."

"Then why rape that woman?"

"We can conjecture all we want," Lieutenant Mize said, interrupting them. "The why of it doesn't matter. We need to find the guy. Reid, you and Hernandez work the rape like any other."

"We talked to the neighbors last night. No witnesses. No one saw or heard anything."

"What about security cameras in the parking lot?"

"Yeah, Hernandez was supposed to get them this morning. The feed is kept off-site."

"Keep me posted on what you find." He flicked his gaze to her. "I've got a buddy at the FBI. I called in a favor."

She gave him a blank look. He wanted the FBI involved in this?

"They've got a safe house we can use. I think, under the circumstances, it's best to keep her there."

She shook her head. "I don't like that plan."

He dismissed her comment. "You see, that's why I don't have to ask whether you like it or not. I'm the lieutenant. You're not."

"But if we keep her hidden, then—"

"Then he can't find her."

"If he can't find her, then we have no chance to find *him*," she countered.

"From what she told us, she only wanted to shadow you for seven or eight days. If we don't find him before she leaves town…well, then it's out of our hands."

She stared at him in disbelief. "So we're just going to cut her loose, knowing she's got this guy—now a rapist—after her?"

"What are we going to do, Harper? Force her to stay here until we catch the guy? You've got a serial rapist that you've been working for six months. You think Danielle Stevens is going to give us that kind of time?"

"But, sir, if he leaves town with her, then we have no chance to solve the rape from yesterday," Reid interjected.

"I know that. So it looks like you've got a week to find the guy." He pointed at Harper. "And you've got a week to babysit at an FBI safe house."

"But Lieutenant—"

"It's not up for discussion, Detective." He looked past them toward his closed door, then back at her. "I've got orders too."

She shook her head, amazed by their decision. "So they'd rather she leave town—and take our rapist with her—than chance having something happen to her here. They don't care if something happens to her on her way back home…or in LA."

"It's not my call, Harper."

"So why not tell her to leave now? Why give her the week?" Reid asked.

"Because they want to save face," Harper answered, knowing it was the truth. "We're trying to find the guy. We're at least keeping her safe. Not our fault that she has to leave. Not on our conscience if something happens to her outside of our jurisdiction," she said sarcastically. "Shame that poor woman got raped and all, but I guess we're not going to solve that one."

"Look, I know this seems like we're bailing on this, but we're not. What other choice do we have?"

"We do like I wanted to in the first place. Make her accessible to him."

"And what if he grabs her? Kills her, for God's sake? Then what? Are you going to stand up to the national media and explain how we used her as bait?" he asked loudly.

"He doesn't want to kill her. At least, not yet."

"You don't know that, Harper." He waved his hand in the air, signaling an end to the discussion. "It doesn't matter anyway. It's done. You're in the safe house. We'll have two units posted along the street. It's an older neighborhood, quiet. Not much traffic."

"And what am I supposed to tell her?"

"What is there to tell her? We're trying to keep her safe, that's all."

CHAPTER SEVENTEEN

Dani blinked stupidly at her. "A safe house?"

"Yes."

She was a little surprised that Harper didn't seem thrilled by it. "But that's good, right? I'll be safe?"

"I'll stay with you, of course."

Ah. That's why she wasn't thrilled. She'd still be on babysitting duty. "I'm sorry, Harper."

Harper frowned. "Why are you sorry?"

Dani waved a hand at her. "Well, obviously you have more important things to do than to babysit me."

Harper smiled and shook her head. "That's not it at all."

"Then what is it?" At Harper's hesitation, she tilted her head questioningly. "What is it you're not telling me?"

Harper glanced over her shoulder, toward Lieutenant Mize's office. "We'll go over it later," she said quietly. "We'll go ahead and take all of your things this time. It looks like we'll be there for the duration."

Dani frowned slightly. "The duration of what?"

Harper met her gaze for a second, then looked away quickly. "Of your stay. The duration of your stay."

"I see." And of course she did. That's what had Harper looking so miffed. Not the fact that she'd be babysitting...but the fact that they were keeping her safe—until they weren't. "The duration of my stay...until I leave town."

Harper sighed. "Yes."

"Well, I don't know what I expected. I know you've already gone above and beyond the call of duty." She folded her arms around herself in a false sense of security. "You're involved in this by default only. I'm sorry."

Harper closed her desk drawer a bit more forcefully than necessary. "Quit saying that. I'm a cop. It's my job." She walked over and picked up two of Dani's bags. "Let's get out of here."

Dani grabbed the remaining two bags and followed her. "What about Detective Springer?"

"He's doing a second interview with the victim from yesterday."

* * *

Harper had no clue if this safe house was stocked with anything. If they were going to be there for several days, it wasn't like they could call room service for meals. She wasn't exactly thrilled with the idea of stopping at a grocery store for supplies. For one, she wasn't really a very good cook. Besides, taking Dani into a store would most likely cause some commotion. Ordering delivery wasn't an option either. She supposed she could get one of the patrol units to pick something up for them each day.

"What's wrong? You're frowning."

She shook her head. "Nothing. Thinking about food."

"Huh?"

"As in, what are we going to eat?" She looked in her rearview mirror, then made a sharp, quick turn to the right before speeding up. No one appeared to be following.

"Ah. In the movies, they always seem to have pizza boxes or Chinese food or something," Dani said.

"Can't allow a delivery to a safe house. I was thinking maybe we could have someone pick meals up for us. We'll have two patrol units assigned." She could feel Dani studying her.

"You're having second thoughts, aren't you?"

"About?"

"About sending me away when you had the chance."

Harper glanced at her and smiled. "Are you kidding? Being toyed with by a stalker is so much fun. Can't wait until we catch the bastard."

"Only they don't really want to catch him, do they?"

Harper sighed. Had she really thought Dani wouldn't see through this so-called plan of theirs? "The number one priority is keeping you safe."

"You mean until I leave here."

"I don't agree with their decision, Dani. They want to make sure nothing happens to you while you're on our watch."

"They don't want any bad press."

"Exactly."

"But he raped somebody," Dani said quietly. "Doesn't that change the game?"

"Springer and Hernandez are working it." She turned at the light, heading into a residential neighborhood. "Without DNA evidence, there's not much of a case." She shrugged. "Clown makeup and white gloves. Not much to go on."

Dani shifted in her seat. "Do you think—if I had stayed home—that he would have escalated it this far?"

"What are you asking? Do I think he would have raped you?"

Dani nodded.

"I don't know. Did his plans change once you got here? Did they change because we found his tracking device? There's no way to know, Dani."

"If he can't find me now, do you think he'll leave? Maybe go back and wait for me at home?"

Harper glanced at her GPS on her phone, then turned left. Yeah, that's exactly what Lieutenant Mize and the others were hoping. Keep Danielle Stevens out of sight, hoping the guy gives up the chase. At least in Dallas. And maybe it wasn't such a bad plan. In a city this size, if the stalker has no way of knowing where she was or when she'd be leaving, then sure, maybe he leaves. So when Dani headed back, he wouldn't be following her. No, he'd already be back in LA. Waiting for her.

"Before you go to your house, you need to call the police there. Tell them he followed you to Dallas. Then you need to hire a bodyguard."

Dani let out a frustrated breath. "I know. And won't that be fun."

Harper watched as the neighborhood changed. Older homes, large, mature trees, big lots. And very little traffic. She glanced again at her phone. She was three blocks away. As she turned down the street, a patrol unit was parked on the corner. She glanced at them as she passed and the two officers gave a subtle nod at her, acknowledging her.

She pulled into the driveway, then drove around the back where the garage was. Her car would be hidden from the street.

"Home sweet home," she murmured. When Dani would have opened the door, she stopped her with a light touch on her arm. "Let me take a look inside first."

"I'm not crazy about staying out here by myself."

"I'll be quick."

When she closed her door, she saw Dani reach across the seat and lock it. She couldn't blame her for being scared. She'd been fighting this stalker for months. She used the key Lieutenant Mize had given her and pushed the door open. The house had a stale, closed-up smell about it. It was dark and quiet inside and she reached to the wall and flicked on the light in the kitchen. It was clean. In fact, nearly spotless. So was the living room, although it was sparsely furnished. There were two bedrooms. Three, really, but only two rooms had beds. The third room was completely empty. She flipped on lights as she went, seeing nothing out of the ordinary.

She went back outside, finding Dani's eyes glued to the door. She nodded at her, indicating she could get out of the car.

She slung her backpack over her shoulder—the pack that she kept in her locker—and picked up two of Dani's bags. She let Dani precede her into the house.

"Clean."

"Surprisingly, yes."

Dani paused in the hallway. "Which bedroom will we use?"

"There are two. Pick which one you want."

Dani met her gaze. "I want whichever one you're going to be in."

"Ah. You want to share."

"Yes. If you don't mind." Then Dani smiled apologetically. "I'm sorry, but I'm—"

"No problem. I don't mind." She laughed quietly. "Can't wait to tell Reid, of course."

Dani went into the larger of the two rooms and placed her bags on the floor against the wall. "What would his reaction be if he found out I was gay?"

"Shock, disbelief. Disappointment. Probably the same as every other guy." She paused. "Why? You want to tell him?"

"God, no. It was hard enough telling you."

Harper shrugged. "You are who you are, Dani. It shouldn't be hard to tell the truth. It seems like it would be easier than living a lie."

"Says the woman who's never been in the closet."

"Yeah, well look at me. I don't think trying to be in the closet would help me."

"Oh, please. You're not *that* gay."

Harper laughed. "Trust me. I'm that gay."

"You were young when you knew, right?"

"Yes."

Dani nodded. "I think that makes a difference. I just assumed I was straight, you know. And when I wasn't, well, I wasn't prepared for it. Hiding seemed to be my only option. Hiding and…and pretending that I wasn't gay. Even to myself, I could hardly dare admit it."

"Until college?"

Dani nodded. "You must think I'm crazy. I mean, in this day and age, still trying to hide it. What's the big deal, right?"

Harper shrugged. "It's your life. I'm not judging."

Dani took a deep breath. "It's scary. For me. To think about being out...open with people. Terrifying, really."

Harper didn't have any advice for her. She didn't know the first thing about hiding or being in the closet. Not with family. Not with friends. And not with co-workers.

CHAPTER EIGHTEEN

"I'm bored."

Dani smiled as that was the third time Harper had made that statement. "I'm starving," she countered.

Harper tossed her the remote. "Yeah. Let's get something. I bet we could get a pizza delivered to the patrol car at end of the block." She paused. "Of course, we just had pizza the other night."

"I don't care. I'll eat anything."

The kitchen had proven to be void of any food items. The fridge did contain four water bottles, so that was a plus. There were two frozen burritos in the freezer, but both were six months expired. Even so, they'd debated whether to eat them or not. She flipped through the channels, absently listening to Harper on the phone—first to one of the cops keeping an eye on their street, then to a pizza place. She turned, chancing a quick glance at Harper. Cute. Attractive. Gay. And even though Dani had confessed to her that she was also gay, Harper had not made even one inappropriate comment or innuendo. In fact, she'd been pretty much all business, all the time.

Which, of course, Dani was thankful for. She was used to fighting off the attention of men. She had absolutely no experience in fending off unwanted attention from women. Of course, she was being presumptuous in thinking that Harper was that kind of woman anyway. She'd given no indication that she found Dani even slightly attractive. Which was a bit disconcerting, she admitted. Here, she finally admitted to someone that she was gay—another lesbian—and that woman apparently could not care less.

She sighed. She was thankful, really. She had no experience with this sort of thing, anyway. And now certainly wasn't the time to be experimenting with it. Harper Jeremiah was attractive, yes. She admitted it was one reason she'd picked her to begin with. The eyes, of course…those serious, trusting eyes…that's what drew her in the first place, but seeing the whole package—the face, the lips, and yes, the eyes—gave her no choice. She hadn't even bothered looking through the rest of the profiles that had been sent to her.

"You're frowning."

Dani looked up. "Am I?"

Harper smiled reassuringly at her. "I won't let anything happen to you. I promise."

Dani smiled too. "No, I don't believe you will." Her smile faded almost immediately. Of course, once she left Dallas, Harper wouldn't be around to protect her any longer. She'd be on her own. Well, she and the bodyguard she was going to be forced to hire.

"So I got two pizzas and some hot wings. And a giant cookie."

Dani laughed. "Starving, huh?"

"Yeah. Pizza for breakfast is pretty good too."

Dani tossed the remote down, not interested in anything on TV. "FBI safe house. What do they eat?"

"I imagine when they use it, it's not on the spur of the moment." Harper sat down beside her. "I guess we should have taken the time to go by a grocery store. Could have gotten some frozen dinners or something."

"Or something. I'm a very good cook, in case you were wondering."

"Oh, yeah?"

Dani nodded. "When I was young, my grandmother lived with us. Both of my parents worked so she tended to the evening meals. When I got home from school, that was my chore…to help with dinner."

She touched the necklace at her neck, absently pulling the locket from under her shirt. Her grandmother had given it to her on the day she died. Her grandfather—a man Dani never knew—had used it in lieu of a ring. The black-and-white picture inside was faded and tattered—her grandmother's wedding day. She didn't recall a time that her grandmother hadn't worn the necklace. When she'd taken it off that morning and given it to her, Dani had been confused. She'd had no idea that she'd been sick, had no idea that she was dying. She let the locket slip from her fingers and she glanced over at Harper, who was watching her.

"This was hers," she said, holding her hand over the locket for a second before tucking it back inside her shirt. "I was fifteen when she died. We were very close. I think if she'd been alive when…well, when I realized I was gay—which was that very next summer—I think I could have talked to her about it." She touched the locket again. "She was my rock. My best friend, really. I often wonder how differently my life would have turned out if she had lived longer."

"Meaning you may not have escaped to California?"

"Escaped. Funny word, isn't it?" She leaned back. "I simply went from one prison to another." She held her hand up. "And you don't have to say it. A prison of my own making, I know."

"What's the real reason you're in the closet?"

Dani frowned. "The real reason? You think there's some underlying issues that I have?"

"I guess most people, especially when they're young, have a fear of rejection. You said your family was very conservative. Is that the main reason? Fear that they would reject who you are?"

Dani pictured her parents—her father's stern face, her mother's disapproving stare. There were rarely any smiles. "Fear of disappointing them," she finally said. "I wanted to be a cheerleader. I was pretty and popular and my friends were all the cool kids. So I wanted to be a cheerleader."

"They didn't want you to?"

"No. My parents were older. My mother was forty-three when I was born, my father almost fifty. They were extremely protective. I wasn't allowed to date until I was sixteen." She gave a quick smile. "Well, he said seventeen, but I eventually talked him down to sixteen. My mother, though, she thought that if I was a cheerleader, then I'd have to fight off the boys. She was terrified I was going to lose my virginity before my wedding night. Terrified that I would get pregnant." She paused. "They... they hated the way I looked."

"They hated that you were attractive?"

Dani nodded. "They didn't quite know what to do with it."

"So? You said you were a cheerleader, right?"

"Yes. And they were both very disappointed in my decision. They never came to any games. My grandmother was still alive and she gave me the money I needed. After she died, well, I quit. My parents were then very happy."

"But you were not."

"No. When college came around, since I was no longer dating the football player and there was no marriage proposal on the horizon, they did pay for that. The university is in Knoxville and thankfully, they allowed me to live in the dorm."

Harper smiled. "Where you finally gave in to your primal desires," she teased.

Dani laughed. "Yes. And after that first year, I found the courage to stand up to my parents and leave." She tried to hold on to her smile. "They were very disappointed in me. Again."

"So you still have this chasm between you?"

"Yes. They won't admit it, but they read the tabloids. I'm sleeping around, I didn't save myself for marriage, I'm not a very good girl." She waved her hand in the air. "They believe it all."

"If there's this divide between you anyway, why don't you just tell them you're gay and get it over with? What do you have to lose?"

"Nothing. I have nothing to lose with them. My decision to stay in the closet has everything to do with my career at this point. Once I'm out of the movie business...does it matter? Is it anyone's business...my personal life? Should I feel compelled to make some big statement announcing that I'm gay?"

Harper shrugged. "It might be a relief to say it out loud. To admit it."

"To not hide it anymore, you mean? From anyone?"

"I'm sure it would be...freeing. Emotionally, at least."

Dani nodded. "I'm sure it would be. I'm just not certain that I have the courage to say it out loud. And I know how pathetic that makes me seem."

"Dani, it's your life. You are who you are. You can't pretend to be something you're not, just to please other people, especially your parents. They have their own life...you have yours," she said matter-of-factly.

"You make it sound so easy."

"It is easy. Whatever you've conjured up in your mind as to what would happen if they knew...it's probably way worse than reality."

Dani smiled. "You obviously don't know my parents. They're old, old school."

Harper stood up. "From what you've told me, your parents aren't a part of your life anyway. What does it matter?"

"It matters because they're all I have."

Harper stared at her. "You don't have a relationship with them, Dani. How can you say they're all you have?"

That statement hit home and almost brought tears to her eyes. No, she didn't have a relationship with them. Nor with her sister. She didn't have any friends. She had no one. She had her "people," that was all. There was simply...no one.

"I'm sorry," Harper said. "I can't really relate to your situation, so I have no right to criticize it or offer you suggestions. I'm sorry."

Dani waved her apology away. "It's okay. I'm used to being alone."

Harper sat down again. "But why, Dani? You're a beautiful woman. Why are you alone? Why are you content with that?"

"I'm not content. I'm...I'm lonely." Dani tilted her head, turning the tables on Harper. "Why are *you* alone?"

Harper clenched her jaw. "Totally unrelated subject." She stood up quickly. "I'm going to check on our pizza."

Obviously, Harper had no intention of discussing her own personal life, despite the many questions she had for Dani. She watched her open the front door, pushing down the panic she felt at the prospect of being alone in the house. Harper stepped out, then turned, glancing over her shoulder.

"Lock the door behind me. I'll be right back."

Dani hurried to the door, doing as instructed as soon as the door closed. She turned her back to the door and leaned against it. She'd hidden her sexuality for so many years, it was strange to be talking about it now, as she and Harper had been doing. And strange, too, that Harper was so guarded about her own personal life. Why *was* she alone? If she had to take a guess, she would assume it was something tragic. Harper's eyes told her that.

She pushed off from the door, then literally jumped when her phone rang. She hadn't even given it much thought the last few days. There were only a handful of people who knew her number and those in her inner circle knew not to call unless it was an emergency. She went to her bag and pulled out her phone, relieved to see that it was Shelly.

"Hey...what's up?" she asked as nonchalantly as she could.

"I was just checking on you," Shelly said. "Everything okay?"

"Fine," she lied. "I've been given VIP treatment here."

"Well, I would hope so. I wanted to let you know that Pamela lined up an interview with *People* for when you get back. And they're still clamoring for you to do one of the late night shows."

Dani blew out her breath. "Put *People* off. We'll schedule something later."

"But Danielle, Pamela said—"

"I don't care what she said. Don't schedule anything without clearing it with me first." She squeezed the bridge of her nose tightly. "We'll talk when I get back. This trip is kinda like a vacation so…let's hold off on anything until I get home, okay?" She heard Shelly sigh, but there was no protest.

"Okay. As you wish. I'll pass it on to Pamela, but you know she dismisses most of what I say."

"Then be firm with her. She's not the boss, Shelly. I am."

She put the phone back in her bag, contemplating turning it off altogether. Despite her instructions that no one was to call her, she knew that Shelly would be the one to break. And of course, she was glad she did. Pamela tended to go a bit overboard whenever Dani wasn't there to rein her in. She picked the phone up again, then flipped it in her hands several times. Without much thought, she held the button in, watching as it powered off. It was something that she should have done days ago. This trip *was* like a vacation to her. Well, except for the creepy clown guy. And the police protection she was getting. That part wasn't so bad.

"God…you really are pathetic," she murmured with a smile.

CHAPTER NINETEEN

Dani pulled the covers up to her neck, pausing to listen to the light rain that was falling. She felt Harper shift beside her. Their dinner had been eaten in relative silence and even afterward, Harper had remained quiet...distant. Dani turned her head, seeing Harper's face in the shadows. They'd left the light on in the bathroom.

"Does this make you uncomfortable?" she asked quietly. "Sharing a bed."

Harper turned toward her too. "No. Should it?"

Dani should just keep her questions to herself. Harper was beyond reluctant to talk about herself. But...

"When's the last time someone's shared your bed?" She heard Harper laugh lightly, but she sensed it was forced.

"You want to know when's the last time I had sex or what?"

Dani rolled to her side. "Okay. Yes."

"Why?"

"You're attractive. You're nice. Most of the time," she added. "Yet you don't have anyone in your life. You appear to be single. Alone." She paused. "Your eyes tell me you've been hurt."

Harper's sigh was so quiet, Dani almost missed it.

"It's been...three years, four months...and a handful of days."

"What was her name?" she whispered.

Harper turned her head to look at her. "Jan."

"Is it...is it something you want to talk about?"

Another sigh and Dani assumed that was her answer. She was surprised when Harper spoke.

"There was a...a serial killer...and rapist...in Tucson. That's where I came from," Harper said. "They called him the Raggedy Ann Killer. He left a doll at each scene."

"Oh, my God," she whispered.

"There were...eight victims. I worked the case. We never got close to him. Jan...Jan was his last victim. At our house...in our bedroom."

"Harper...I'm so sorry." She moved her hand under the covers, finding Harper's. She squeezed her fingers tightly.

"The victims were all random. Except for Jan. He picked her. Because of me." Harper turned her head. "He left a note. Said his thirst had been quenched...for now. She was the last one. I guess he moved on."

"Oh, Harper. I don't know what to say."

"There's nothing to say." Harper turned away again, staring at the ceiling. "I couldn't stay there, so I transferred here about five months after it happened."

"Do they know? Does Reid know?"

"No. I haven't told anyone." Harper gave her fingers a final squeeze, then pulled her hand away, rolling over to her side, her back to Dani.

Dani wasn't really shocked by her confession. She had sensed it somehow...the heartbreak that Harper had suffered. It was the doll. Not so much the first one at the hotel, but the one left at Detective Springer's apartment. There had been a look in Harper's eyes that hinted at something buried deep inside... something that was being called to the surface. Not a Raggedy Ann doll, no, but still...leaving dolls behind as a calling card, she imagined that conjured up all sorts of terrible memories for Harper.

Dani rolled to her side, facing Harper's back. No, she didn't know what to say. It made more sense now, though. Harper was still grieving. She was an attractive, single woman still grieving. She had no lover. And if Dani had to guess, she'd say that Harper had no friends either. She'd probably left Tucson—and her friends and family—with the intention of starting over. However, Harper couldn't leave her memories behind. Those followed her here. And three years, four months and a handful of days later…those memories still haunted her.

She let out a quiet, weary breath and closed her eyes, very sorry that she'd brought her own troubles with her to Dallas… and to Harper.

CHAPTER TWENTY

The breaking of glass had Harper sitting up in bed, wide awake.

"What was that?" Dani asked beside her.

"Stay here."

Dani sat up. "Was that a window?"

"Sounded like it." Harper pulled on her jeans, then watched as Dani got out of bed, picking up her jeans as well. "I'll check it out. You stay here."

"The hell I will."

Harper grabbed her gun and her phone, then paused at the bedroom door, listening. All was quiet. She turned to Dani. "Stay close to me."

"Like glue," Dani murmured.

She used the flashlight on her phone, shining it down the dark hallway. Dani's hand was clutching her T-shirt from behind and she could almost feel the fear emanating off her. She heard nothing out of the ordinary and her gut told her there wasn't anyone in the house, yet she used caution as she crept down the hallway and into the living room. She found the offending window—the curtain was moving from the breeze. Dani brought her attention to the floor.

"A baseball."

Harper flipped on the lights, making sure there was nothing else disturbed other than the broken window. She kicked the ball with her foot, seeing a smiley face drawn on its white surface.

"So he found us again," Dani stated.

"Looks that way." She called Fender, the officer parked at the corner. It was four. Shift change wasn't until six. "Yeah, hey…it's Detective Jeremiah."

"Yes, ma'am. Is everything okay?"

"No. We had a baseball thrown through one of the front windows. You got any activity?"

"No, ma'am. It's been quiet. Haven't seen a thing."

"Okay. Go ahead and come up to the house, park in the driveway. I'll let you take the ball back to the lab when you get relieved."

"Be right there."

She turned to Dani. "He didn't see anyone."

"I know we keep asking this same question…but how did he find us?"

"If I didn't know that this guy followed you to Dallas, I'd suspect we had a leak in the department, like you suggested." She studied Dani. "Let's do a body scan."

"Excuse me? I mean…it sounds kinda fun, but…"

Harper smiled and shook her head. "We've checked your luggage, your clothes. Let's do a body scan. When we first checked for bugs, they didn't scan the clothes you were wearing. Shoes. Watch."

"Okay. So you still think he's tracking us."

"He's either been given the information, or yes, he's tracking us."

* * *

"A body scan?"

"Yes. They're doing it now."

Reid leaned closer. "And…you slept in the same bed?"

Harper smiled. "We did. She likes to snuggle."

"Oh, my God! Say she didn't."

Harper winked. "I don't think she knows that she likes to snuggle."

"Damn…you lucky dog. I still can't believe you got this assignment."

Lieutenant Mize walked over to them, motioning with his head for them to follow him. He closed the door to his office, then stood at his desk, facing them.

"A baseball, huh? Are we sure it was him?"

"No way of knowing for sure," Harper said. "There was smiley face drawn on it, like the balloons had."

"Could it have been a neighborhood kid?"

"At four in the morning? I suppose it could have been, but you indicated it was a quiet, older neighborhood…retired folks, mostly."

"Yeah, that's what I was told." He turned to Reid. "You interviewed the victim again. Anything new?"

"Actually, yes. He wore white gloves, but she said she saw a tattoo on his wrist. Partial, anyway, where the glove slid up. It was red. She said it looked like an arrow. Had a feather."

"Like a bow and arrow? Cowboys and Indians?"

"Yeah, I guess." Reid shrugged. "Other than that, no, nothing new. But she's holding up pretty good."

"She'll make a good witness then," Mize said. "Provided we could find him, which looks doubtful." He turned back to her. "This safe house is out, obviously. I've requested another one."

"So we're just going to keep moving around, hoping we lose him one of these times?"

"It would help if we knew how he was finding you in the first place. And no, there's no leak here, Harper. There aren't enough people in the loop. Even the safe house, no one knew who we were keeping there, not even the patrol officers."

"It's no secret that Danielle Stevens is here and is supposed to be shadowing me. I'm fairly certain everyone knows who's in the safe house with me."

"It's rumors, nothing more. Now what? You're scanning her stuff again, looking for a bug?"

"Yeah. Full body scan."

"Yeah, I heard. I'm sure you just made their day down there."

"What if they don't find anything?" Reid asked. "Then what? Maybe it *is* a leak."

"There's no goddamn leak," Mize said quickly. "How would he have a contact in the police department anyway? He followed her here from Los Angeles. However the hell he's finding her, it's not because of a leak," he insisted.

While Harper tended to agree with him, she thought they should at least keep the possibility open. Unless, of course, the body scan produced something.

He walked around his desk and sat down. "Now…four more days. That's all we have to worry about. Surely you can elude this guy for four days, Harper."

"That's right. Four more days. Then we send her on her merry way," she said sarcastically.

"Well, since he seems to keep finding you, maybe you'll get the opportunity to catch him. Just make sure nothing happens to Ms. Stevens in the process. We want her alive and well when she leaves Dallas. And the sooner, the better." He handed her a piece of paper. "That's the address. We'll put a unit on the street, right out front. You won't see him tonight."

"Thanks," she said dryly, wondering if even that would keep him away.

"What about me?" Reid asked.

"I think you and Hernandez have a serial rapist you're working on, right?"

CHAPTER TWENTY-ONE

"So you didn't tell me how much fun the body scan would be," Dani teased.

Harper raised her eyebrows. "How so?"

"Patti Jennings. She was quite thorough."

Harper laughed. "You're very bad, Ms. Stevens." Then she winked. "Maybe I should have done one too."

Dani laughed, but she sobered quickly. "But they found nothing, huh?"

"No. However he's finding us, it's not because of a tracking device." Harper surprised her by turning into a grocery store parking lot. "So we don't have a repeat of last night," she explained.

"You're going to let me go shopping with you, right?"

Harper reached into the backseat and brought out a dark blue baseball cap with DPD emblazoned on the front. "Sunglasses?"

"I have some, yes."

"Don't look at anyone, don't smile. If you have to talk, use your Tennessee twang."

She pulled her hair into a ponytail and secured it through the back of the cap, then turned to Harper and smiled. "How's this?" she asked as she shoved sunglasses on.

"Don't smile. You're too pretty when you smile. And that cap can't hide it."

Try as she may, Dani couldn't keep the grin from her face. Too pretty, huh? "Okay, I'll try not to smile." She made a face, giving a sideway, crooked grin and widening her eyes dramatically. "How's that?"

Harper laughed. "Okay, that'll work."

"What are we shopping for? Will I get to cook?"

"I was thinking frozen dinners or something. Simple stuff."

Dani got out and followed her to the door. "What did you do with the leftover pizza?"

"Gave it to Reid." Harper held the door open for her. "But if you were going to cook something simple, that didn't require a lot of stuff, what would it be?"

Dani paused. "What are you in the mood for?"

Harper grinned. "Mexican food."

"Okay…so no. What else?"

"A good steak. Medium rare. Baked potato. Vegetable is optional."

Dani laughed. "So we're buying frozen dinners, I guess."

"What about Hamburger Helper or something?"

"Gross. Really?"

"I've always been kinda fond of casseroles."

"I grew up on casseroles," she said as she pushed the cart down an aisle. "My grandmother had three or four that she rotated."

"So let's do a mini-casserole then. Pasta, cheese…some creamy stuff."

"I guess we could do something. A pseudo stroganoff maybe. That wouldn't be too hard."

Harper nodded. "I'll even help. I'm a great chopper."

They got everything she needed to make a dish that at least resembled beef stroganoff, although she doubted once she added the shredded cheese—Harper's insistence—that anyone would dare call it stroganoff. To be safe, Harper had also picked up a few frozen dinners…just in case. They also got a couple of frozen breakfast burritos and a bottle of orange juice.

When they got to the checkout, Dani offered to pay, handing over a credit card. Harper glanced at it and shook her head.

"Probably not a good idea."

"Oh." She saw her name—Danielle Stevens—stamped across the front. "Sorry. I forgot."

"Forgot you're a big star?"

Dani smiled. "Yes. And I like it very much. But I have another card. In my real name."

"That's okay. I got it."

Harper leaned closer as she carried their bags out. "So are you really like…a big shot?"

"I wouldn't go that far. I only have four movies. And I'm rather reluctant to give interviews. I hate doing the talk show circuit." She shrugged. "Again, I'm not a very good celebrity."

"You're obviously good enough to warrant a stalker."

"Or bad enough." She got in beside Harper and closed the car door. "I'm being honest here. I'm not all that good. As an actress, I mean. It's totally based on my looks and I don't pretend that it's any other reason. And if I was really into this whole lifestyle, then yes, I could milk it for years, I'd guess. But I'm not into it. At all."

"Which is why you want to do the drunk cop movie."

"Exactly. I'll be exposed. It'll be a damn good reason to get out."

"That's got to be disappointing, though…going out on a low note."

Dani shook her head. "Not for me. Maybe disappointing for Danielle Stevens but not for Dani Strauss."

"What about going back to Tennessee and trying to reconnect with your family? Is that in the cards?"

"I don't know." She turned to look at Harper as she drove. "You mean going back as their lesbian daughter?"

Harper smiled. "Yeah…the real you."

"I would imagine they'd prefer I stay away if that was the case. What about your family? Since you left Tucson, do you still have a relationship with them?"

"We talk on the phone some. Not a lot." Harper glanced at her quickly. "They didn't like me being a cop to begin with. The thing with Jan...well, they blamed me. So did her parents."

"Did you blame you?"

Harper nodded. "Yes."

"Still?"

"Still."

* * *

"This place is certainly nicer than the other one," Harper said as she inspected the master bath. "Wonder how long it'll take him to find us?"

"Well, he certainly wasn't tailing us. You made me dizzy with all the turns you made."

Harper followed her into the kitchen. "Yeah, I almost got lost myself." She caught the onion that was about to roll off the counter. "I'm a great onion chopper. But let me check in with the unit out front. I'll be right back."

"Okay."

The patrol car was parked across the street from the house. She jogged over to them, smiling at Ja'wan Freeman as he lowered his window.

"Hey, man. You've got an easy job tonight."

"Detective Jeremiah...good to see you," he said with a quick handshake. "Bill Ford, this here is Harper Jeremiah."

Harper looked past him to his partner and nodded. "Ford.... yeah, I've seen you around."

"You got Danielle Stevens in there?" Ja'wan asked with arched eyebrows. "Got all kinds of rumors swirling around."

"Like what?"

"Like she's linked to that rape the other night. The case Springer caught."

Well, so much for Mize thinking there wasn't much speculating going on. She didn't see the point in lying to them. "Yeah, she's in there. She's got some guy stalking her. He keeps finding us."

"Yeah, I heard about the baseball last night. We'll keep a good eye on the place, Detective. You won't have a disturbance tonight. Not on my watch."

"I hope not." She tapped the side of his car. "Thanks for having my back."

"Sure thing, Harper."

Ja'wan Freeman was one of the first officers she'd met when she'd transferred to Dallas. He'd worked the scene of her very first assault victim—a scene that brought back all sorts of nightmares—and for some reason, he'd taken a liking to her. He was big and black and brawny and she admitted she was a little intimidated by him. But it was as if he'd sensed the war going on inside of her. He'd stuck by her all night, helping with the questions, prompting her when she'd stumbled over some of them. Afterward, they'd gone out for drinks when his shift had ended. He hadn't asked any questions and she never felt the need to explain, but they'd bonded over drinks. They hadn't seen each other socially since that night, but whenever she saw him—like now—he was friendly with her, more so than he might have been with other detectives. She always tried to give him the same respect that he showed her.

She turned back around, finding him watching her. She gave him a quick nod, wondering if he was remembering that night too.

She went back inside the house, locking the door behind her. She heard Dani call from the kitchen.

"Harper? That's you, right?"

She smiled. "It's me."

"Good. Come chop the onion. I'm ready for it."

The kitchen smelled divine and she inspected the pans on the stove before going to the cutting board and the onion.

"Toss it in the pan. Then add the mushrooms."

"So you sliced the mushrooms but not the onions?"

Dani laughed. "Mushrooms don't make me cry."

Harper made quick work of the onion, a task that brought back pleasant memories. Jan was quite the cook, but she hated chopping veggies. She always teased Harper, calling her the sous-chef as Harper peeled and chopped whatever Jan needed. She paused a second before adding the onions to the pan with olive oil, realizing that this was the very first time she'd participated in cooking dinner since Jan had died.

"You okay?" Dani asked quietly.

Harper nodded. "Yeah. I used to...I used to do this a lot."

"For Jan?"

"Yes. She didn't like crying over onions either." Harper held her hand up. "And don't say you're sorry. It's a...it's a nice memory." She put the knife down. "Too often when I think of Jan, I think of that night...of how we found her." She swallowed, pushing those images away. "I don't think of the good times nearly enough."

"How long were you together?"

"Six years. We'd met a couple of years before that, but we were both dating other people." She pushed away from the counter. "I was on patrol when we first got together. I made detective...a couple of years before, well, before the..." Before the what? The rape? The murder?

"Harper?"

She turned, meeting Dani's eyes.

"Can I...can I hug you?" Dani asked quietly.

"You think I need one?"

"Yes. I just don't know if you want one." Dani moved closer. "Do you ever allow yourself to be comforted?"

"No. That might push my guilt away. Guilt is all I have to hold on to."

"Guilt is an awful thing to hold on to. Memories—love, laughter—that's so much better than guilt."

Harper tilted her head. "You don't speak from experience."

"No. I speak from wishing. Wishing I had love and laughter in my life." Dani took another step closer, not asking this time as she wrapped her arms around Harper and pulled her close.

Harper gave in to the hug, closing her eyes as their bodies made contact. It had been so very long since she'd been this close to another woman. Jan's memory was still fresh in her mind, but she knew it was Dani whose arms were wrapped around her.

It felt nice.

CHAPTER TWENTY-TWO

Dani had to admit—even though it only vaguely resembled stroganoff—that it was a delicious dinner. Judging by Harper's moan, she agreed.

"Adding cheese to this dish was sinful."

"Adding cheese to this dish was a good idea," Harper countered. "My idea. Good idea."

"A bottle of red wine…something with just a touch of sweetness would go good with this," Dani mused.

"I could go for that." Harper smiled. "I could go for a beer. Or some of your Tennessee whiskey."

"Actually, I could go for a beer too." She put her fork down. "My parents didn't drink a drop of alcohol. So when I got to college, I experimented. A lot. I was warned that beer was an acquired taste." She laughed. "Well, I was also told good wine was as well, but we couldn't afford good wine."

"But beer?"

"Yes. I like beer. When I worked at the real estate place, we used to go out to local microbreweries quite a bit. I enjoyed that. There's so many unique beers out there."

"I would pick you for a light beer kind of gal."

"You'd be wrong," she said as she took another bite of the pseudo stroganoff.

Harper paused, lightly tapping her plate with her fork. "Listen, about earlier."

Dani raised her eyebrows. "Earlier?"

"You…me…the hug."

"Oh. Are hugs not allowed?"

"No. I mean, no, that's not it, however…hugs probably aren't allowed." Harper put her fork down. "What I mean is, I don't talk about Jan. Ever. To anyone." She picked her fork up again, stirring the food on her plate. "I don't know why, really. Reid…he's the closest thing I have to a friend here and I've never mentioned her."

"And you're questioning why you've told me about her?"

"Yeah."

Dani folded her hands together, wondering what Harper was thinking. "Did it feel good to talk about her?"

Harper nodded. "I feel responsible for her death. I carry that with me. But I also feel…cheated. Cheated out of love. Cheated out of a life with her. We were happy. We had a good relationship. So I carry this guilt with me—because she's dead—yet I still have a sense of selfishness. I feel sorry for myself for what I've lost."

"From what you've said, you not only lost her, but you lost your family, her family. You left friends behind." Dani waited until Harper met her eyes. "You don't have any friends, do you?"

"No. I don't have anyone."

Dani reached across the table and covered Harper's hand with her own. "We're kinda in the same boat for completely different reasons," she said quietly. "I'll be your friend, Harper… if you'll be mine."

Harper turned her hand over, letting their fingers entwine. "Thanks. I think I'd like that."

"Me too."

* * *

Harper took her time in the bathroom, trying to give Dani some privacy as she changed clothes for bed. She admitted that the evening had been...well, it had been nice. Dinner was good. She'd even had seconds. They'd cleaned up the kitchen together, then they'd gone into the living room, flipping through channels on the TV before Dani found another cooking show to watch. They'd chatted some but mostly, it was a quiet—but companionable—evening. By ten o'clock, Dani was fighting yawns and Harper had to remind herself that they'd been woken up at four that morning by a baseball thrown through the window.

She'd looked out the window, seeing Ja'wan still parked across the street. It comforted her knowing that he was there. Before going to the back of the house, she checked all the doors and windows, making sure everything was locked. Maybe they'd have a peaceful night for once.

Dani was under the covers, the overhead light already out and the lamp turned on beside the bed.

"I know this is the opposite side of the bed from what we've been doing, but I wasn't crazy about sleeping next to the door."

"This is fine." She didn't think it mattered anyway. Each night, Dani seemed to find her way into the middle of the bed. She had exaggerated a bit with Reid, but yeah, Dani liked to snuggle. So far, it hadn't been anything blatant...only holding Harper's arm in a death grip while she slept. Harper doubted Dani even knew she did it.

"I also have a confession to make," Dani said.

Harper paused as she drew back the covers. "Oh, yeah? Got another bombshell to drop on me?"

Dani laughed. "No, nothing quite as shocking as me being a lesbian."

Harper got in beside her. "Shocking to some, I suppose. I had no preconceived notions about you so it wasn't *that* shocking." She reached out to turn off the lamp. The light from the bathroom cast enough glow into the room for her to still see Dani.

"Oh, come on. You were surprised."

"Okay. A little. But only because you're the most attractive lesbian I've had the pleasure to meet."

Dani smiled at her. "Thank you."

"And your confession?"

"Oh. Well, you seem like the kind of person who likes her personal space."

"I do?"

"Yeah. You kind of keep your distance. You're not a touchy person, at least not that I can tell."

"Okay. I guess."

"Yeah...so I...I kinda got into your space. Last night."

Harper stared at the ceiling, a smile on her face. "Last night, huh?"

"Yes. I woke up and I was...well, I was kinda...well, I was using your arm as a clutch pillow or something."

"And you thought you should confess that to me?"

"In case I did it again, you know. So you wouldn't be shocked."

Harper laughed. "Dani, you've done that every time we've shared a bed. Last night wasn't the first."

"Oh, my God! You *knew*?"

"Of course. I'm a very light sleeper to begin with."

"I'm so sorry. I don't know—"

"It's okay. If it bothered me, I would have said something. Or at the very least, moved away from you." She turned her head to look at Dani. "I know you're scared. I know I'm the only one you trust right now. If you need that reassurance, if you need physical contact like that...I'm okay with it."

"Thank you. You *are* the only one I trust."

"I know. It's okay. I think you're safe here."

Dani sighed. "Until I have to leave. You don't happen to know any good bodyguards, do you?"

"I know this whole situation is...is crazy. The idea that we're protecting you while you're here, only to send you off on your own is ludicrous, in my opinion."

"What would you do differently?"

"I would try to draw him out."

"Use me as bait, like you said?"

"Yes. But it could be a dangerous game, and I know why Lieutenant Mize, the captain, I know why they won't hear of it. There are so many things that could go wrong."

"Then why do you want to do it?"

"Because when you leave here, he's going to follow you. Provided, of course, that he can find you."

"Which he's been able to do so far," Dani said as she rolled toward her. "Use me as bait how?"

"Not try to hide you, for one thing. He's getting bolder. He's obviously showing up, leaving dolls, slashing my tires, throwing baseballs. He's getting close, but he's not trying to come inside. Most likely because he knows I'm here."

"You're not suggesting I stay somewhere alone, are you?"

"No. But somewhere where he would think you're alone." She shook her head. "It doesn't matter now. It's too late for that. We've already tried to hide you. If we reverse course, he'll know."

Dani fidgeted with the covers for a second, then sighed. "Harper? Do you think I should just leave now?"

"Why?"

Dani sighed again, this one almost painfully loud. "I have another confession to make."

"Okay."

"When I picked you...your eyes, I told you that I knew I could trust you just from looking at your picture." Dani turned toward her. "When I came here, I had a sense that he might follow me. And I knew if he did, that you would protect me. It was like, I would bring him down here and you would catch him for me."

"You thought all of that just from looking at my picture?"

"Harper, I don't want to leave here only to take him back with me."

"Oh, Dani...I don't know what I can do. Mize knows what my reservations are about this. That doesn't seem to matter. He's got his orders too."

"Which is to make sure nothing happens to me while I'm on your watch, regardless if you catch him or not."

"Yes."

Dani nodded. "So again…do you know any good bodyguards?" Then she smiled, wiggling her eyebrows teasingly. "Or better yet, are you available?"

Harper laughed. "You mean leave this glamourous job of mine to follow you around? I don't know. What does it pay?"

Dani laughed too. "Oh, honey, I'll pay whatever you want."

CHAPTER TWENTY-THREE

Harper jerked awake, listening. She turned her head slowly, finding Dani next to her, both hands wrapped around Harper's left arm tightly. She listened to her breathing for a moment, then tried to determine what it was that had awoken her. There were no sounds out of the ordinary, but something didn't feel right. Sixth sense perhaps, but she knew something was wrong.

"Dani," she whispered. She moved her arm slightly, nudging her awake. Dani opened her eyes sleepily.

"Hmm?"

"Wake up. I think...I think I heard something."

Dani's eyes popped open. "What is it?"

"Don't know."

She sat up and pulled on her jeans, not bothering with her shoes. Her weapon was beside the bed and she picked it up. She heard Dani dressing too and she knew better than to suggest she wait here in the room alone.

At the door, she held a finger to her lips, indicating to Dani to be quiet, then she slowly opened the door. There was a lamp on in the living room. She frowned. Had she forgotten to turn it off? No. No, she remembered plunging the room into darkness after she'd checked the locks.

She turned to Dani. "I need you to stay here," she whispered. "Don't argue with me."

"But—"

"Stay right here in the hallway where you can see me." She pointed. "Someone's been inside."

"Oh, Jesus." Dani clutched her arm. "He could still be inside," she whispered.

"Yes. Stay here."

Thankfully, Dani didn't argue. She pressed against the door and nodded. "Be careful."

Harper felt her heart pounding in her chest as she crept down the hallway. She nearly gasped when she saw it; a lone balloon—bright red—was tied to the lamp. It bobbed harmlessly overhead, the message mocking her.

Have a Nice Day!

She went to the front door, finding it still locked by a deadbolt. So were the windows. She flipped on the lights, then went into the kitchen. The back door was also locked. With a deadbolt. From the inside.

"What the hell?" she murmured. How had he gotten inside? Then her eyes widened. She'd left Dani in the hallway, but she'd never checked the spare bedroom...the hall closet. The other bathroom.

She turned and nearly ran to the back of the house, relief flooding her when she found Dani standing where she'd left her, her eyes swimming in fear.

Harper once again held a finger to her mouth, then went to the spare bedroom and pushed the door opened. It was dark and quiet. She turned the light on, finding the room undisturbed. She opened the closet door, then paused to look under the bed. The bathroom was also empty. Other than the damn balloon, there was no indication that anyone had been inside.

She blew out her breath, then went back out to Dani.

"All clear."

She took Dani's hand and led her into the living room. Dani gasped when she saw the balloon.

"Oh, my God." She turned to Harper. "He was inside. He was really inside the house." She sat down heavily on the sofa, staring at the balloon. "Just like before. At home. He would come during the night while I was sleeping."

Harper pulled out her phone from her jean's pocket, calling Ja'wan. After four rings, it went to voice mail. "Come on, come on." She called again, as she went to the window and looked out. The street was empty. There was no sign of the patrol car, no sign of Ja'wan and Bill Ford.

"What the hell?" she murmured as she ended the call.

"What is it?"

"Looks like our backup is gone."

"*What?* Why?"

"I have no idea," she said abruptly. She grabbed Dani by the shoulders, holding her in front of her. "We pack our things. We go through the garage. We get in the car and get the hell out of here."

Dani nodded but there was fear in her eyes. "He was inside. What if—"

"He's not inside now." She motioned out the window. "Without backup, I feel like we're sitting ducks. We need to get out of here."

Dani nodded. "Yes. Okay. Yes." Dani took her hand. "But don't leave me."

"I'm not going to leave you. I promise."

It didn't take them long to pack the few things they'd taken out. Harper shoved her clothes haphazardly into her bag without thought. She kept Dani behind her as they went through the kitchen and to the garage door. It, too, was protected by a deadbolt, locked from the inside. Still, she was cautious as she opened the door. The deadbolts hadn't seemed to deter him from entering the house.

Her small flashlight was enough for them to see by and she felt Dani clinging to her back as they stepped into the garage. It was eerily quiet, so quiet she could hear each rapid beat of her heart as she flashed the light around. The garage was empty, as it had been yesterday when she'd parked there. No boxes, no clutter. No place for anyone to hide. She shined the light inside the car, hearing Dani gasp behind her. In the backseat was a doll, dressed in a police uniform. There was a knife stuck in the chest.

"Son of a bitch," she muttered. "He was in here. How the hell did he get in here?"

"Harper...let's get out of here," Dani said urgently beside her.

They ignored the doll as they tossed their bags in the back. She jerked open the overhead garage door, expecting to find someone outside waiting for her, but the driveway was empty. She paused, looking around. The street was dark, quiet. Then a lone dog barked a few houses down, breaking the silence.

She hurried around to the car, getting in and slamming the door. She took off with a squeal of her tires, busting down the dark street at breakneck speed.

CHAPTER TWENTY-FOUR

"I know it's three in the morning!" she said loudly into the phone. "I'm telling you, there was no unit there. Freeman and Ford were *not* out front. They were supposed to stay the night. He got into the house. He left a freakin' balloon for us. And now I've got a goddamn doll dressed in a police uniform—with a knife stuck in its chest—riding with us in the car!"

"Calm down, Detective."

"I am trying to be calm," she said as she turned the corner, seeing headlights behind them. "He's like a damn ghost. The house had deadbolts, Lieutenant. How the hell did he get inside? And who the hell pulled Freeman and Ford?"

Dani tugged at her arm. "I think someone's following us."

"I know." She turned again, taking the corner too fast and missing the curb by inches.

"What?" he asked.

"Someone's tailing us."

"Then go to the station. He won't follow you there."

"We're too far away. And I'm telling you, there's a leak. Someone is feeding him information."

"And I'm telling you that's ridiculous."

She glanced in the mirror, seeing the car behind her slowing. She sped up, then turned again. A few more blocks and she'd hit the freeway.

"Let me call you back," she said.

"Did you lose him?"

"More like he lost us," she said.

"Go to the station, Harper. I'll get there when I can."

"Yeah," she said as she disconnected. "But…no, thanks."

"What is it?" Dani asked.

"He wants us to go in." There was little traffic as she took the ramp onto the freeway. A car or two ahead of her, another coming up from behind, that was it. "I don't think that's a good idea."

"What'll we do?"

"I'm going to call Reid. Have him meet us somewhere. Let him take this damn doll out of here," she said as she glanced over her shoulder, seeing those lifeless eyes staring at her.

"So he quit following us, right?"

"Looks that way." She glanced at her phone, finding Reid's number. It rang a four times before his sleepy voice sounded in her ears.

"Do you know what time it is?"

"I do. Get up. I need you." She heard covers rustling.

"What's wrong?"

"I need you to meet us somewhere. Now, Reid."

"Jesus, Harper, what's going on? I thought you were at a safe house."

"There's an IHOP off Mockingbird Lane. Meet us there."

"Okay, okay. I'm up."

"Thanks." She put her phone in her lap, then looked over at Dani. "You okay?"

"Are you?"

"I don't think I've processed it yet. He was in the house with us. A house with deadbolts that lock from the inside." She shook her head. "If he'd wanted, he could have killed us tonight."

"I'm sorry, Harper."

"It's not your fault, Dani. I'm the one who's supposed to keep you safe," she said, her voice shaky. "And I'm sleeping as if nothing is going on."

"We were supposedly at a safe place. We had two cops sitting on the street in front of the house. Why wouldn't we go to sleep?"

Harper glanced at her. "What is he doing? Is he just fucking with us?"

"It's a game," Dani said. "Since the beginning, that's how I always felt, like he was playing a game with me."

"Yeah. A game that he's definitely winning."

* * *

Dani was too nervous to enjoy the coffee, but she took a sip anyway. Harper sat beside her in the booth. Her eyes were glued to the door and she had yet to pick up her cup. As if feeling her watching, Harper glanced over at her.

"You okay?"

It was the third time Harper had asked that question, and Dani wasn't sure how to answer. It was her fault, of course, that she'd brought this guy to Dallas with her. And yes, it was her fault that an innocent woman had been raped. Now Harper was on the run as well. Her fault too. Harper's expression softened as their eyes met.

"You have guilt written all over your face," Harper said quietly. "For no reason. You're as much a victim as anything."

"But I brought him here."

"No. He followed you here." Harper sighed and finally reached for her coffee cup. "I just don't know what to do about it."

"Do you think we should go in?"

"I don't know. He's getting his information from somewhere." She rubbed her head. "I don't know what to do anymore." She glanced to the door. "There's Reid."

Detective Springer came inside, yawning. There were only three other tables occupied, and he smiled when he spotted them.

"You look an awful lot like Danielle Stevens," he said with a wink. "Do you get that often?" His smile faded when neither she nor Harper returned it. He slid into the booth opposite them. "What's going on?"

"Our guy showed up again."

"At the safe house? No way."

"He got inside. Left a balloon for us. Left another damn doll inside the car." Harper cleared her throat. "The unit out front, it got pulled off. We were there alone, without backup. And he got inside the goddamn house while we were sleeping."

"Jesus Christ," he whispered. "Who pulled the backup?"

"I don't know. I called Mize," Harper said. "He wanted us to come in, but we were being followed. I tried to lose him but... it was more like he gave up the chase. That's when I called you."

"Jesus...Harper, what's going on here?" Detective Springer murmured. "I can't believe he was inside the house."

"I know. There's got to be a leak, Reid. How else could he know where we were? And he's as slippery as a damn ghost. The house had deadbolts, locked from the inside. When I checked everything, all was still secured, yet there was a damn balloon tied to a chair in the living room." Harper leaned on her elbow, running her fingers through her hair several times. "I don't know what to do, Reid. He's escalating everything. Raped a woman, for whatever reason. And while we were sleeping, he was in the goddamn house with us."

Dani could tell how tense Harper was, and she leaned closer, letting her shoulder touch hers. Harper pressed against her too and took a deep breath.

"So what do you want to do?" he asked.

"Mize said to go in. He was on his way."

"But you're afraid to go in?"

"Hell, we don't know who this guy is. The only description we have of him is a creepy clown face. He could walk right into our squad room and we wouldn't know it."

"I still think that's the safest place for you two to be." He leaned closer. "It's like he's playing mind games. The dolls. The balloon. Hell, he was in the house with you. He could have—"

"I know." Harper glanced at her quickly. "I know what he could have done." She took a deep breath. "I guess we have to go in, don't we." Harper conceded.

"That's really your only choice," Detective Springer said with a nod, then he smiled politely at the waitress who brought him a cup of coffee. "Thanks."

"Are you ready to order?" she asked, looking between the three of them.

"Just coffee for now," Harper said dismissively.

"I couldn't possibly eat anything," Dani said. She was having a hard enough time swallowing the coffee. She picked up the cup, absently glancing out the window toward the parking lot. The scream got lodged in her throat as she dropped the cup, spilling coffee across the table. The clown was pressed against the window, his nose smashed on the glass as he peered inside, looking for her.

Harper jumped up, running for the door. Dani was paralyzed with fear as Detective Springer jumped up too.

"What the hell's going on?"

She pointed, her hand shaking. "He was...he was there... looking in."

"The clown?"

Dani nodded. "Yes...the clown."

Their waitress hurried over with a towel and started cleaning up the coffee. "Don't you worry about the mess. I just hope your friend didn't get scalded," she said with a smile. "You probably hear this all the time, but you look just like Danielle Stevens."

Dani smiled back at her, summoning up her best Tennessee twang. "I've heard that before, but she's much prettier than I am."

"Oh, honey, I don't think so. She wears too much makeup. I like the fresh look myself."

"Well, thank you."

"Should I bring you another cup?"

"No, no," Dani said quickly. "We're leaving. But thank you."

Detective Springer pulled out some bills and tossed them on

the table, then he took her elbow and led her toward the door. Harper opened it, then motioned them out.

"No sign of him," Harper said, directing the statement at her.

"I'm not surprised."

"I didn't even see him," Detective Springer said.

"I swear, he's like a goddamn ghost. Come look what he left us."

Tied to the car was a balloon, identical to the one left in the house.

"Have a nice day? Really? I'll give him this, he's got a sense of humor," Detective Springer said.

"Yeah. Same balloon that we found in the house," Harper said.

Dani grabbed Harper's arm and squeezed. "Look," she said, pointing to the car. "The doll is gone."

Harper tried the back door, but it was still locked. "Like I said…a ghost. Maybe there was a tracking device in the doll. That's how he found us here."

"Then why take the doll?"

"I don't know. Hell, I don't know anything anymore."

"Well, let's get out of here," Detective Springer said. "You're not safe out here in the open. The guy could be anywhere… watching."

Dani looked to Harper for direction and she nodded. "Yeah. We should go. Lieutenant Mize was on his way in." Harper then turned to Reid. "You follow us, okay? Close."

"You got it."

Harper hesitated, glancing back toward the window where the clown had been, wondering if it was worth sending out a forensic team. He'd had white gloves on. His nose was the only thing that touched the pane.

"What is it?" Reid asked.

"Nothing. Let's go."

CHAPTER TWENTY-FIVE

"I get the feeling that you don't really trust your lieutenant right now."

Harper glanced over at Dani. "Besides Reid, I don't trust anyone right now."

"You don't think your lieutenant—"

"No, I'm not saying he's involved, but besides us, he's the one who has been privy to everything. He's the one who set up both safe houses." She looked in the mirror, feeling somewhat comforted knowing Reid was right behind her. "I don't know. Maybe it's somebody close to him." She knew that didn't make sense though, seeing as how Dani had brought her stalker with her.

"It's all kinda...surreal, isn't it?"

Harper nodded. "Yes. You're being awfully calm about it, though."

"I don't know how else to be. I'm too scared to think, really."

"It's going to be okay, Dani."

"You think so?" Dani wrapped her arms around herself. "How does he keep finding us? He was staring in the window.

He knew where we were. He was just watching us." She turned her head to look at Harper. "A creepy clown. We've got a creepy clown chasing us."

"We'll get him. Don't worry."

"It's hard not to worry. I don't want anything to…well, I dragged you into this. I don't want anything to happen to you." She held her hand up. "And don't say it's your job. All of this…" she shook her head. "This is not your job. It's turned into babysitting, something you feared at the beginning, right?"

"It's turned into a protection detail, yes, but it's still my job."

"You haven't let me out of your sight since the moment we met. You took me to your home. You let me share a bed with you because I was scared. Is all of that your job?"

Harper wasn't sure how to respond to that. Dani was right, of course. She was going way above and beyond. And for a moment there, she had actually considered disobeying Mize's orders. For a moment there, she'd considered taking Dani and going on the run to try to lure the clown to them. So she could then what? Kill him? Arrest him?

Why? Why was she doing all of this? She looked over at Dani, admitting that in only a few short days, she'd gotten under her skin. She was no longer Danielle Stevens. Hell, she didn't even know who Danielle Stevens was. No…she was Dani Strauss. A beautiful woman with a stalker—a creepy clown. And Harper intended to keep her safe by whatever means necessary.

Again…why? Did she think that by keeping Dani safe she could somehow make amends for what had happened to Jan? In her mind, she'd failed Jan. She hadn't protected her. Jan's murder wasn't random, like the others. Jan was selected. And how easy must it have been? Harper wasn't home much. She'd been consumed with catching the killer…the Raggedy Ann Killer. Consumed with it, following dead-end lead after dead-end lead. That last night included. She was out chasing a lead and he was at her house, slaughtering her lover.

"Harper?"

Harper pulled her eyes from the road, glancing over at Dani. Dani raised her eyebrows.

"You've got a death grip on the steering wheel."

She relaxed her hands a little. "Sorry."

Dani reached over and rubbed her arm lightly. "Jan?"

Harper wasn't really surprised that Dani could read her that well. She nodded. "Just making sure my guilt was still intact," she said truthfully.

Dani said nothing else. She simply nodded and leaned her head back.

* * *

"There's not a leak, Harper. Get that out of your mind."

"Then how—"

Lieutenant Mize held his hand up. "Enough of this. Let's move on." He glanced at a note on his desk. "The patrol unit claims to have gotten a radio call, pulling them off duty. Said it sounded like any other radio call."

"What are you saying? There wasn't really a radio call?"

"No. At least not one that was initiated by us. Someone hacked the frequency. It's not unheard of." Mize leaned back in his chair. "I know you think that there's a leak somewhere, that this guy's got an informant or something, but that makes no sense, Harper. This guy showed up out of nowhere. Danielle Stevens coming here was only two weeks in the planning and even that was kept quiet. You didn't even find out until a day before."

"I know it makes no sense, Lieutenant, but how else is he finding us?"

"There's a tracking device that we've missed."

"We've scanned everything. Twice." Harper held her hands up. "The only thing I can think of is if it's something that's not detectable."

"What about her phone?"

Harper shook her head. "No. We left her phone here as a precaution."

Mize folded his hands together, tapping his index fingers together. "So…there's something we haven't discussed," he said carefully.

She raised her eyebrows. "Such as?"

He opened his hands up. "Such as...did this start out as a publicity stunt by her?"

Harper stood up. "Are you seriously suggesting that she staged this whole thing?" She narrowed her eyes. "Seriously?"

"It was mentioned...yes."

"What? Like she hired a stalker? For publicity? And then had him rape a woman? *Really*? You think this was staged?"

"It was mentioned as a possibility. Hell, everybody's just looking for answers."

She tried to keep her temper under control, but the words were out before she could stop them. "Answers? Nobody took this seriously at the beginning. You certainly didn't." She took a step closer to his desk, pointing at him. "You had no interest in catching this guy! You wanted to hide her until she left town and took her stalker back with her. Even *after* he raped a woman!"

Mize glared at her. "Detective..." he warned. "Sit down and shut up before you say something you'll regret."

Harper ran her hands through her hair. "He was in the goddamn house with us! He could have killed us so easily because we're sleeping, thinking we have backup outside!" She turned her back to him, taking a deep breath, then stared up at the ceiling. Was that it? He'd been in the house while they were sleeping. Had he opened the door and peeked in at them?

"Do you want me to take you off of this detail?"

She spun around quickly. "No, sir."

He studied her, his eyes narrowed. "This one is getting a little personal for you, isn't it?"

She frowned as she sat back down. "What do you mean?"

"The note targeting you...the doll in the police uniform... the knife. It's been suggested that we turn Ms. Stevens over to Springer, get you out of the way."

She was surprised at the panic she felt. Reid was her partner. She trusted him to have her back. But she didn't trust him—or anybody else—to keep Dani safe.

"No, sir. I'm okay." She swallowed down her panic. "I think that Ms. Stevens would prefer I stay on."

"Is that right? Based on what?" He spread his hands out. "I'm not trying to place blame or anything here, Harper, but you haven't exactly kept her out of harm's way."

She was too shocked to respond to his statement. Was she to blame?

"I'll give her the opportunity, at least," he continued. "She wanted a female officer to shadow based on an upcoming role of hers. Now that she's apparently in real danger, she may prefer a man on this assignment. We'll let her decide."

Harper had no doubt as to what Dani's decision would be. Did she? Or was she being presumptuous? Maybe Mize was right. She hadn't exactly kept this guy away from Dani.

"Go ahead and send her in, Harper. And ask Springer to come in too." He paused. "You can take a break. Grab some coffee or something. I know it's been a rough morning for you."

My God, was he really so blatantly patronizing her? Suggesting a man could do a better job? Telling her to take a break because she'd had a rough morning? But she nodded obediently before taking her leave. Arguing would do no good. Dani was sitting at her desk, and she looked at her questioningly. Reid was just walking in with a cup of coffee.

"Lieutenant wants to see you," she said to Reid. She turned to Dani. "And you."

Dani's brows drew together. "What's going on?"

Harper shrugged. "I'm not really sure, to be honest with you."

CHAPTER TWENTY-SIX

Dani sat down next to Detective Springer, uncomfortable in the room without Harper. Lieutenant Mize offered her a reassuring smile, but she thought it looked forced.

"Ms. Stevens, we're thinking about making some changes."

"Changes?"

"Yes. I thought perhaps you might feel more comfortable—safer—if we placed you under the care of Detective Springer."

Her eyes widened. "In place of Harper?"

"Yes. It's been a rather eventful few days for you. Detective Jeremiah...well, she hasn't been able to totally shield you from this guy. I think—"

She stood up quickly. "No. I don't want to change." She glanced at Detective Springer. "No offense to you, but I would not feel more comfortable or safer with someone other than Har—I mean, Detective Jeremiah." She glanced out of the office window, hoping to see Harper, but she was not at her desk. She felt her hands shaking and she feared she was about to have a panic attack. What if they really made the change? Then what? Would she be forced to do it? What were her options? Leave Dallas?

"Ms. Stevens, I assure you, Detective Springer is fully capable of—"

"I don't care." She met his gaze. "I prefer to stay with Detective Jeremiah."

"Are you sure, Ms. Stevens? Because—"

"I'm sure."

He stared at her a moment, then finally nodded. "Very well. It's your decision, of course, but I wanted to give you the opportunity to change."

"Thank you, but I'm fine with her."

He stood. "Well, I guess we need to get Harper back in here then. Thank you," he said dismissively, waving a hand toward the door. "I'll come get her in a moment, if you could let her know."

With a quick glance at Detective Springer, she left them, closing the door behind her. She was relieved to find Harper back at her desk. She sat down beside her, flicking her gaze toward Lieutenant Mize's office.

"You won't believe what he wanted," she whispered to Harper.

Harper smiled. "So does that mean you're not ready to ditch me yet?"

"You knew?"

Harper nodded. "He thinks that…well, that a man could do a better job of protecting you."

Dani rolled her eyes. "He said he thought I'd be more comfortable with Detective Springer…safer." She met Harper's gaze. "He sort of insinuated that you're not doing your job."

"I know."

"Why? It's not your fault the guy keeps finding us."

"I know."

Dani lowered her voice even more. "I don't like him very much."

Harper laughed. "Good. Because he doesn't like me very much."

"Why?"

Harper shrugged. "His wife left him for another woman."

"What does that have to do with you?"

"I guess I'm a reminder. The woman she left him for was a detective."

"Oh. But still…"

"Doesn't matter." Harper glanced toward the office too. "So what did you say?"

"I told him I preferred to stay with you. I hope I didn't offend Detective Springer. It's nothing against him."

"Reid will be disappointed, not offended."

She leaned back in her chair. "So what do you think the new plan of action will be? I'm kinda hoping they've run out of safe houses. How about a five-star hotel?"

Harper smiled. "That would be nice. But I'm not sure anything has changed. Keep you safe is the goal."

"Until I leave."

"Until you leave."

"I wonder if—"

"Harper? In here."

Their eyes met at the sound of Lieutenant Mize's voice, then Harper stood, pausing to touch her shoulder as she walked by her. Dani turned, watching her until Harper closed the door. She took a deep breath, wondering what she would have done if he'd insisted that she change from Harper to Detective Springer. For that matter, she wondered what Harper would have done.

CHAPTER TWENTY-SEVEN

Harper kept her face expressionless as Mize stared at her. She could feel Reid shifting uneasily in the chair beside her.

"So, Ms. Stevens wants to stick with you. Apparently, for some crazy reason, she's been charmed by you or something." He folded his hands together. "Is all of this weighing on your conscience, Harper?"

She frowned. "Are you insinuating this is my fault somehow?"

"Well, we've been playing this your way. It hasn't worked so far."

Her eyes widened. "*What?* You were the one who sent us to the safe house. That wasn't *my* idea," she stressed.

He looked over at Reid, then back at her. "The rape victim notwithstanding, we need to get her out of Dallas without anyone getting hurt. Or killed. Priority number one."

"Then let's catch this guy. We're not acting like goddamn cops! We're on the defense. Hiding. Let's go after this guy."

"We're not using her as bait. She's a Hollywood actress, not a cop. We're not putting her in the line of fire."

"You don't think she's going to be in the line of fire when she leaves here? Are we going to just wave goodbye to her at the city limits and hope she gets as far as Fort Worth before he's upon her? Then it's no longer our problem."

"Watch your tone, Detective," he warned. "You're on thin ice as it is."

God, he was being a goddamn prick and she didn't know why. It was as if he had no intention of catching the stalker. They weren't even trying.

He pointed at her. "You are on babysitting duty only. That's it. They're working on finding a place for you to stay for a few days. Reid will be there for backup. What the plan is—without putting her out there as bait—is to occupy the two rooms adjacent to yours. If this crazy son of a bitch tries something, you'll have backup. There will only be one entry. There'll be cameras. So if he finds you, no way he gets close. We'll be monitoring the parking lot. We'll have eyes everywhere. So we're not just sitting back playing defense, Harper. If the guy comes around, we'll get him. If he doesn't…well, then it's out of our hands, seeing as how she'll be leaving town and all."

She nodded. She didn't like what he was insinuating, but at least they were doing *something* to try to catch the guy.

"What should I tell our rape victim from the other night?" Reid asked. "She's called to see if we had any suspects yet."

"Tell her the truth. There are no suspects."

Harper wanted to contradict him. That wasn't the truth. They had a suspect. An unnamed, unknown clown who was stalking Danielle Stevens. They could try to hide them away again, however she didn't believe for one second that Dani's stalker wouldn't find them. He always did. Maybe this time, they'd be ready for him.

* * *

"A hotel? Is that safe?"

"I guess you got your wish. They must be out of safe house options." Then she shrugged. "Not that they've been all that safe, right?"

"So we're back to square one? Hiding me away until I leave town?"

"Not exactly, no, but it won't be a five-star hotel. More like a small motel." Harper sat down at her desk. "All the details haven't been worked out yet. It'll take a few hours to get set up."

Dani scooted her chair closer. "I'll get to stay with you, right? I mean…"

"In the same room or in the same bed?"

"I'd prefer both, actually." Their eyes held. "If it's okay with you," she added quietly, hoping that it was.

Harper nodded. "Yes." Then she smiled. "We just won't tell Reid. He'll be next door, eaten up with envy."

"Speaking of eating…"

"I know. I'm hungry too. We'll pick something up on the way." She looked at her watch. "I've got a briefing scheduled in a half hour. I'm sorry you have to hang around here. You're probably bored out of your mind."

"No. I've been watching…observing. It wasn't exactly what I had in mind to prepare for my role, but it'll have to do." Then she smiled. "Besides, I'm getting some really good, hands-on training with you."

Harper laughed. "Is that what you're calling it? Half the time we've been running away from this guy."

"I'm still in one piece, thank you very much. My nerves may have been frazzled some but I'm safe."

"Well, maybe it'll all be over with very soon. Things can get back to normal for you."

"My normal or real normal?" Dani shook her head. "I can't say I'm looking forward to either." Then she smiled. "I'd rather hang out with you."

CHAPTER TWENTY-EIGHT

"There's a hole-in-the-wall barbecue place," Harper said, motioning to an aging white building. "We're about four blocks from the motel."

"You think it's safe?"

"I think so. It's still daylight. I haven't seen anyone following us." Harper glanced into the rearview mirror again. "If it's a real dive, we can just take our food with us," she offered.

Dani contemplated a plate full of barbecue and her stomach rumbled. "You think they'll have ribs?"

"I imagine so. Is that a favorite?" Harper asked as she turned into the parking lot.

"Back in the old days, yes." Back in the really old days, when she was still young and innocent, she added silently. Smoke swirled from the back of Donny's Pit Barbecue and the smell brought back all sorts of memories from her childhood.

"My uncle had a place like this," she offered. "Nearly every Sunday after church we'd make the drive over to Townsend and spend the day with them. It's very near the Smoky Mountains, just west of Gatlinburg, if that means anything to you."

Harper shook her head. "Afraid not. I could find Nashville on the map, that's about it."

"Townsend is just enough off the beaten path that it doesn't get the tourists like Gatlinburg and Pigeon Forge."

"Is that where you grew up? You said you went to college in Knoxville."

"We lived just south of Knoxville, yes." Harper held the door open for her and Dani smiled her thanks. "I hope no one recognizes me."

"The ponytail, the ball cap—I think you're fine."

Harper was right. No one paid them any attention as they sat down in a booth. She felt safe enough here, she supposed. Harper must have felt comfortable enough too, because they decided to eat their food there instead of taking it with them. Harper had a view of their car out in the lot as well as the front door.

"The ribs are excellent," she admitted as she bit into her second one. "Different from what I grew up on so I wasn't sure I'd like them. My uncle's ribs were generally drowning in sauce."

"Coming from Tucson, I'm not an expert on pork ribs. From what Reid has taught me, these have a dry rub and a mop sauce."

"Do you go out to eat with him much?"

"When we're working, riding together, yeah. After hours? Not so much."

"You keep to yourself." It was a statement, not a question and Harper nodded.

"We put in long hours as it is. I think we're sick of each other's company by the end of the day."

Dani knew it was an excuse as much as anything. It had been over three years since Jan—her lover—had been killed. Just how deep was Harper's guilt? Like this morning in the car, she wondered if perhaps that guilt was starting to slip away and Harper had to remind herself of it sometimes. What was it she'd said? Making sure her guilt was still intact?

Dani knew nothing of that kind of guilt, but she still harbored her own, didn't she? There were many different facets of it, she knew. Mainly, it was the fact that she'd let her relationship with her family deteriorate to where it was. If she'd been honest with them all these years—if she hadn't pretended to be someone she wasn't—would it be different?

Probably not. Her father was rather set in his ways. Old-fashioned. He still lived by the rules he'd been taught as a child...rules he'd passed on to her. Rules that he thought she'd broken many times over. And she had. She'd broken those rules and more. He would be devastated to find out just how many she'd broken.

Well, once this was over with, once she had her life sorted out, she was going to go back home. She would talk to them. She would tell them the truth about herself, let them know the real her. Then, she supposed, it would be up to them to decide if they wanted her in their life or not. Same with her sister.

"You okay?"

Dani looked up, realizing she had stopped eating. She smiled quickly. "Yes. Lost in thought."

Harper just nodded, saying nothing else. Dani nodded too as she picked up another rib.

CHAPTER TWENTY-NINE

Harper thought it was a little anticlimactic as they pulled into the motel's parking lot. No one was following them and nothing suspicious had happened. In fact, it had been a rather uneventful dinner, so much so that they'd taken the time for a piece of pie for dessert.

"So they're all here already?"

"Yes. We're to check in like normal. The guy behind the desk is a cop. The room we're assigned will be between two already occupied."

"And Reid will be in one, right?"

Harper smiled as she got out of the car. "Yes. And I think that's the first time you've referred to him as Reid and not Detective Springer."

Dani walked beside her toward the office. "That's because I didn't want to get too friendly with him." She nudged Harper's arm affectionately. "But you I can call Scout and get away with it."

Harper laughed. "Please don't call me that in front of Reid. He wouldn't let it go."

She recognized the guy behind the desk, but she couldn't place his name. He smiled at her then turned his attention to Dani. No...he turned his attention to Danielle Stevens, she noted as he blatantly stared at her, his eyes traveling up and down Dani's body in awe. Harper had to tap on the desk several times to force his gaze back to her. He cleared his throat before speaking.

"Welcome to the Eastside Budget Inn," he said with a wink. "Looking for a room?"

He was playing his part well, but Harper wasn't in the mood to reciprocate and she didn't return his smile. "Key?"

He nodded. "Of course." He slid it across the desk. "Detective Springer is in room twelve. Detective Hernandez is in fourteen."

She arched an eyebrow. "Really? We're in room thirteen? *Thirteen?*"

"What? You superstitious, Detective?"

"Yeah, I'm getting that way." She snatched up the key. "You here all night?"

"Yes, ma'am. I'll be relieved at seven."

"Good. Don't fall asleep."

"Of course not. You and Ms. Stevens have a good evening. We got the place locked down." He cleared his throat again. "Umm...I don't suppose I could get an autograph, could I?"

"No, you cannot," Harper said sharply and led Dani out of the door. "And stay alert."

Dani laughed quietly. "You were mean."

"Yeah, well, he needs to take his assignment seriously." She handed Dani the room key, then opened the back door of the car, taking out both of their bags. "He probably thinks he's got a cushy deal going. He gets to ogle you for a bit, then sit in the office and watch TV all night as if he doesn't have a care in the world."

"Ogle me?" Dani laughed again. "Is that what he was doing?"

Harper wiggled her eyebrows. "Should I show you?" she teased, the question out before she could stop it.

Dani smiled at her. "Are you flirting with me, Detective?"

Harper felt a blush light her face. "No, of course not." No, because she didn't flirt. Ever. Because there was Jan.

Dani squeezed her arm. "It's okay to flirt, Harper," she whispered.

Harper met her gaze, wondering if it really was okay. Because…there really wasn't Jan, was there? Jan rattled around in her mind, that was all. But flirting? Where had that come from? And who was she flirting with? Dani Strauss or Danielle Stevens?

She finally gave Dani a quick smile. "Sorry. Out of practice, I guess." She walked along the sidewalk stopping when she came to room thirteen. She looked at the black numbers nailed to the door, noting the "1" was crooked, the paint chipped off in spots. "Well, home sweet home," she murmured.

Dani was still holding the key, and Harper stepped aside, letting her unlock the door. The stale smell of the room made her wrinkle up her nose. Dani looked at her with a shrug.

"I guess it could be worse."

There were two double beds in the room and Harper tossed both of the bags onto one of them. The only furniture was an oversized chair with faded upholstery and a small dresser. A TV was on top of the dresser, and her eyes were drawn to the scratch marks that littered the top.

"I'm not sure they could have found anything worse."

"I suppose there's a reason they picked this place, huh?"

"Yeah. They only have two or three rooms booked a night. I'm sure the owner was happy to hand over the place for a few days." She walked into the bathroom and flipped on the light. The shower appeared clean, but there was a moldy smell. "This place is such a dump, I'm sure your stalker friend will know it's staged. No way Danielle Stevens stays at a place like this."

"Or he'll think we're staying here just to confuse him. Provided, of course, that he finds us again."

"I have no doubt that he will." She sat down in the chair with a sigh.

Dani sat on the edge of the bed. "We've asked this question a hundred times, but how is he tracking us?"

Harper had no answer. If there wasn't a leak, how *was* he following them? "It has to be something that's not detectable on a scan." She pointed to Dani's bag. "Something in there, maybe. That's the only thing that's constant."

"Do you want to look through it? There's not much in here. I carry it more out of habit than anything."

Harper leaned forward and took the purse, knowing it had been scanned twice so far. As Dani had said, there wasn't much inside. A black leather wallet was the first thing she picked up. She opened it, finding two credit cards and some cash. She saw five or six one hundred dollar bills and a couple of twenties. She glanced up at Dani.

"You can buy dinner tomorrow."

Dani smiled at her. "I offered to buy dinner tonight."

Her fingers wrapped around a shiny gold tube. She spun it around, then opened it, revealing a light-tinted lipstick. She looked at Dani. Did she wear lipstick? As if reading her mind, Dani nodded.

"I was never really into makeup. Bare minimum when I'm being me. A whole lot more when I'm Danielle Stevens."

Harper inspected the case, wondering if something could be hidden inside. "At your house, where did you keep this?"

"The lipstick? It stays in the purse. And I usually always took my purse into the bedroom."

Harper sighed. "So probably this wasn't left out where he could have access to it."

"No."

Harper handed it back to Dani. "You live alone, I know... but do you have...well, you know, 'your people' around much or what?"

Dani laughed. "My people? No, not really. My assistant, Shelly, came over almost daily, whether I needed her—or wanted her—or not. She takes care of the little things that I no longer feel comfortable doing, like shopping."

"So if you'd go out to...say, a grocery store, you'd get bombarded with autograph seekers?"

"Not so much that. I mean, I'm not this huge megastar that would get swarmed if I went out in public. It's not that." Dani leaned back on the bed, resting on her elbows. "People would stare and point and whisper. And cell phones would be pointed at me. And eventually someone would come up and ask for an autograph or ask to take a picture with me."

"All things you hate."

"Yes."

"You also said you hated the talk show circuit. Do you have to do it anyway?"

"When a new movie comes out, yes. Promotion. I hate it. I'm really rather shy and I don't like talking about myself. And I hate the personal questions that come up. I mean, you can only be so evasive without it raising eyebrows."

"How do you come across? Cool? Disinterested?"

Dani smiled and shook her head. "It's a game. I've been coached. I know all the right answers. I know how to fake it. I smile and laugh at the appropriate spots and I make up just enough little tidbits to be entertaining."

Harper shook her head. "I can't imagine having to do that, telling strangers things about myself."

"No. Some people love it. For me, though, it's the least enjoyable aspect of the business. Well, losing my privacy probably ranks higher, but you know what I mean."

Dani closed her eyes, and Harper wondered what she was thinking about. She let her gaze roam freely over her. Dani was extraordinarily beautiful and Harper imagined the camera loved her. She had an itch to see one of her movies, to see if the Dani she'd come to know was anything like Danielle Stevens. Dani had told her once that she wasn't really acting, that she was simply being herself. Harper wondered if that was really the case.

Her gaze traveled back up to Dani's face, finding blue eyes looking back at her. Harper didn't pull away from Dani's stare… she couldn't.

"What?"

The question was whispered quietly, and Harper finally blinked and looked away. She cleared her throat before speaking.

"Sorry."

"For what?"

Harper shrugged. Yes. What was she sorry for? For blatantly roaming her eyes over Dani's body when she thought Dani wasn't looking? For ogling her? She smiled slightly.

"You're very beautiful."

Dani had a soft blush on her face. "Thank you."

Harper raised an eyebrow. "But it's a curse?"

Dani smiled at her. "I think you're very attractive too. Is it a curse?"

It was Harper's turn to blush. "Reid says I'm cute in a tomboy sort of way. But you...well, you're—"

"I told you I was quite a tomboy growing up. I learned when I got older, though, that my looks...well, that I could pretty much get whatever I wanted. Kinda sad, really."

"To use your looks while pretending to be something you're not?"

"Yes. Pretense. Like the movies. I had lots of practice."

"I don't get the impression that you're pretending with me. Am I wrong?"

Dani wasn't afraid to meet her eyes, holding her gaze once again. "For the first time in...well, forever, I guess...I feel completely comfortable around someone—you. I don't have to pretend to be Danielle Stevens with you." Dani sat up and leaned forward, resting her arms on her thighs. "I like you a lot, Harper. You're...you're real to me. You don't know me and you don't owe me anything, yet, here we are...together. Because you care." She smiled. "You probably wished you didn't care, but I know you do."

Harper smiled too. "Yes. Guilty."

Dani surprised her by moving closer and kissing her on the cheek. "I'm very, very glad I chose you," she whispered before pulling away. "You have the most honest eyes I've ever seen."

Harper sat still, paralyzed as Dani's hand—her fingers—touched her cheek.

"You're a good person, Scout. I'm so lucky."

Harper swallowed, not knowing what to say. Then Dani smiled and took her hand away.

"Sorry. I didn't mean to get so melodramatic with you."

"It's okay," Harper said with a quick nod. "I'm glad we can talk like this."

"Yes. Like friends."

"Yeah…like friends."

Later, however, while she lay wide awake, listening to Dani's even breathing, she felt the fingers of attraction start to claw at her. Dani was on her side, facing her. Her head was touching her shoulder, her hand holding lightly to Harper's arm. Dani hadn't started out in that position, no. She'd first laid on her back as idle chitchat passed between them. Then she'd rolled away from Harper. In a matter of minutes, though, she turned again, moving closer to Harper. In sleep, she'd moved closer still to where she was now.

Harper closed her eyes, trying to find an image of Jan in her mind. It was a struggle, but finally one came—the mess of unruly brown hair, the laughing eyes, the teasing smile. Jan. Then the image slowly faded, replaced with another: blond hair, guarded blue eyes, a hesitant smile. Then that changed too…blue eyes that now twinkled, a smile turning into a laugh.

She opened her eyes, moving her head a fraction to look at Dani. The light from the bathroom made a streak across the bed, illuminating Dani's hair. Her lips were slightly parted, and Harper's gaze locked on them for countless seconds before she made herself look away. She blew out a heavy breath, wishing sleep would claim her already.

CHAPTER THIRTY

Dani woke with a start, which was odd for her. She lifted her head from Harper's shoulder, quite embarrassed for having been caught using it as a pillow.

"I heard it too," Harper whispered. "Stay here."

Dani scooted up to the wall, covering herself with the blanket as if it could offer some protection. Harper didn't bother with her jeans, simply walking quickly to the window. She moved the curtains aside—hideous faded yellow ones—and looked out. Dani was comforted to see the gun in her hand. With the security chain still in place, Harper opened the door and peeked outside. Dani could see Harper relax as she closed the door again.

"Nothing."

Dani let out a relieved sigh. "It was loud enough to wake me up. Whatever it was."

Harper got back in bed. "I know. You normally sleep through anything."

"It was a bang or something."

"Yeah, sounded close. Let's hope Reid doesn't have a hooker in his room."

Dani smiled at that as she scooted back down into her spot and settled beside Harper again. "Umm, I guess I was using you as a pillow. I'm sorry."

"Yeah, I'm getting used to it. You're quite a snuggler."

Oh, God. Dani felt a blush light her face, and she was glad it was too dark for Harper to see. She was embarrassed, yes, but she was also a little frightened. Frightened by the noise that had awoken her so suddenly…and frightened by the attraction she felt to Harper. She decided to focus on the former rather than the latter.

"Do you think the noise was from one of our neighbors?"

"Probably not."

"So that noise could have been…it could have been him, right?"

"Maybe. Are you worried that it was?"

"I don't know," she said quietly. "I just…"

"Are you scared?"

"Yes."

"I think we're okay here, Dani. We've got detectives on each side of us. The officer at the desk—if he's not watching TV—is supposed to be monitoring the parking lot. I think it's covered."

"I guess so." She could feel her thundering heartbeat, and she wondered if it was still the fear of the stalker that had it beating so. There was a chill in the room, but she could feel the warmth from Harper's body. She longed to know what it would feel like to be held by her. Despite the warnings dancing through her mind, she moved closer to her, the whispered words out before she could stop them.

"Would you hold me?" She could sense Harper hesitating, and she mentally slapped herself. "I'm…never mind," she murmured, although she couldn't bring herself to move away from Harper.

"No…I'm sorry, Dani. I…"

Dani stared at the ceiling. "You're still in love with her, aren't you?" She heard Harper take a deep breath.

"I probably always will be."

Dani nodded in the darkness. "I'm so sorry, Harper. I didn't mean to make you feel…well, uncomfortable."

"I know. You're scared."

"Yes, I'm scared." She bit her lower lip. "I'm scared of my stalker, and I'm…scared of…well, it's been so long since I've had physical contact with anyone," she admitted. "It's been a rather lonely life, to say the least." She turned to glance at Harper, deciding to be honest with her. "It's probably best that you don't hold me. I'm already attracted to you. You should probably keep your distance."

"Oh, Dani," Harper whispered. "I don't have anything to offer you. Inside…I'm just, I'm just empty still. You don't need that kind of a complication in your life."

Dani squeezed her eyes shut. *God, what were you thinking?* She'd been attracted to the woman in the photo from the start. She told herself she'd picked Harper Jeremiah because of her eyes—those honest, trustworthy eyes—but she knew that wasn't the sole reason. Still, she shouldn't have said anything. She should have left things as they were. She managed a quick nod, wishing she could take back her words. "You're right. And again, I'm sorry."

She waited what she thought was an appropriate amount of time before rolling onto her side, her back to Harper. Harper said nothing else, but a few minutes later, Dani was surprised to hear the covers rustle, surprised to feel Harper shift beside her. An arm snaked around her waist, pulling her back into a sturdy, warm body. She sucked in a quick breath of air as Harper spooned behind her.

"How's this?"

With her heart still hammering in her ears, Dani's only answer was to take Harper's hand and pull it more tightly around her.

CHAPTER THIRTY-ONE

Harper feared it would be awkward between them. Or worse, she feared her guilt would be eating her alive this morning. After all, she'd just spent the night holding another woman in her arms—a beautiful, vibrant woman who said she was attracted to her. But there was no guilt. Jan wasn't haunting her. And Dani seemed perfectly normal, not mentioning their talk at all. She sat at the edge of the bed and stretched her arms over her head with a pleasant moan.

"I slept like a rock." Dani glanced over her shoulder. "Thank you, Harper. You make a great security blanket."

Harper smiled at that. "My pleasure," she said with a wink, hoping to keep things light between them.

"Can I have the bathroom first or would you rather?"

"No, go ahead. I'm going to take a look outside, make sure everything's okay."

Dani raised both eyebrows. "You won't go far, right?"

"No. Promise. I'm just going to check in with Reid."

She went to the window and slowly moved the curtains aside. The sun was barely up and she saw no activity outside. Not that she expected much. There had been only five vehicles in the parking lot when they'd gone to bed, three of which were police. She did a quick count now and saw six. She heard a door slam down the way from their room and she watched as a man hurried to a truck. He was hunched over with his collar turned up, most likely to avoid the wind. On impulse, she touched the windowpane, surprised at how cold it was. She hadn't bothered with a weather forecast in days and she assumed a front had come in during the night.

She let the curtain fall back into place and went to the door. She opened it as far as the chain would allow. She wouldn't have been shocked to find a doll leaning against the door, but there was nothing. She grabbed a sweatshirt off the chair, slipped it on then went outside. It was definitely colder than it had been last night. She was about to go over to Reid's room when something in the parking lot caught her eye. There, on the windshield of one of the cars was a doll. It was the tangled mess of red hair that made her gasp—a Raggedy Ann doll.

She hurried back to their room, slammed the door quickly and locked it, then took three or four steps away. Her heart was pounding loudly and she sucked in several deep breaths. It was a coincidence, of course. He probably had to buy a doll and this was all he could come up with.

She ran her fingers through her hair nervously. Right? A coincidence?

"Yes, surely," she whispered to herself. Jan's killer was still out there somewhere, but she had no illusions that she'd stumbled upon him. The Raggedy Ann Killer didn't stalk, he didn't play cat and mouse games. The Raggedy Ann Killer forced his way into bedrooms, then raped and tortured his victims before killing them.

"Harper?"

She turned toward Dani, seeing the frown on her face.

"You're as white as a ghost. What is it?"

Harper cleared her throat. "There's a…there's a doll out there, on one of the cars."

Dani's shoulders sank. "Oh, no. So he did find us." She came closer and touched her arm. "Something else is wrong. What is it?"

Damn, but Dani could read her. She pointed to the door. "The doll…well, it's different. It's a…it's a damn Raggedy Ann doll."

"Oh, my God." Then Dani's eyes widened. "Oh, no. You don't think—"

"No, no. It's a coincidence only. It's got to be. It just freaked me out there for a minute." She held her hand up. "And don't say you're sorry."

"Okay. So now what?"

She picked up her phone. "Call Reid. Then check with the desk guy, see who came in last night. Check security tapes." She took a deep breath. "Damn."

* * *

"You didn't see *anything*?"

"No. One guy came in about ten thirty for a room. Older guy in a truck. He's on his way to Lubbock. He left already this morning."

Harper nodded. "Yeah, I saw him." She stared at him, narrowing her eyes. "So if no one came in, how the hell did a goddamn doll get on one of our cars?"

"I don't know. I swear, I was…I was alert all night."

"There was some kind of a noise, it was after midnight," Reid said and Harper nodded.

"Yeah, we heard it too. I looked out. I didn't see anything."

"Me either."

Harper stepped back, knowing that Officer Sorrell—the desk clerk guy—was technically off duty. His replacement was already behind the desk, idly flipping through his phone.

"I guess we look through the surveillance video and see what the hell it was you missed."

"I swear, nobody came in. At least not in a vehicle."

They'd chosen this particular motel not only for its meager occupancy rate but because it was horseshoe-shaped with only one entrance. Apparently, if Officer Sorrell was to be believed, their stalker had slipped in on foot.

Harper rubbed her eyes as they went back outside. The doll was still on the car, and she turned away from it.

"Do you have an evidence bag?"

"Yeah, there are some in my car." He touched her arm. "What's wrong? You look a little freaked out by that thing."

She glanced back at the doll. "Had a case in Tucson. Serial killer. Left a Raggedy Ann doll at each scene." She turned away from the doll again. "Bad memories."

"Okay. I'll take care of it. You want to watch video with Hernandez?"

"No. I want to check on Dani. I'll meet you back in the office. Have Hernandez take this thing to the lab. Maybe we'll get lucky this time."

She watched Reid for a minute, then turned away when he reached for the doll. She tapped quickly on their door, hearing Dani on the other side.

"Is it you?"

"Just me."

Dani released the chain, then opened the door, her eyes first meeting Harper's before traveling to the lot...and the doll. She then took Harper's arm and tugged her inside.

"I'm so sorry about the doll, Harper. Of all the dolls he could have picked—"

"I know. Reid is going to get Hernandez to take it to the lab. I'm fine."

Dani nodded and Harper knew she didn't believe her. "If you say so."

Harper held her questioning gaze, softening her expression some. "Dani...I'm fine. It just...it was a shock, that's all. It's a doll, part of his game, nothing more."

They stared at each other for a long moment, then Dani surprised her by moving closer and pulling her into a tight hug. There was nothing professional whatsoever about their relationship any longer and she didn't pretend that it was. The position that she found herself in at that moment was far too intimate to pretend. She relaxed, letting Dani hold her for as long as she wanted. There was no guilt, no images of Jan flashing before her eyes. There was just this woman who was offering her comfort...and something more.

She closed her eyes, pulling Dani a little tighter against her, then she gently pushed her away. Now wasn't the time to explore this.

Dani seemed almost embarrassed by the hug and she wouldn't meet Harper's eyes. Harper didn't say anything. Dani had her own demons to deal with.

"We're...we're going to look at the video from last night. Do you want to come with me or stay here?"

Dani looked at her then. "I'll go with you, if you don't mind."

CHAPTER THIRTY-TWO

Dani stood behind Harper and Reid, who sat near the desk, the security surveillance video already up and running. She watched the dark, shadowy entrance to the motel for several minutes, then found her attention shifting from the stalker to Harper…and the hug they'd shared. She fingered the locket at her neck absently, her mind replaying the events of last night and this morning. Things had changed between them in a matter of hours, it seemed. Changes that she was responsible for, not Harper. She never would have thought she'd be bold enough to initiate any physical contact between them, but it had come so naturally, she hadn't had time to think it through.

She also hadn't had time to really sort out these feelings she was having. Was the attraction she felt for Harper simply a result of the situation she found herself in? Harper was a cop, her protector, her security blanket. Was that why she was feeling this affection for her? Or did it still stem from when she'd first seen her picture? She thought back to that day when she'd been flipping through the profiles of the female detectives they'd sent her. Her intention had been to select someone who had a lot of experience, someone who was well-seasoned, someone she could learn from. No one jumped off the page at her until she came to Harper Jeremiah. She remembered staring into her eyes, wondering what she'd been thinking in that instant when her picture was snapped. She'd dutifully gone through the profiles of each one, but she kept going back to Harper. She knew then that even if Harper had been a rookie, she'd still have chosen her.

"Fast forward to midnight," Harper said. "It was after that when we heard the noise."

Reid nodded and Dani forced her attention back to the monitor, pushing her thoughts of Harper away...at least for the moment.

"There! Did you see it?"

Reid shook his head. "It was just a shadow."

"Right. Go back. Play it again." Harper pointed at the bottom left of the screen. "Watch here."

Dani kept her eyes glued to where Harper had pointed, anticipation making her heart beat just a little fast. Reid played it at real speed and it was just a blur on the screen, as if a shadow flew by the camera.

"That's nothing," Reid said.

"Slow it down. It's a person."

Reid played it again, this time in slow motion. He paused the video as the shadow materialized. "Son of a bitch," he murmured.

Harper tapped the screen. "A person. Half a head, shoulder."

"Too dark for any ID."

"What's the timestamp?"

"Twelve twenty-two."

"Okay. Let's check the parking lot feed at that timestamp. See what we get." Harper glanced back at Dani. "You okay?"

Dani nodded. "Just trying to stay out of your way."

But Harper scooted her chair over. "Come sit with us. You might catch something that we miss."

Dani seriously doubted that, considering Harper had been able to spot the shadow of half a person—a shadow that was on the screen for all of a nanosecond. She pulled up a third chair anyway, sitting down beside Harper. Their knees touched as they both leaned forward, closer to the monitor. Neither of them pulled away and she wondered if it was only her imagination that she felt Harper press a little harder against her.

"There he is!" Reid said excitedly.

Dani's eyes widened as the shadow of a man came into full view. He was dressed in black, head to toe. From inside his jacket, he pulled out the Raggedy Ann doll and placed it carefully on the car. Then, as if it had been planned all along, he balled his hands into fists and banged them loudly against the car's hood.

"And there's our loud noise," Harper said.

The man took off in a flash, disappearing from the camera's view. Reid backed the video up and replayed it, slower this time. When he enlarged the frame, the man's face was distorted, clearly covered by a ski mask or something.

"So he made the noise on purpose," Dani said. "Why?"

"Maybe he wanted us to find the doll last night."

"But he didn't hang around. He took off," Reid said.

"Has to know there're cops here," Harper said as she leaned back in her chair, her eyes staring at the ceiling now. "Or maybe that's how he dresses when he's out and about."

"He was in clown makeup when he found us at the IHOP," Dani reminded her. "That's not to say he doesn't have it on under the mask."

"He made the noise, hoping to wake us up and have us find the doll. Maybe hoping we'd take off again like we did the night before."

"And when you didn't—"

"He's got to think we feel safe here...and that we've got cops here," Harper finished for him.

"Or else you never woke up," Reid said. "He could have been sitting all night, across the street or something, waiting. He may have seen us this morning when we were inspecting the doll. In which case, he knows for sure there are cops here."

"That's a dangerous game he's playing." Harper stood up. "Dangerous or stupid."

"Not so stupid," Reid countered. "He obviously made the cameras. He's covered up. We can't ID him. He was in and out of here in forty-five seconds, if that."

"Again, for what purpose? Just to rattle us? Just to let us know that he found us again?" Harper spun around quickly. "And how the *hell* is he finding us?"

"The million-dollar question," Reid said. "I'll let Mize know the timestamp on these, let the experts go over them. Maybe they'll get something else."

* * *

"How is it?"

Dani nodded. "Good. Yours?"

Harper nodded too. Their breakfast—tacos that Hernandez had brought back with him—had been a rather silent affair. She finally put her egg and bacon taco down, wrapping it up again.

"Do we need to talk? Clear the air?"

Dani put hers down too. "I don't know what to say, really. I...I've overstepped the boundary. Several times," she added. "You are just doing your job. And I've...well, I've let my personal feelings...I've—"

"Dani, yes, this situation we're in, it's not normal. We've become close in a short period of time." She gave Dani a small smile. "We've been sharing a bed since day two, I think. Sharing everything." She stood up, walking away from Dani. "I'd be lying if I said I wasn't attracted to you," she admitted. She turned back around to face her. "I know what your life has been like. I know you've had two very secret relationships where you weren't emotionally invested in either one." She closed her eyes for a moment. "I...I'm not at a place where I can offer you anything—emotionally."

"Harper—"

"I can't give you anything, Dani. I don't even know if I could give you a physical relationship, must less emotional." She went closer, meeting her gaze. "I like you, Dani. As a person. And I find you attractive—incredibly so. But right now..."

"It's okay," Dani said, her words not much more than a whisper. "You don't have to feel responsible for this, Harper. I'm the one who crossed the line. And I'm sorry."

"Dani—"

"No. We've talked. Consider the air cleared." She pointed at Harper's taco. "Finish your breakfast. The way our track record has gone, we may not eat again today."

Harper stared at her a moment longer, watching as Dani averted her eyes, making a show of unwrapping her own taco. The words they exchanged may have cleared the air on the surface, but down below, where it really mattered, she suspected it was as muddy as ever.

She sat down again, silently chewing the taco, her eyes drifting to Dani time and again. Dani wouldn't meet her gaze and Harper guessed she was embarrassed. Embarrassed by what she'd said last night. Embarrassed by the hug they'd shared. Embarrassed for opening up to Harper, only to be rebuffed.

Harper took a deep breath, looking inward for a moment. Had she rebuffed Dani? In a manner of speaking, yes. But why? Well, there was Jan, of course. There was her guilt. No. If she were being totally honest with herself, it was the absence of guilt. The guilt she'd carried with her these last few years was starting to slip away. Was she afraid it would disappear altogether? Was she afraid that if it disappeared, Jan would fade away too?

When had it happened? She couldn't remember a time when Jan wasn't the first thing she thought about each and every morning. Now? No. The last week, Jan hadn't been there. She'd had to force thoughts of Jan into her mind. Like now. It wasn't Dani's fault, though. It was this assignment...it was being together with her all the time, it was sharing meals...sharing a bed. It was sharing her personal space with someone again. It was sharing all of that with a beautiful woman who said she was attracted to her.

Dani didn't have to come right out and say the words. If Harper were willing, they'd be sharing more than just a bed at night. Harper looked over at Dani, seeing her staring at the wall. What thoughts were running through her mind? Did she wish this case was over and done with so she could get away? Get away from Harper? Get away from these feelings that were springing up between them? Is that what Harper wanted? For Dani to leave? For Dani to leave and take those feelings with her? Leave her in peace…alone again with only her guilt—and Jan's ghost—for company?

Harper let out a quiet sigh and closed her eyes for a moment. No. That wasn't what she wanted at all.

CHAPTER THIRTY-THREE

Dani stared first at the dozen red roses, then at the doll that Officer Fadden held—another Raggedy Ann doll. She then slid her gaze to Harper, whose own stare was on the doll.

"So? What should I do with them?"

Harper looked up at him then. "A kid delivered them?"

"Yes, ma'am. And get this. He said a guy dressed as a clown gave him twenty bucks to bring them here."

Harper clenched her jaw. "Did he happen to say where this clown guy was?" she asked, her words clipped.

He shook his head. "He said the guy took off down the street, but he wasn't sure where he went. I asked him to wait in the office if you want to go talk to him."

Harper nodded. "Leave the roses. Take the doll. We'll send it over to the lab with the others." She looked at Dani then. "There's a note. I'll be right back. Let me go talk to the kid."

Dani nodded, but Harper must have sensed her hesitation.

"I'll have Reid come over."

"Okay."

When they left, Dani reached for the note, but she didn't open it. Instead, she touched a rose petal with her finger, wondering why he'd sent beautiful live roses this time. The last few times he'd left roses for her, they were either black ones or ones that were old and spent, the petals falling from the stem at the touch. With a quick sigh, she opened the note, glancing over the words there. Nothing too threatening this time.

"Hey, Harper told me to keep you company," Reid said as he walked in the open door. "I hear you got a delivery."

She stepped aside, showing him the roses. "And another doll."

"What kind?"

"Raggedy Ann again."

"Damn. That one kinda threw Harper. Said there was a serial killer who would leave them. I don't guess they ever caught the guy."

Dani wasn't really surprised that Harper had only skimmed over the case with Reid, leaving out the part about Jan and the real reason the doll had "thrown" her. She handed him the note. "This was left with the roses."

He read it silently, then raised his eyebrows. "Kinda lame."

She shrugged. "I guess he thinks he's a poet."

Reid smiled. "This kind of stuff is not freaking you out anymore?"

"Well, beautiful roses, a rather sweet note...it beats the threatening ones, doesn't it?"

"I guess. What do you take it to mean?"

"I don't know. I think maybe he knows who Harper is. Did some research, found out about the serial killer in Tucson. I think he's leaving the Raggedy Ann dolls for her, not me."

"You think so?"

"The first one, Harper thought it was just a coincidence that it was a Raggedy Ann doll. A second one? I'm not so sure."

"Not so sure of what?" Harper asked as she came inside, her glance going between Dani and Reid.

"The doll," Dani said. "I'm not so sure it's just by chance that it's a Raggedy Ann. I think he's leaving the dolls for you, not me."

"Yeah, that's crossed my mind too." She motioned to the note. "What did it say?"

Reid handed it to her, and she read it out loud. "You can't hide from me, Danielle. All I have to do is follow your heart. It will always lead me to you."

Harper read it again, silently this time, with a frown. "What the hell does that mean?"

Dani smiled. "I'm not sure it means anything. At least he wasn't threatening your life this time."

"Well, there's that." Harper handed the note back to Reid. "Put this in a safe place, would you?"

"Yeah, I'm just one giant evidence bag. So…did the kid know anything?"

"The kid was an eighteen-year-old who works at that donut place down the block. He said the clown came in for a bag of donut holes. He offered him twenty bucks to make a delivery for him." Harper shrugged. "He took the flowers and the doll, headed this way. The clown walked down the street in the opposite direction."

"Any chance we can still find him? I mean, a clown is bound to stick out, right?"

"Yeah. I called it in. They're sending some units out to the area, but I'm sure he's long gone by now."

"Pretty smart, though. No one can ID him as long as he's got makeup on."

"Do you think he's just playing with us now? Toying with us?" Dani asked.

"He's got to know we're all cops here. I'd guess he's going to wait us out until we move you somewhere."

"Or until I head back home and resume my life. Obviously I can't stay here indefinitely under police protection."

"They haven't found any prints at all on any of the dolls or notes," Reid said. "He's been very, very careful."

"Like he's done this before," Harper agreed. "You said once that he was almost like a professional. I don't believe there are professional stalkers, but maybe he's a professional in another area."

"Like a thief who's been able to avoid arrest? Leave no prints, no evidence," Reid said. "Or like our serial rapist." He turned to her. "Five women. Not one shred of evidence at any of the scenes. People who can pull that off...they're either very, very good, or very, very lucky."

"Our guy is not only careful with evidence, but with surveillance too. At Dani's hotel that first day, he knew where the cameras were and he knew how to avoid them without calling attention to himself. Like last night. He knew exactly where the cameras were. He gave us nothing."

"You talk to Mize?" Reid asked.

"Briefly. He says to stay put. We'll meet tomorrow to reevaluate the situation." Harper turned to her. "He's going to want to know your plans."

Dani met her gaze. "Meaning...when am I leaving?"

Harper nodded.

Dani gave her a quick smile. "I don't even know what day it is."

"It's Saturday," Reid offered.

Dani bit her lip. "So my seven days are about up." She looked at Harper. "I can't believe it's been six days already."

"Tell him three more days," Harper said. "Maybe we'll get lucky."

"And if we don't?"

Harper didn't shy away from her stare. "I don't know, Dani. I honestly don't know."

Dani nodded, then turned away, focusing her attention on the roses. Would Harper really let her leave, knowing her stalker was still out there, following her? Would she be on her own to face this? Fear—and something else—nearly choked the breath from her. She heard a phone ring, heard Harper answer, heard her murmured "we'll be right back," but Dani never turned. She was afraid Harper would see her tears.

CHAPTER THIRTY-FOUR

Harper sat in the lone chair, trying to keep her eyes on the TV and not Dani. Dani was on the bed, propped up against the pillows. Things had been rather strained between them, so much so that Harper had invited both Reid and Hernandez to their room to share dinner, just to keep the conversation going. She wasn't sure if Dani's silence was the result of them "clearing the air" or the prospect of her having to leave Dallas soon.

Once again, Harper glanced at Dani, finding Dani's attention on the TV. Harper wasn't even sure what they were watching. A sitcom with bratty young kids was all she'd gotten out of it. There had been no reaction from Dani during the entire episode. She simply couldn't stand the silence any longer.

"Do you want to talk?"

Dani gave her a weak smile. "I'm okay, Harper. I just…well, it's been an emotional few days. I guess it's caught up with me."

"I'm sorry, Dani."

"What are you sorry for?"

"This silence between us, for one. It's my fault."

"It's not your fault. I appreciate you being honest with me, Harper. Someone else, they may have…I don't know, taken advantage of the situation. Thank you for not…pretending."

Harper stood up, pacing in the small space between the bed and the door. She didn't know what to say to Dani to make it right. She stopped pacing, turning to face Dani.

"I…I liked the hug." She swallowed. "That was the first contact I've had with anyone since…well, in over three years." She swallowed again. "I liked it." Dani didn't say anything, she simply stared at her. Harper took a deep breath, wondering how to continue. "I'm having a hard time holding on to my guilt," she admitted truthfully. "And that scares me because guilt is all I have left of Jan."

"Oh, Harper, the guilt is something you've forced on yourself. That's not all you have left. Jan is in your heart, in your mind. You said yourself, she always would be."

"I feel like she's slipping away from me," she admitted.

Dani tilted her head, her eyes gentle. "Is it…is it my fault?" Harper nodded. "Yes. I think it is."

"Then I should say I'm sorry." She forced a smile to her face. "I guess it's a good thing that I'll be leaving in a couple of days, huh?"

Dani's attempt to lighten the mood seemed to have the opposite effect. For both of them, it seemed. Harper couldn't believe how quickly Dani had become a part of her life, as if she belonged there. She was having a hard time remembering her days—and her lonely, solitary nights—before Dani popped in.

A quiet tap on their door interrupted her thoughts and she turned to it, thinking it must be Reid.

"Got another delivery, Detective."

She looked at Dani with raised eyebrows. She didn't recognize the voice and she wondered if Officer Sorrell's shift was starting later than usual. She went to the door but kept the chain on as a precaution. She'd barely turned the doorknob when it was forced open in a rush, throwing her against the wall. She turned, only to have the side of her face smashed with the blunt force of a gun. She tried to hold on even as her eyes were swimming in blackness. Her knees buckled and as she hit the floor, Dani's scream echoed in her muddled brain.

She squeezed her eyes shut, trying to ignore the pounding in her head. *Get up! Get up! Get up!* She struggled to her feet, blinking her eyes to try to clear the stars that were blinding her.

"What the hell's going on?"

"Reid...thank God!" Harper grabbed his arm. "Come on! He's got her."

Reid should have been the one driving, she knew that as she sped out of the parking lot. It was a nondescript smallish black car that she'd seen Dani being thrown into. Dani had been limp, dangling in his arms like one of his lifeless dolls. Had he knocked her out? Had he smashed her face too? Had he drugged her?

"Jesus Christ! Slow down, Harper!"

Reid held on to the dash with one hand, the other was on the door as he braced himself against the wild turn she made. The neighboring car honked several times at her as she cut in front of them. It was still relatively early in the evening—eight thirty, maybe?—and there was enough traffic for him to get lost in. That was probably his plan all along.

She pounded her fist against the steering wheel angrily. How could she have been so lax? Why had she opened the door without knowing for sure who it was?

"Slow down!" he yelled again. "He's only three cars ahead of us. We got him."

"If he gets to the freeway, he'll disappear in traffic. We'll lose him!"

Reid was thrown against the door as she changed lanes, cutting off two cars in the process.

"Goddamn it, Harper, you're going to kill us both!"

"I am *not* going to lose him," she said tersely.

"How the hell did he get inside the room? Where was Sorrell?"

"He kicked the door in. And I don't know where the hell Sorrell was." She slammed the steering wheel again with her fist. "That son of a bitch! I swear, when I catch him, I'm going to put a bullet in his head!"

CHAPTER THIRTY-FIVE

Dani blinked slowly, struggling to focus, her mind still cloudy...foggy. There was a sweet taste in her mouth and she tried several times to swallow it away. What had he used? Chloroform? Did people really do that? She was tossed back against the seat as he swerved in traffic. A loud horn honked beside them. She was stretched out on the backseat, her hands unbound. What should she do? What *could* she do? Was Harper looking for her? The last thing she remembered—before the clown had grabbed her—was Harper falling to the floor. Was she still lying there? Was she hurt? Had Reid heard the commotion and found her? She closed her eyes and braced herself as he slammed on his brakes, only to speed up again. He was driving fast. Was Harper following him?

God...what should she do?

Her hands were free. She could jump up, grab the wheel. Yes, and maybe flip the car, killing them in the process. She could open the back door and jump out. And probably kill herself in the process.

She finally dared to open her eyes. She looked up, finding him watching her in the rearview mirror. She gasped as he smiled…the evil grin of a creepy clown. A real, live creepy clown.

"Gotcha!" he said, snapping his jaws together as if taking a bite out of her.

She shrunk back from the sound of his voice, then nearly rolled to the floor as he took a sharp turn. "*Gotcha.*" Yes, he definitely had her now. Harper would never find her. He would disappear with her. He would kill her. He would…he would probably do all sorts of…of *things* to her first.

Then he would kill her.

She eyed the door. It was obviously locked, but she thought she could pull up on the manual lock and open the door at the same time. And then what? Fall into traffic?

Yeah…great idea, Dani.

He changed lanes yet again as horns blared around them. Had he run a red light? She felt the car slowing, albeit slightly. Was there a curve coming up? Dare she try it? She looked in the mirror again, but he was focused solely on the road. Stupid idea, she thought as she sat up and pulled the lock free before opening the door. It swung out wide as he turned the corner and she fell out, instinctively covering her head as she landed hard on the pavement. She rolled more times than she could count and she came to a final, abrupt stop against a concrete barrier. The roar of traffic, the squealing of tires, the blasting of horns all faded as she curled into a ball, praying she wouldn't get hit.

* * *

Harper saw a flash of…of something as it was thrown from a car. It rolled up against the concrete barrier that separated the road from a construction site. She swerved to miss it, then slammed on her brakes. Horns blared around them and she braced herself, the car behind them missing her by mere inches.

"Are you out of your mind? He's getting away!"

Harper had a moment of panic. Should she follow the car? Or? She started going again, thinking she would lose him if she hesitated any longer. But something…something wasn't right.

"Come on, Harper!"

"Hang on."

She spun the car around, scraping the barrier with her fender. They were now facing oncoming traffic and the sound of horns honking seemed to surround them. Her headlights landed on the object up against the concrete and she spotted a mass of blond hair.

"Oh, my God. How did you see her?"

Harper didn't answer him. She got out, running toward her. She knelt down beside her, trying to prepare herself for what she might find. She touched Dani's shoulder, rolling her over. She gasped as Dani's eyes met hers.

"Harper," Dani murmured before sobs took her breath away.

"It's okay. I got you now." She pulled Dani into her arms and she felt Dani cling to her, felt—heard—her sobs as Dani buried her face against her chest. "I got you now."

She stood, taking Dani up with her. She wrapped Dani tight against her and walked over to the car.

"Is she okay?"

"I think so. You drive."

She opened the back door and put Dani in, then got in beside her. Dani immediately clutched her arm. The overhead light was bright enough for her to see the blood on Dani's forehead. She touched it lightly, seeing the scrape of skin. Her cheek was also bruised. Then Reid closed the door, plunging them into darkness.

She winced when Dani touched the bruise on her own cheek.

"Are you okay?"

Harper nodded. "Just blacked out for a second there," she said quietly. "Are you?"

"I think so."

Harper took Dani's hand and squeezed it tightly. "I'm so sorry. I...I promised to protect you and I failed." She felt tears threatening, and she closed her eyes, trying to ward them off. "I thought I'd failed again. I was so afraid it would be like..." She couldn't go on as her tears closed up her throat. She'd failed Jan. Jan was dead. She'd failed Dani. If Dani hadn't fallen from the car, what would have happened? What if she couldn't have stopped the car? What if he'd gotten away with her? Harper would never have found her. And she would have failed Dani too. Dani would have most likely met the same fate as Jan.

Her heart broke all over again as Dani pulled her into her arms, offering her comfort. Harper should be the strong one, Harper should be comforting Dani, not the other way around. But here they sat, in the darkness of the backseat, holding each other, mixing their tears—soothing their fears.

How many minutes they clung to each other, she didn't know. When she felt in control again, she gently pulled away, still keeping a hold of Dani's hand. She looked up, finding Reid watching them in the mirror, eyebrows raised in a question. She had no answer for him.

"Take us back to the motel," she said, her voice still thick with emotion. "I want to get our things."

"We need to call Mize. He'll want us to go in."

Harper had no intention of going in. Not now. "Motel first."

Reid eyed her in the mirror for a second, then nodded.

She felt Dani lean against her shoulder, eyes closed. Harper moved closer to her.

"You okay?" she whispered.

Dani nodded but said nothing. Harper noted that their fingers were still linked, and she leaned back against the seat, letting her own eyes slip closed.

CHAPTER THIRTY-SIX

Emergency lights flashed all around the motel and Reid slowed as they approached.

"What the hell? Did Hernandez call in the troops?"

They were stopped at the entrance and Reid showed his badge to the officer. "Detectives Springer and Jeremiah," he said. "What's going on?"

"Officer down. Sorrell."

Harper leaned forward. "Down? Dead?"

"Yes, ma'am. Stabbed in the throat."

"Oh, my God," Dani whispered.

Reid maneuvered the car between an ambulance and a squad car. Hernandez was standing off to the side, talking to two women. Detectives from Homicide, no doubt. He stopped in front of their rooms and Harper turned to Dani.

"Stay here. I'll get our things."

"What are we going to do?"

"I'm not sure yet."

When Reid would have gone over to talk to Hernandez, Harper stopped him.

"I'm going to get our things, then we're out of here."

"Out?" He shook his head. "Harper, no. We go in. We report what happened. We let Mize decide the next course of action."

"No offense, Reid, but every damn plan that Mize has come up with so far has ended badly." She pointed toward the office. "And now he's killed a cop. So no, I'm not going to hang around for Mize's next brilliant plan."

"Harper—"

"No. This ends. He wants Dani. He's proven—by taking out Sorrell—that he'll go to any lengths to get her."

"You don't even know how he's finding her."

"Doesn't matter anymore. He finds her. And the next time… it ends."

Reid leaned closer. "What are you going to do? Kill the guy?"

She met his gaze. "Yes."

Reid grabbed her arm. "Harper, you can't go out without backup."

"Backup has done no good whatsoever."

"Let me go with you."

"No."

He lowered his voice. "What the hell is going on with you?"

"Tired of this damn game we're playing."

He motioned with his head toward the car. "And her?"

"What do you mean?"

"Hell, Harper…you know what I mean."

"Just doing my job."

"What I saw in the car, that wasn't your job." He leaned closer again. "Hell, Harper, you were crying, for God's sake."

"Don't worry about me. I'm fine."

He released her arm. "Okay. Whatever you say." He shrugged. "What the hell should I tell Mize?"

"Tell him the truth. Tell him I took off. Tell him you don't know where I am."

She brushed past him and went into their room, the door hanging open by one hinge. She glanced at the floor where she'd fallen, then to the bed where Dani had been. It had happened so fast, she hadn't even had a chance to offer a warning to Dani, hadn't had a chance to call out before he'd hit her. She touched her cheek now, feeling it starting to swell under her eye. The whole situation...damn, it could have been so much worse. He could have killed Dani right then if he'd wanted to. But that wasn't his game. Not yet. He apparently wanted to play with her before he killed her.

She pushed her thoughts away and went about collecting their things. Neither of them had unpacked. Perhaps unconsciously—with their recent track record—they knew they'd be leaving in a hurry once again. She zipped up her bag and tossed it over her shoulder, then picked up Dani's purse and her clothes bag and left the room without looking back.

Reid was talking to Hernandez and the two female detectives from Homicide. He looked over and she nodded at him before opening the back door to the car. Dani was still sitting there with her arms folded around herself. In her left hand was the locket she always wore.

"It...it broke again. I guess in my tumble." She wiped at a tear on her face. "My grandmother's. It would have killed me to lose it," she explained.

Harper took it from her fingers and closed her fist around it. "I'll keep it." She put it into her jeans pocket. "Come sit in the front with me."

"Where are we going?"

"I don't know yet."

CHAPTER THIRTY-SEVEN

"You think this is safe?" Dani asked as soon as the elevator doors closed.

"As safe as anything we've had so far." She smiled. "You said you wanted a five-star hotel."

Dani nodded. "So I did." She leaned against Harper's shoulder and gave a weary sigh. "And a car chase and a murder scene." She looked up at her. "Are you in trouble with Lieutenant Mize?"

"No doubt."

"Will they find us here?"

"Eventually, yes. I chose this area because there are six hotels within walking distance."

"They'll find the car."

"I doubt they'll find it in this area. I left the keys in it."

Dani's eyes widened. "You think someone will steal an unmarked police car?"

"Yeah. Windows are down, the keys are in the ignition, and it's in a dark alley. I would imagine it would be gone by midnight."

"You're pretty sneaky, Scout."

Harper smiled at the nickname Dani sometimes called her, but she said nothing else. She was tired—emotionally. She knew Dani was too. She didn't think now was the time to voice her fears to Dani…not now, riding up in an elevator to the twenty-first floor.

When the doors opened, she stepped out first, looking in both directions of the hallway. She motioned for Dani to follow and she led them down to their room. It was large, plush and so, so different than the tiny, dirty motel they'd been in.

"Very nice," Dani said. "Thank you."

Harper dropped her bag on the floor. "You want to shower?"

"Yes. Actually, I'd love a soak in the tub."

"You sore?"

"A little." Then, "Yes, a lot."

Harper nodded. "How about you let me shower first, then you can have the bath. Take as long as you like."

"Okay. Thank you."

Harper took longer than she intended in the shower, but the warm water felt too good on her skin. She knew Dani was waiting though, so she finally made herself get out. While robes weren't normally her thing, she couldn't resist the thick, soft one she found. Walking barefoot out to the main room, she found Dani sitting in one of the chairs, her eyes closed. She opened them, her gaze drifting slowly over the robe. Their eyes met for a second and Harper felt the energy between them. She looked away quickly, trying to ignore the heat she felt.

"All yours," she said as lightly as she could. "Take your time."

Dani didn't say anything as she walked past her and Harper turned, following her progress until Dani closed the bathroom door. She stared at the door long after it was closed, then turned away, heading to the minibar to see what overpriced treats it held. She contemplated room service and a bottle of wine, but she wanted something stronger than that. A tiny bottle caught her eye. Scotch. She ignored the price as she snatched it up. She twisted off the cap and took a sip, savoring the taste before swallowing. It seemed to clear her head somewhat and ease the throbbing ache in her cheek.

She gathered her dirty clothes, then remembered the locket she'd taken from Dani. She pulled it out of the pocket of her jeans and held it in her hand. The engraving on the back was faded—*My Love*. She felt a lump form in her throat. She and Jan had those same words engraved on the rings they'd exchanged. She folded her hand up, hiding the locket from her gaze. Jan's ring was buried with her. Harper's ring...she'd ripped it off in a fit of fury—and tears—one night when Jan's ghost had been sharing a bottle of whiskey with her.

After a few seconds, she opened her palm again. She wondered if Dani kept a photo inside and thought briefly of opening it to see, but decided she wouldn't invade her privacy. Instead, she laid it carefully on the dresser. Obviously it was something Dani cherished.

She turned the lights out, leaving on only the lamp, then she took the tiny bottle of scotch and sat down in the comfy, oversized chair. She stretched her legs out with a tired sigh. She should be formulating some sort of plan. She should be doing *something*, but she was too drained to contemplate anything. She hadn't told Dani but she'd turned her phone to vibrate. It had buzzed in her pocket more times than she could count. A quick glance had told her Mize and Reid had tried to reach her, both leaving messages. She hadn't bothered listening to either. She turned her phone off and pulled out the SIM card, just to be safe. The first thing they would do to find her was track her phone. She didn't need to listen to the messages anyway. Mize would be threatening her, demanding to know where she was, demanding that she come in. Reid would be issuing a warning about Mize and his anger.

And she simply didn't care.

She closed her eyes, trying to clear her mind of thoughts of Mize and Reid...and the stalker. The stalker who had managed to snatch Dani up in a matter of seconds. Harper hadn't been prepared. She'd let her guard down. And Dani? Dani had thrown herself out of a moving vehicle to avoid capture. How much courage had that taken? She was damn lucky she wasn't hurt. Or worse.

She opened her eyes when she heard the bathroom door. Dani stood there, her hair damp and tucked behind her ears. Like Harper, she was wearing a matching white robe. She looked so...so young, so innocent. Vulnerable. Her face was fresh and clean, no makeup to mar her natural beauty. The sight of her simply left Harper breathless. As their eyes held, Harper could see the sadness in Dani's, the remnants of tears. What was making her sad? Was it the stalker, the events of the day, the week? Or was it something else? Was it her lonely life? Her only brushes with intimacy were stolen moments with a roommate in college, and again, stolen moments with a married woman. Two affairs that were physical, never emotional.

Had anyone ever truly made love to Dani?

The answer to that question was hidden in Dani's eyes. Hidden in plain sight and it nearly broke Harper's heart to see it. She didn't think about Jan—not for one second—as she stood and walked slowly toward Dani. Their eyes were locked together as Harper stood in front of her. She reached out to gently touch the scrape on Dani's cheek, feeling the slight swelling beneath her fingers. She moved her hand lower, along the front of the robe. She could see Dani's pulse throbbing in her neck, could sense her uneven breathing...could almost hear Dani's thundering heartbeat. Or was that her own she was hearing?

It didn't matter which. Like the matching bruises on their cheeks, their hearts were beating the same tune.

She opened Dani's robe, thankful there were no undergarments covering her. Her breasts were full, her nipples erect, but Harper paused when she would have reached out to touch them. She looked back up, making sure this was what Dani wanted. She was shocked to see tears in her eyes.

"I'm sorry," she whispered immediately, moving to close Dani's robe again, but Dani stopped her.

"I need you," Dani whispered back to her. "Now. I...I need to be—"

"Loved," Harper finished for her. She wiped a tear at the corner of Dani's eye. "Please don't cry."

Dani nodded bravely as another tear escaped and Harper caught that one as well. Then she leaned closer, brushing her lips against Dani's so softly, she barely felt them. It was enough, though, to make Dani suck in a quick breath, enough for Dani to reach out to her, drawing her back to her mouth. Incredibly soft lips met her own and Harper felt a tremor course through her body at the contact. It was only then that she thought of Jan—a twinge of guilt surfacing—but she pushed the ghost away, not wanting to spoil the moment. Dani needed her now. Jan did not.

Gentle hands brushed her skin as they parted her robe and Harper sucked in a breath at the contact. Dani wasn't the only one who had been without love—intimacy. She had too. She deepened the kiss, pulling Dani closer to her, their opened robes no longer a barrier. Dani moaned against her mouth as their breasts touched, the sound causing Harper to utter her own quiet moan.

She didn't hesitate any longer. She pushed Dani's robe from her shoulders, letting it fall to the floor. Dani's chest rose and fell with each deep breath she took and Harper would have sworn that she saw her trembling under her stare. She wanted to say what was foremost in her mind—how utterly beautiful Dani was. But she kept the words inside. How often must Dani have heard them in the past? Yes, but how often had she heard them from a lover?

She touched Dani's face, her fingertips gently grazing her skin. Dani's eyes slipped closed, her face relaxing as Harper's fingers traced her lips, then her chin, moving slowly down her neck. She paused only slightly before touching her breasts. Dani's breath caught and her eyes fluttered open. Harper held her gaze as she brushed her nipples, seeing Dani's blue eyes darken, hearing her own quickened breath. The words she'd wanted to keep in slipped out.

"You're so beautiful." Dani's expression didn't change, and Harper wished she had not spoken. She leaned closer, kissing gently on the bruise on Dani's cheek. "I'm sorry."

Dani took her hand and brought it back to her breast. "Make love to me." Her voice was hoarse with unshed tears.

"Yes."

The sheets were cool against her skin as she drew Dani down to her. Harper didn't understand Dani's tears, the tears that fell gently from her eyes. Harper rolled them over, kissing the tears away as they fell.

"It's okay," she whispered. "Everything's okay."

* * *

Dani couldn't explain her tears...not to Harper, not to herself. Her emotions felt raw, exposed. She'd cried in the tub, unable to stop them then. She'd felt so alone and all she'd wanted was for someone—Harper—to hold her. She'd gotten herself under control by the time she'd stepped from the tub. But then there Harper was, looking at her like...like she cared. Like Dani mattered to her...like Dani was the most important thing in her life.

"Everything's okay," Harper whispered against her lips.

Yes, at that moment, everything was okay. She closed her mind to her doubts, her fears. Harper was here. Harper would make everything okay. Harper would take her away from it all, if only for a few hours.

She gave in to her kisses, opening her mouth, allowing their tongues to play together finally. It had been forever since anyone had touched her like this. She arched against Harper, feeling her weight press down on her. Moans mingled in the quiet room and soon, the world faded away. It was only them—no past, no stalker, no future. Just them in that moment—touching, kissing.

She opened her thighs, inviting Harper inside.

CHAPTER THIRTY-EIGHT

Harper smiled as Dani teased her nipple—again and again, her long blond hair brushing against her skin with each pass of her lips. She was exhausted and her eyes remained closed, but her body still responded to Dani's touch. They'd slept fitfully, in and out of sleep, interrupted by touches that grew bolder, more familiar, more demanding as the night wore on. She'd found Dani to be a passionate lover, as interested in Harper's pleasure as in her own. Harper had given in to her each time, surprised at how easily Dani could bring her to orgasm. She hadn't been riddled with guilt, she hadn't dwelled on it. She simply gave what Dani wanted—needed—and took what Dani offered her. There had been no words spoken between them. What was there to say? Neither knew what tomorrow would bring...or the day after that. She would have plenty of time to reflect on it all when Dani left and went back to LA.

Her hips jerked now as Dani's mouth kissed its way down past her stomach. As she had the first time, Harper moaned in anticipation, her eyes still closed as Dani spread her thighs. She rose up, meeting Dani's mouth as she buried herself in Harper's wetness...once again.

* * *

Dani moaned when Harper entered her. Long fingers curled inside of her, stroking her slowly, sensuously...taking her time. Dani's hips rolled with each stroke and she pulled Harper down to her mouth, kissing her fervently as the rhythm of Harper's fingers accelerated, little by little, until the cadence was such that Dani found her hips slamming into Harper, urging her on.

Harper pulled her mouth from Dani's, their breaths coming in quick gasps. Dani stared into her eyes, wondering how many times they'd made love...wondering how much time they had before dawn. Dawn would signal a new day, an end to these stolen moments. As if reading her mind, Harper slowed. She lowered her mouth again, kissing Dani thoroughly before moving to her breasts. She captured a nipple between her lips, her fingers delving deeper inside, faster again. Teeth raked against her nipple, then Harper's tongue swirled rapidly against the rigid peak. Dani's eyes slammed closed as she arched her hips high, opening herself to Harper. She felt her nipple being sucked into Harper's mouth and her world came to a stop for a breathless moment, then all her senses seemed to explode at once, bursting around her. Harper's mouth caught her scream and she squeezed her thighs tight around Harper's hand, holding her inside until the tremors subsided.

Harper gathered her close and pulled the sheet over them. Dani snuggled against her, once again wondering how much time they had until dawn. She felt herself falling into a deep sleep even as her hand moved between Harper's thighs, resting in her wetness.

* * *

Harper blinked several times, seeing daylight sneaking in behind the curtains. She closed her eyes again, ignoring it. Dani was sleeping beside her—nearly on top of her—and Harper pulled her closer. What a night it had been...what a morning. It was as if neither of them could get enough of each other's touch. Even now, as exhausted as she was, Harper wanted to wake Dani, wanted to make love just one more time. One more time before real life reared its head.

Where had this insatiable appetite come from? Three years of self-induced celibacy? Three years of letting her guilt run her personal life? She opened her eyes again. And just where was her guilt now? Where was Jan?

Harper opened her eyes, waiting for the inevitable fingers of guilt to claw their way into her heart again. She was holding another woman—a very naked woman—in her arms, a woman she'd made love to more times than she could count. Where was the guilt? Where was the disappointment in herself? Where was the shame? In the darkness of night, had she pushed it all away?

Dani shifted in her arms, rolling onto her back, the sheet slipping down to her waist. Harper's gaze traveled over her breasts, remembering how sensitive they were, remembering how soft...how responsive. Remembering how they tasted. She turned away from the sight, waiting on the guilt of daylight to descend upon her.

It never did.

"Are you still sore?" she asked Dani.

Dani's eyes never opened, but her mouth lifted in a smile. "In more ways than one."

Harper smiled too, and it occurred to her that those were the first words spoken between them since...well, since before. She didn't know what she was supposed to say, if anything. Dani surprised her by breaking the ice first.

"Are you beating yourself up?"

"I keep waiting on the guilt to hit me," she said honestly. "But...no."

Dani rolled to her side, facing Harper. "I feel like we should talk, but I don't know what to say."

"I know. Me either."

"Harper, I...I needed you, I needed *that*. I hope...well, I hope that you're not sorry."

"No. It was…it was a perfect night," Harper said, again waiting on guilt to strike. It was perfect, yes. Was that saying that things with Jan—in bed—weren't perfect? No. Things with Jan—sex with Jan was good. It always had been. Maybe last night, well, they were both riding on emotions; they *both* needed that, not just Dani. So maybe it was the fact that Harper needed that physical contact too that had her reeling.

"Do you feel guilty for not feeling guilty?"

Harper nodded, wondering how it had come about that Dani could read her so easily. "Honestly, after Jan died, I didn't think I'd ever be able to touch another woman. Or if I did, I assumed Jan would be there with me, that I would be thinking of her." She moved her hand under the cover, touching Dani's hip, before sliding it up to her waist. "It wasn't like that at all." She met Dani's eyes, trying to read them. "It was only you, never her."

"Thank you for telling me that. I was afraid that…well, I thought maybe—"

"No. I knew exactly who I was making love to. She wasn't with me last night." She sighed and lay back, staring at the ceiling. Did that mean Jan would never be with her again? Had her ghost finally left?

"I'm sorry," Dani whispered.

"No. Don't be." She turned her head to look at her. "Why were you crying?"

Dani blinked several times and Harper again saw a misting of tears there.

"I felt…all alone. I felt like I was on an island and no one was coming for me."

"I was right here."

Dani blinked at her tears again. "You were here, but you were still so far away. I needed to be touched and hugged and… and loved. You'd made it clear that you couldn't be that person for me."

"Oh, Dani…I'm sorry. That was my guilt talking. That was how I thought I *should* feel." She stared back at the ceiling, trying to reconcile her feelings now. Despite her telling Dani that she had nothing to offer her, that she felt empty inside...was that truly the case? Dani had awakened feelings inside of her that she thought were long dead. Feelings that she didn't think she'd ever have again...feelings that she thought Jan had taken with her to the grave. She looked back at Dani again. "I was attracted to you from the start."

Dani smiled and wiped at a tear on her face. "I was attracted to you just from looking at your picture. The real thing proved to be even better."

Harper smiled too, then sobered. "I almost got you killed."

Dani shook her head. "We felt safe there. Neither of us was prepared."

"I was terrified that I wasn't going to be able to keep up with him. I was afraid I'd lose him in traffic...then, then I'd never find you."

"I didn't know if you were following. He was driving erratically so I hoped you were, but the last thing I remembered was him hitting you, you falling to the floor." Dani touched the bruise on her cheek. "I knew if I didn't get away from him, then he'd kill me. I knew that."

"So you threw yourself out of the car." Harper took her hand. "I saw it happen, but I wasn't sure it was you, I wasn't sure. But I stopped. Something told me to stop."

"Maybe there was a guardian angel watching over us," Dani whispered.

It was Harper's turn to try to blink away tears. Could that be? Could Jan have somehow...? No. She didn't believe in that sort of thing.

Did she?

CHAPTER THIRTY-NINE

Dani held the broken clasp in her hand, thinking back to when she'd had it repaired two months ago. The jeweler had told her to replace the clasp then, but she'd asked him to fix it instead. She'd wanted the locket—the gold chain, the clasp, all of it—to remain intact, just as her grandmother had worn it all those years. Nothing else appeared to be damaged, at least.

"You said that was your grandmother's?"

Dani turned, finding Harper standing behind her, her hair still damp from her shower. She didn't know what liberties she could take now...now that they'd slept together. She would take as much as Harper would allow, she supposed. Because yes, last night had been perfect. So different than the affair she'd had with Tara. And certainly different than the fumbling teenagers she and Traci had been. When she'd dared to dream about having a lover...a lover she didn't have to hide...those dreams were never as vivid as what she'd experienced with Harper. She hesitated going to her, though. It was now the light of day; they were no longer in bed, naked, touching. Harper tilted her head, studying her. Could she read her mind? Did Harper sense her uncertainty? She must have. She leaned closer, touching her lips lightly, then lingering there, enough for Dani to feel the heat spring up between them again. What liberties could she take? She opened Harper's robe, finding her naked, as she'd hoped. Their kiss deepened and Dani felt herself being pulled closer, her clothed body pressing against Harper's naked one. She wanted to rip her own clothes off. She wanted to pull Harper back into bed. She wanted to turn the lights out and pretend it was still the wee hours of the morning, pretend that they had all the time in the world.

But they didn't. They had a stalker.

Still...Harper was the one to end the heated kiss, the one to take a step back...not her. Harper tightened the robe again, cleared her throat, and repeated her question.

"So...your grandmother's?"

Dani nodded, only then realizing she still had the heart-shaped locket in her hand. She looked at it, the shiny surface worn smooth by years and years of being touched, of being rubbed between fingers. The inscription on the back was all but worn away. *My Love.*

"She never had a wedding ring. Or an engagement ring, for that matter." She smiled, remembering the story her grandmother had told her many times. "They eloped. Drove all the way to Vegas to get married. They couldn't afford rings so he got this for her. She never took it off, not even after he died." She looked at Harper. "So when she gave it to me...when she took it off and gave it to me...well, I guess I should have known something was wrong."

"I'm sorry."

Dani nodded. "I was always closer to her than to my parents. It's hard to believe that my mother was raised by her. My mother was so completely different than she was." She held up the pendant. "It broke a few months ago. I asked him to fix the clasp instead of replacing it. I guess that was a mistake. It would have killed me if I'd have lost it." She squeezed her hand around it. "This locket means more to me than anything."

Harper was staring at her, her eyebrows drawn together. "And you never take it off," she murmured, almost to herself.

Dani opened her hand, looking at the locket. "No. Why?"

"'All I have to do is follow your heart,'" Harper said. "The note he left. All he has to do is follow your heart."

Dani's eyes widened. "Oh, my God. You don't think…?"

"How did it break the first time?"

Dani shook her head. "I don't know, really. I was at my house. The detective was there, I remember. It just fell off."

"Okay, let's start at the beginning." Harper guided her into the chair, then sat down next to her. "Your stalker was already in the picture when it broke?"

"Yes." Dani held up her hand. "And no offense, because I love you in the robe and you know, you're naked and everything… but if you want to have a serious conversation with me, you should probably put some clothes on."

* * *

Harper came out of the bathroom—fully clothed—her mind reeling with questions. Could it really have been the locket all along? But they'd scanned it. They'd scanned everything.

"You're frowning."

"I know." She held her hand out. "Let me see it."

Dani handed over the locket and Harper tried to pry it open. "Is it usually this hard?"

"No. But then, I rarely open it. There's not much left of the picture inside."

Harper finally got it to open and she spread the heart apart, revealing an old, faded picture. It was so old and frayed, she couldn't make out the image. "Your grandmother?" she guessed.

"Yes. Her wedding day."

Harper went over to the desk and, using a pen, pushed the picture out of the locket. Behind it was a tiny square of blue, not much bigger than a piece of glitter.

"Oh, my God," Dani whispered. "Is that…is that something?"

"I imagine so." She put the locket down, leaving the tracking device inside. "Okay, it broke. You did what? Took it somewhere to get it fixed?"

"Yes. I would normally have sent Shelly but…well, honestly, I didn't trust her with the locket. It was all I could do to leave it to be repaired. It's that precious to me."

"How long was it out of your possession?"

"Not long. I think three or four days."

Harper paced alongside the bed. "How did your stalker get ahold of your locket?" She stopped pacing. "He's watching your house. He sees you go to the jeweler, you take something in. How does he know what it is? How would he get access to it?"

Dani shook her head. "I don't know."

"And if that thing is a tracking device, the scans should have picked it up." She paused. "Of course, it could be an on-demand type of device."

"Meaning?"

"Meaning it only transmits a signal when it's asked to. He could have left it dormant anytime he knew you were in the station with me. There was no need to track you, he knew where you were. He probably assumed we were scanning everything."

"What do you want to do?"

"First things first. Let's call your jeweler. I'm assuming he'll remember you."

Dani flashed a smile. "I would hope so. He took a picture with me. He was going to hang it on his wall."

It was barely ten thirty. Eight thirty in LA. Would the jeweler even be at his shop yet? Instead of turning her phone on and using her cell, Harper had Dani use the room's phone. Until she had some more information, she wasn't quite ready for Lieutenant Mize to find them yet. She did think briefly of calling Reid, though. Now that she knew how he was tracking Dani, she thought they could use that to their advantage.

"Hi, Mr. Chandler. It's Danielle Stevens." Dani nodded. "Yes, I'm fine. Thank you. I'm actually calling about the locket— the clasp—that I had you fix." A pause. "No, no, it's fine. Well, actually, it broke again but that's not why I'm calling." She held her hand up, as if speaking to him in person. "I'm not in the area right now, no." She looked at Harper and rolled her eyes. "Of course. As soon as I can. Now…about the locket. You remember when I left it with you. Did anyone come in, asking about it? Did anyone ask to see it or anything?"

Harper watched as Dani's brow furrowed in a frown.

"A cop? Really?" Dani met her gaze. "A detective? Was it Detective Zapalac?" Dani nodded quickly. "I see. No, no. Everything's fine. Yes, as soon as I'm in the area, I'll come by." Dani nodded again. "Thank you." She put the phone down, then stood up and backed away from it as if it was threatening her.

"Who is Detective Zapalac?"

Dani wrapped her arms around herself. "He was…he was the detective assigned to my stalker." She met Harper's gaze again. "You don't think *he's* the stalker, do you?"

"He's the one who didn't believe you?"

"Yes."

"And did he know about your security camera?"

"Yes."

Harper shook her head. "I don't know, Dani. If he's your stalker, what are the chances that he's going to be assigned to your case?"

Dani's eyes widened. "What if he wasn't assigned to me?"

"What do you mean?"

"I mean, I called the police. Several times. Uniformed officers always showed up. Then one day, I get a knock on my door. He's there. What if he wasn't assigned? What if he did it on his own?"

"You're thinking he pretended he was working your case?" Harper shrugged. "I guess. Why would you have cause to doubt him?"

"Exactly. After that, I always called *him* whenever something was left. He…he always came out by himself." Dani leaned her head back and stared at the ceiling. "Oh, God. I can't believe it."

"Look, let's don't assume all of this. We know our stalker is here. Let's call LAPD and check. If he's there, then he can't be your stalker."

"It's him," Dani insisted. "In the car last night, there was something familiar about him. He only said one word to me: 'Gotcha.'" She shook her head. "But if it's him, why go to all this trouble? He had me in LA. I let him into my house, for God's sake!"

"Remember, it's a game to him. That's all."

"He's much more than a stalker, isn't he?"

"Yes. He could be a serial killer, for all we know."

"God, Harper, you're not helping ease my fears here."

"Sorry. But you know what I mean. You're a celebrity. Celebrities get stalkers. Perfect cover for him." She held her hand up. "Again, let's don't jump to conclusions. Let me call LAPD."

CHAPTER FORTY

"A cop? You can't be serious." Reid looked between her and Dani and shook his head. "He pretended to be a cop?"

"A detective, to be more precise," Harper said.

Reid looked at Dani. "What did he do?"

"When I first suspected someone had been in my house—pictures moved, books out of place—I called the police. When I had flowers left inside for me, I called the police. Uniformed officers always showed up, took my statement, suggested I get a security camera, a bodyguard, that sort of thing. Then one day, this detective knocked on my door. He had a badge. He had a card, it looked official." Dani tucked her hair behind her ears in a nervous gesture. "He told me he was taking over the case and that I should call him from now on if anything happened." Dani looked at her. "The first time I called him was when a doll was left in the kitchen during the night. I was totally freaking out and I called him. He came right away. But it was always the same. No evidence. Nothing on the security camera. I got the impression that he didn't believe me." She shook her head. "How funny that must have been to him, huh?"

"I called LAPD," Harper said to Reid. "Verified that they have no Detective Zapalac and they've never assigned anyone to Danielle Stevens."

"What about the jeweler? Maybe they've got him on a security camera. We should check. We need to get Mize involved."

"No. If we go in, then they'll take Dani away, I'll be removed from the case. LAPD will get involved. The FBI will get involved."

"Hell, Harper, you'll be lucky to still have a job. You know you're looking at a suspension. I'm telling you, he was *pissed*. They found your car in Five Points. It was stripped so bad, the dash wasn't even in one piece."

"I don't care about that right now."

Reid looked at Dani. "What do *you* want to do?"

"I stay with Harper," Dani said firmly. "I don't trust anyone else."

Reid sighed and shook his head. "You're right, Harper. As soon as you go in, they're taking your service weapon and shield and putting you on paid leave. They'll whisk Dani away. And yeah, they'll get LAPD involved, the FBI too. We'll be out of the loop."

"That's not going to happen. Not until we get this bastard."

Reid met her gaze. "What do you want me to do, Harper?"

"Be my backup."

He stared at her for a long moment, then let out a deep breath. "Sure. We might as well both be suspended at the same time, right?"

She reached across the table and squeezed his hand. "Thank you. And I'm assuming they're running a trace on my phone."

"They are."

"So as soon as I put the SIM card back in, they'll get me."

"They will."

"So when we really need the troops, I'll do that. Until then, it's you and me."

He nodded. "So? There's a plan?"

She stood up. "Working on it."

"Working on it?"

"You said before that this guy was a professional. I think he is. He's done this before. Sorrell wasn't his first kill."

"And you think you can take him down?"

She and Dani exchanged glances and Harper nodded. "I've got to."

"Okay, Harper. I'll go with you on this, but I don't like it."

"Fair enough."

He nodded, then turned a circle, looking around the room. "Nice place. What did this set you back?"

Harper smiled. "Don't have a clue. I let Danielle Stevens pay for it."

Reid laughed, then opened the minibar, snooping inside. "I notice there's a bottle missing."

"Yeah, that little bottle probably cost her fifty bucks."

Dani smiled at her. "And you didn't even share it with me."

His gaze drifted around the room again, finally landing on the unmade bed...the *only* bed in the room. He looked at her and raised an eyebrow. She met his gaze, then grinned teasingly. He rolled his eyes.

"As if," he mouthed to her.

Harper met Dani's amused expression and gave her a subtle wink.

CHAPTER FORTY-ONE

"This is a stupid idea. It's never going to work."

"You've said that. I don't know why. He's following the locket."

"You do look kinda cute as a blonde. I'm not crazy about the long hair, though."

"Shut up," she said as she adjusted the wig.

Reid laughed. "You look like you're in drag."

She turned and glared at him. "Seriously...shut up."

"I can't believe you're trusting me with her. You've been kinda possessive with Danielle."

"I know. And if anything happens to her, I'll shoot you myself."

"If I didn't know better, I'd say you've got a little bit of a crush happening here, Harper."

A crush? Harper wanted to tell him that what happened last night was way more than a crush, but she wasn't certain Reid could handle that bit of information. Besides, Dani was still Danielle Stevens. What happened between them last night couldn't ever get out.

"We've…kinda become friends," she said instead.

"Look, I saw you last night in the car. I think that was a little more than you being friends." He shrugged. "But hey, you falling for a straight chick—Danielle Stevens—nobody would blame you. Hell, if I was the one guarding her day and night… Jesus, I'd have already made a fool of myself. I mean, that woman is gorgeous. Even after all she's been through, looking at her today, she's like—"

"I get the picture."

"Yeah. And like, you're really sleeping in the same bed?"

"Really."

"*Man*…I'm so jealous!"

They both turned when the bathroom door opened, and Dani came out. Harper stared, wondering how in the world she'd managed to get all her hair shoved under the wig. She was wearing Harper's shirt. Harper was wearing one of Dani's blouses. It was a little tight, but she could manage. They'd even gone so far as to have Dani wear Harper's shoes—a half size too large.

"Well? Do I look like you?"

Harper shook her head. "No. You're much too pretty to pass for me."

"I'll say," Reid added.

Harper pointed at her wig. "How did you hide all your hair?"

"Pin curls and a wig cap." Dani tugged at the wig. "How bad does it look?"

"It looks great. Not that I think you should keep that style or color. I kinda like…" She stopped, nearly forgetting Reid was there.

"Yeah…I'm not crazy about you in that look either," Dani said, not trying to hide her smile.

Reid looked between them, obviously confused by their familiarity. Harper finally cleared her throat.

"So? Are we ready?"

Reid held his hand up. "Let me just go on record as saying—"

"Yeah, yeah…stupid idea. You got a better one?"

"I'm sure Lieutenant Mize would have a better one."

Harper shook her head. "No. We do this, we get it over with."

"And we'll probably both lose our jobs."

"So you keep saying." She had to admit, it was risky. How far were they willing to go? Into New Mexico? Arizona? All the way to California?

"We should at least fill Mize in," he continued, harping on his earlier suggestion.

"The answer is still no. Now…let's go over it again."

"Risky plan," Reid mumbled. "We'll never pull it off."

She ignored him. "Got your burner phone?" They both nodded. "I go to the front desk, you follow behind. Dani, keep Reid between you and the doors. The rental car will be out front, waiting. We'll go outside together. Again, Dani, make sure Reid is a buffer. Turn your head. Don't give him a clear view of you."

"Provided he's even watching," Reid said.

"He's watching. Biding his time, but he's watching. We'll say our goodbyes. A handshake. I get in the rental and drive away. You go in the opposite direction. Ditch the patrol car. Hop in the second rental."

"Meet up with you north of Fort Worth."

"We should know by the time we get to Decatur whether he's tailing me or not."

"You check into a motel in Wichita Falls," Dani added. "Alone. And hope he comes knocking."

Reid shook his head. "Crazy plan. If he's as good as we think, he's going to recognize us tailing you too."

"I think our guy is so focused on Danielle Stevens that he's not going to see anything. He had her. She got away. I imagine he's filled with rage at this point. Her escaping wasn't part of his game."

"Then why didn't he try something last night?"

"We're in a fancy hotel, with security, twenty-one floors up. I know he went into her hotel room that first day, but that was different. It's one thing to pretend to be delivering room service to an empty room. Quite different when that room is occupied. Even if he did get in and disabled me, he's still got to get her down twenty-one floors. He's obsessed with her, but he's not crazy."

"And you think he'll feel safe enough trying something in a little two-story motel in Wichita Falls?"

"Yes. He'll think she's alone. Game over."

Reid still shook his head. "I don't think you can pull this off. You look *nothing* like Danielle Stevens."

"It's dark. When we get to Wichita Falls, it'll be almost midnight. The only thing he'll see of me is blond hair. Remember, he's following the locket."

"Look, I hate to be the cynic here, but you don't know for sure that the thing you found in the locket is a tracking device."

"What else would it be?" Harper threw her hands up. "Reid, if you want to back out, tell me now. I'll think of something else. Hell, Dani and I can go alone. Let him think I'm escorting her back to LA."

Reid met her gaze. "I just think this is a bad idea, that's all. We've gone to so much trouble to hide her, why would we let her sneak out of town in the dead of night?" Reid paced between her and Dani. "Harper, think this through logically, okay? For one thing, he's killed a cop. You have no business going after him alone. And two, you're a Dallas cop—a rogue Dallas cop—in Wichita Falls. Everything about this is wrong."

"It was the only idea that made sense." She could tell by the look in his eyes that he wasn't all in with this. In fact, he wasn't really *in* at all. Did she blame him? If it were reversed, would she agree to this crazy scheme? She let out a frustrated breath. Maybe it was a bad idea. She turned, looking at herself in the mirror. She didn't recognize herself, no, but she wasn't Danielle Stevens. And Reid was right. Would they really let Danielle Stevens leave town with such little fanfare?

Hell.

She ripped the wig off.

"Harper?"

She moved closer to Dani, studying her profile. No, it would never work. She reached up and touched the wig, then shook her head. "Reid is right. It's not going to work." She met her gaze. "Don't ever dye your hair brown," she murmured.

"I take it we're going with Plan B?"

"Yeah." She turned to Reid. "Dani and I will go alone. That'll keep you out of trouble with Mize."

"That's Plan B? No, Harper. Plan B should be going in to the station. Plan B should be you—"

"No. Tell Mize I took off and wouldn't tell you a thing. If it ends badly, they'll have someone to blame."

"It's going to end badly. You think you can take this guy on by yourself? Hell, Harper, he already killed a cop. He's a pro. He's not going to just waltz into your room and let you arrest him."

"I don't plan on arresting him," she said pointedly. "As you said…he's killed a cop. I doubt it's his first time."

"Harper, let's go in. Tell Mize about the locket. Let them—"

"No," she said firmly. "I don't trust anyone right now. Not with her."

CHAPTER FORTY-TWO

"Nervous? Scared?"

Dani nodded. "Not going to lie, yes. But I'm glad we're together."

"That was a stupid plan," Harper conceded. "Although the hair salon in the hotel was very accommodating."

She laughed. "Yeah, but that blond wig was so not you." She leaned back against the seat, trying to relax. "You're going to get into a lot of trouble with Mize, aren't you?"

"I imagine so. I'll worry about it later."

Dani reached to her neck, noting the absence of the locket. Harper must have seen her.

"It's in a safe place."

Dani glanced at her and smiled. "It feels weird without it. It always does when I take it off."

"Is that the only thing you have from your childhood?"

"Yes. When I left home, I didn't take much with me. I told you, my parents weren't in favor of the move and they didn't help at all. I think they were hoping that the move would be too much for me—too big—and I'd change my mind." She took a deep breath, remembering that time in her life. "There was always friction between us, but that was probably the thing that drove the biggest wedge. After I moved...well, our relationship deteriorated quickly. I was truly on my own." She paused. "I think, secretly, they were glad I left. They didn't know what to do with me; I was so different from my sister."

"Well, like you said, they were older when you were born. They probably didn't know how to relate to you."

"Add in the fact that the pregnancy was a big shock to them...yes. What about you? You said you had older brothers?"

"Four and six years older."

"Any contact?"

Harper glanced at her. "They try."

"And your parents?"

"We talk occasionally. They're not quite sure how to handle the topic of Jan, so we sort of dance around it. It's just this big elephant in the room that we ignore."

"You should go see them. Reconnect." Harper gave her an incredulous look and Dani laughed. "I know, I'm a fine one to be offering advice, aren't I?"

"My parents are younger. Yours are what? In their seventies?"

Dani nodded. "My dad was fifty when I was born so yes, he's seventy-eight, seventy-nine." She turned to Harper. "I haven't seen them since that day I left home. I was nineteen. I remember thinking how old they were then, how out of touch they were with me...with life."

"Ten years?"

"About, yes. I've changed a lot in ten years. If not for the gay thing, they might actually like me better now." She reached across the console to touch Harper's arm, letting her hand rest there. "Are you okay doing this on our own?" she asked, changing the subject.

"I wish we had some backup, but I can't blame Reid for not wanting to get his ass busted just because I decided to take off with you—unauthorized." Harper raised her eyebrows. "Are *you* okay with it?"

"I trust you."

"Why? I almost got you killed."

"Because you're concerned about *me*. You're not concerned with proper protocol or saving face if something goes wrong. Your only interest is protecting me."

"So many things could go wrong, Dani. This guy, whoever he is, knows what he's doing. He's a pro at this. Our only advantage is that we now know how he's tracking us."

"Meaning the locket will be used as bait, not me."

"Exactly. It's still risky."

"If we had gone in, would they really have brought in the FBI?"

"Yes."

"And you would have been off the case?"

"In a heartbeat."

"Even against my wishes?"

"A cop was killed. They don't care quite as much about you as they did before," Harper said bluntly.

"Which is why I'm glad I'm with you and not them."

She squeezed Harper's arm where her hand had been resting, then pulled it away. Were they on the run now? Was it like a bad movie? Now that her stalker had resorted to killing a police officer, were they even concerned where she and Harper were? Were they truly on their own?

"Second thoughts?"

Dani gave a hesitant smile. "No. A lot could go wrong, I know, but I agree with you. If we'd stayed in Dallas—if I were surrounded by police and the FBI—he wouldn't make a move. He'd disappear."

"Like a ghost."

"But I'd know he was still out there. He might show up later, maybe months later, after I'd let my guard down. If I leave here and he's still out there, I have no choice but to get a bodyguard." She turned to Harper. "It's what I probably should have done in the first place. Then you wouldn't be mixed up in all this. A woman wouldn't have been raped. A police officer wouldn't have been killed."

"Dani, you can't take the blame for that."

"I *should* take the blame for that. I brought him here." She folded her hands together. "And yes, I am scared and nervous. I got used to having a stalker, I guess, but not all of this." She leaned her head back. "And then...after last night...God, I just wish we'd met...well, without a stalker in the picture." She looked at Harper then. "Of course, things might be different between us. I doubt we'd have grown this close."

Harper nodded. "Yeah, I doubt we would have been sharing a bed. Which I quite liked, by the way. There was never anything uncomfortable about it, even that first night when we were still strangers."

There were too many shadows in the car for her to read Harper's expression, but she didn't doubt the sincerity of her words. Yes, comfortable. From the moment she'd met Harper, she'd felt comfortable with her, as if they'd been old friends reuniting after years apart. Which was odd, of course. She had no old friends.

She had no friends at all.

Feeling suffocated again by her loneliness, she wanted to curl into a ball and cry. As if sensing this, Harper reached across the console of their rented car and took her hand, squeezing it tightly. The hand was warm and soft, and Dani's fingers entwined with Harper's, feeling comforted by the contact.

Yes, she did have a friend.

CHAPTER FORTY-THREE

Harper was struggling to stay awake, and she'd already made up her mind to stop at the first motel she came to. As far as she could tell, there was no one following them. Once they'd left Decatur, traffic had been light. By the time midnight rolled around, the nearest car to her was at least a mile behind as the headlights faded in and out of her view. As they approached Wichita Falls, even at this hour on a Sunday night, there was a little more traffic than she would have imagined. It made it harder to judge if someone were following, especially at night as cars' headlights seemed to merge and blur with every blink of her eye. Still, she felt confident that if he had been following, he wasn't right on their tail. And he didn't have to be, did he? He was following the locket.

She glanced over at Dani and couldn't help but smile. She was curled against the seat, facing Harper. She'd tried to stay awake, tried to keep the conversation going but as the miles ticked by, she'd given up the fight.

"Hey...wake up," she said softly. "We're here."

Dani shifted in her seat, then jerked her head up. "Oh, my God. I fell asleep. Why did you let me?"

"I tried tickling you, but that didn't seem to help," she teased. "Besides, you didn't get much sleep last night."

"Neither did you," Dani said around a yawn. "You must be exhausted."

"I am."

She pulled into a well-lit parking lot, following the blinking arrow to the office. There were ten or more cars in the lot of the Coyote Motel and—at least on the outside—it appeared to be clean and meticulously maintained. Large pots of colorful flowers glowed under the lights and gave a welcoming appearance.

"Will this do?"

"It's fine with me," Dani said. "Will you be able to sleep or..."

"I've got to get a few hours, yes."

"Will it be safe? I mean—"

"We'll get two rooms—adjoining. One for us, one for the locket. I'm not sure he'll try anything tonight. We've left Dallas, probably threw him off his game a little. I'd guess he's going to see what we've got planned."

"Cat and mouse."

"Yes. When we head out again tomorrow, he's bound to think I'm taking you back to LA."

"But couldn't he decide to follow along and wait until I'm back home to resume his stalking?"

"I don't think so. He's past that. What fun would it be for him to walk up to your door, pretending to be Detective Zapalac? You'd let him in. There'd be no fight, no chase."

"I hope you're right."

Harper could hear the apprehension in her voice. "Dani... I'm not going to leave you until we've got this guy. If I've got to take you all the way to California, I will."

Dani nodded. "I'm ready for this all to be over with, you know. But...it'll be hard to say goodbye to you, Scout."

Harper smiled. "Not that I want to say goodbye just yet, but I'm really sick of this bastard."

* * *

Dani sat down in the chair, feeling somewhat detached from the situation she found herself in. It could have been a movie set; the gun felt odd in her hands. The whole last week could have been a movie, she thought. Especially last night. She'd been abducted by the stalker—the clown. Thrown, unconscious, into the backseat of a car. Then, with recovered consciousness, she threw herself out of that same speeding car, more scared of her fate with him than that of tumbling out onto a busy street. And then Harper was there, picking her up, holding her, telling her everything was okay. And later, Harper had been there when she'd needed her, when she'd been at her lowest, when—emotionally—she was as drained as she'd ever been. Harper had been there. She glanced over at her now, letting her gaze linger on her face, feeling somewhat comforted by simply looking at her.

They'd entered the motel room and Harper had quickly turned on all the lights. She'd placed the locket on the dresser. After locking the door and sliding the chair in front of it, they'd gone into the adjoining room, turning no lights on at all. Harper had pulled the drapes closed tightly, only then turning on the bathroom light. She'd given Dani her backup weapon, then had literally crashed on the bed. She'd been asleep within seconds, it seemed.

Harper had told her she needed at least a couple of hours of sleep. She'd also told her if she heard anything suspicious or if she was scared to wake her immediately. Of course every little noise she heard outside had her fidgeting nervously.

Scared? Yes, she was. Scared that he would come. Scared that he wouldn't and they'd have to deal with it all again another day. And also scared that it could be over soon, for completely different reasons.

She needed to come to grips with the fact that what they'd shared last night was the result of the circumstances and nothing more. They would say their goodbyes and get back to their respective lives. And in a few months' time, she would return to Dallas, this time definitely as Danielle Stevens, about to shoot her final movie.

Then what? Would she and Harper see each other while she was there? Could they grab dinner, maybe? Would Harper even want to see her? Or would she be riddled with guilt and want nothing to do with her? Or worse, there would be no guilt at all and Harper would be playing the dating game. Perhaps Dani was nothing more than a bridge for her...a bridge taking her from Jan onto the next woman she could fall in love with.

She sighed, again looking over at Harper as she slept. Her face was in the shadows, but Dani knew every curve of it. She'd memorized it long before she'd actually met Harper. She wondered if that's how it would be...a memory in the back of her mind, a memory she took out from time to time, a memory that was real and not just the etching of a photograph.

A slamming of a door brought her back to the present and she jerked to attention, her gaze darting around the room. She heard a car start up then drive off, and she relaxed again. As relaxed as she could be, sitting on guard, holding a gun in her hands.

CHAPTER FORTY-FOUR

Harper woke with a start, disoriented for a moment as she reached a hand out next to her. Finding the bed empty, she sat up. In the darkness, she could see Dani in the chair, watching her.

"What time is it?" her voice still thick with sleep.

"Nearly four."

She groaned and lay back down. "You were supposed to wake me at two."

"I know, but you were sleeping so soundly, I couldn't bring myself to."

Harper patted the bed beside her. "Come here. You're bound to be tired."

"Yes, I am."

Harper took the gun and placed it on the table beside the bed—and the other gun. As Dani lay down next to her, she wished they could get undressed and under the covers, but she didn't want to let her guard down. It was four though. If he hadn't come by now, he probably wasn't going to. Still, she didn't completely relax. She leaned back against the pillow and pulled Dani closer. Dani snuggled next to her with a tired sigh.

"We don't have to leave early, do we?"

"No." She closed her eyes. "You can sleep."

Dani snaked an arm across her waist and burrowed down beside her. Harper was surprised at how familiar it all felt—holding Dani this way. Not Jan, but Dani. She opened her eyes a little, seeing the mass of blond hair spread out around her. She closed them again and pulled Dani a little closer.

* * *

They didn't have time for this. They should get up. They should shower and get on the road. But Harper couldn't bring herself to open her eyes, to wake Dani, to end the peaceful slumber she'd fallen into while Dani snuggled against her.

They didn't have time for this. *She* didn't have time for this. Not for these few precious moments when things felt…normal. And it had been so very long since things had felt normal in her life. Once she opened her eyes, that feeling would end. She was lying here with Danielle Stevens while a stalker was hunting them. A stalker who had turned into a cop killer. A stalker who was now hunted—most likely futilely—in Dallas. Or maybe they weren't hunting the stalker at all. Maybe they were chasing her and Dani. Maybe Mize finally realized that Dani was like a magnet for the stalker.

And maybe she shouldn't have run. Maybe she should have done what Reid had wanted; go in. Let Mize take over. Let Homicide take over. Hell, let the FBI take over. It wasn't too late. She could turn around and head back to Dallas today. Hand Dani over to them. Most likely hand over her gold shield and service weapon too. How long would her suspension be? A couple of weeks? A month? Six months?

But no, there wasn't any need to go back to Dallas. It wouldn't take long to find them, even if they were using cash. The rental car was in Dani's name. Dani Strauss, that is. They would most likely find that out before too long. She figured they maybe had one more day before the FBI swooped in. One more night, if they were lucky. Their guy hadn't made a move yet. Would he be able to hold out much longer? She didn't think so.

They'd drive up Highway 287 toward Amarillo. There were a handful of small towns along the route. They'd grab a motel…a motel with easy access. He wouldn't be able to resist, would he? He'd make his move. And she'd—

"You're frowning," Dani murmured. "What are you thinking about?"

Harper took a deep breath, finally forcing her eyes opened. "Lots of things," she admitted.

"Like?"

"Like I'm hungry, but I don't want to get out of bed."

Dani leaned up on her elbow, meeting her gaze. Harper was thankful for the shadows in the room. Even so, she knew Dani could see through her lie.

"Second thoughts?"

Harper nodded. "It won't matter much anyway. I figure we'll only have one more day at the most before they find us. I just hope our clown friend makes his move before then."

Dani sat up completely and brushed her hair back, away from her face. "They? Meaning FBI?"

She nodded. "Yes."

"Do you think my name has been leaked yet?"

"I think they'll try to find us first before your name is associated with Sorrell's death. If at all. It'll just be a media frenzy. I'm sure they'd like to avoid that."

"What does that say about me that I'd rather face our clown friend than be in the middle of a media circus?"

Harper smiled. "It says that you think I can protect you against the clown but not the circus."

Dani studied her for a moment, then leaned closer and lightly kissed her lips. Harper's eyes closed, but Dani took it no farther.

"I feel like I've known you for years," Dani whispered. "How can that be?"

Harper wished she had an answer. She, too, felt closer to Dani than a week warranted. Even without the intimacy they'd

Bella Books, Inc.

Women. Books. Even Better Together.

P.O. Box 10543
Tallahassee, FL 32302

Phone: 800-729-4992
www.bellabooks.com

shared, she still felt that closeness. Making love had only deepened it. So yes, how could it be that the familiarity between them was fostered by days and not years? Was it the stress of the situation? Was it the state of affairs they found themselves in? Life or death? Did they bond out of necessity?

Or was it something else entirely?

Her answer was to touch Dani's face, caress the smooth skin, get lost in her eyes. She had an aching need to be close to her, to take the time to connect on a more physical level—emotional. She could see in Dani's eyes that she wanted the same. But...

"We should get up. Shower. See what the day holds."

"We should make love," Dani countered in a whisper.

"I don't think we're afforded that kind of time."

"Time is all we can control, Harper. Let's get out of these clothes. Let's take the time."

CHAPTER FORTY-FIVE

They went into the adjoining room and Harper picked up the locket. She held it in her hand for a second before slipping it into her pocket. She slung her bag over her shoulder, then glanced at Dani who was already by the door, waiting. She had a smile on her face; her skin still flushed from their lovemaking, even after a shower. Harper returned her smile.

"Thank you for forcing me to get naked."

Dani laughed. "Yeah, it took all of two seconds to persuade you."

"Did it take *that* long?"

Dani came closer, close enough for them to touch. "I like you, Scout. Through all of this craziness, you've kept me sane." Dani gave her a flirty smile. "As an added plus, you're a very good kisser."

"That's a bonus, huh?"

Dani ran her hand up her chest, pausing to cup her breast before moving higher, circling her neck and pulling Harper closer. The kiss left Harper breathless. Breathless and wanting

more. Breathless and wishing they were…where? Anywhere but here? Wishing that this was a real road trip? Wishing she was taking Dani back to California? Wishing they didn't ever have to stop?

Those thoughts startled her. She had a house in Dallas, a job. That was her life…her lonely life where her only company was when Jan's ghost came to visit. As she stared into Dani's eyes, she realized that she hadn't given Jan a thought since… well, she couldn't remember when. Certainly not yesterday and certainly not this morning…not this morning while they were making love.

She pulled Dani into her arms, soaking in her closeness for a few seconds longer before gently pushing her away.

"I wish we had a day…to play. But we don't."

Dani nodded. "I know. Back to the real world." She paused, again smiling at Harper. "The real world sucks."

"That it does."

Harper motioned for Dani to get behind her as she opened the door, leaving the security chain still attached. The sun was bright, the sky clear, the air cool. There were no cars parked near their rental. She closed the door and removed the chain.

"Stay close to me."

"Like glue."

Harper smiled when she felt Dani's fingers link with a belt loop of her jeans. The smile was short-lived, however. A doll—a damn Raggedy Ann doll again—was propped against the small flower pot on the sidewalk. To her surprise, Dani walked over to it and, without much ceremony, gave it a quick kick, sending it flying out into the parking lot.

"I really *hate* this guy." She turned to Harper. "And I'm beginning to really hate dolls."

Harper laughed, glad Dani had disposed of the offending doll. "Come on. Let's get out of here."

* * *

"You probably don't want to talk about this, but do you think there's any significance to him using a Raggedy Ann doll?"

"Significance? Even if he was able to somehow get my name, I doubt he'd have the resources to find out that I was assigned the case in Tucson. I still think it's just a coincidence. I don't think he's leaving them for my benefit."

Dani nodded. But if this were a movie, it wouldn't be so farfetched that Harper's serial killer—the one who murdered her lover—would show back up in her life. But it wasn't a movie. It was only a coincidence that her stalker left dolls—a variety of dolls, to be sure. The fact that he had resorted to using Raggedy Ann dolls of late was of no consequence. The only impact it had—for Harper, at least—was bringing the tragedy in Tucson back to the forefront.

She tried to relax as the miles sped by. There wasn't much in terms of scenery as they headed west toward Amarillo. By the time they'd left the motel, it was closer to lunch than breakfast. The aroma of burgers and fries filled the car and they'd eaten—almost ravenously—in silence as Harper drove. Now, lunch was gone—wadded up in a bag on the backseat floor—and her watery Coke sloshed in the cup, the ice all but melted.

She passed the time by checking the mirrors, trying to decide if someone was following them. There wasn't a lot of traffic, mostly eighteen-wheelers and pickup trucks. The bright sunshine had given way to clouds, dropping the temperature a few degrees. The country music radio station they'd picked up had warned of drizzle and a freeze was in the forecast for that evening. She wondered if Harper had even packed a jacket. When she'd packed a bag for their stay in a safe house, she wasn't intending for it to last over a week. She supposed the rest of her things were still piled by Harper's desk. With that thought, she wondered if her belongings had already been pilfered, perhaps out of curiosity or maybe Lieutenant Mize had them searched.

"Did you bring a jacket?"

Harper shook her head. "No. I hadn't planned on a cross-country trip. This sweatshirt is fine, though. Are you cold?"

"No, I'm okay." She glanced over her shoulder. "Anyone following?"

"Not that I can tell. You worried?"

Dani smiled. "Not any more than I've been for the past week. Honestly, I don't know that it's all sunk it yet. I mean, he smashed the door in, knocked you out, knocked *me* out—was it chloroform? We did a car chase, I lost my mind and jumped out of said speeding car. You were there to save me—in more ways than one. Now we're on the run, from both the clown and the police." She laughed nervously. "Really? Are we really on the run?"

"I'm afraid so."

"You're going to get into so much trouble, aren't you?"

"Yes." Harper glanced at her. "But don't worry about that. Mize doesn't like me anyway, remember."

"Oh, yeah. Because of his wife." She leaned back. "You think they'll find us today? Tonight?"

"It shouldn't take long for them to know that Dani Strauss and Danielle Stevens are the same person. If they find us before your stalker does, then it's game over, I'm afraid. He'll disappear into the wind. The only hope of finding him would be if you could give a sketch artist a good enough description. Who knows? Face recognition may pop up something."

"The problem is, when I think of the man pretending to be Detective Zapalac, I see a guy in clown makeup looking back at me in the mirror…like he was in the car."

"The only definitive thing we've got so far is from the rape victim. She said he had a tattoo on his wrist. Red feather, she thought."

Dani's eyes widened. "Yes! I remember it. He always had on a suit when he came but I remember one time he moved his sleeve to look at his watch. I saw it then, but I couldn't make out what it was. It was definitely red." She leaned back again, trying to picture Detective Zapalac's face. Or rather the man *pretending* to be a detective. Short dark hair, nearly black. Clean shaven. He was a handsome man. But now that she thought

about it, he was a little standoffish. Not friendly. Nothing warm and fuzzy about him. She hadn't thought anything of it at the time. He was simply a cop answering her call, coming to her aid…because of a stalker.

And he had been the stalker all along.

CHAPTER FORTY-SIX

"This place rivals the Eastside Budget Inn," Harper said as she stood inside the motel room. There was a lone queen bed, a small dresser—the corners chipped—and a dirty, dingy chair that had a rip in the seat.

"It might actually be worse, I think," Dani murmured. "There's a stain on the bedspread. I'm afraid to even guess what it might be."

"I'm sorry. Do you want to go somewhere else?"

"No. It's not like we're planning on sleeping. Same plan as last night?"

"Yeah." She placed the locket on the dresser, then went to the adjoining door and unlocked it. Like last night, she left the lights off. The room reeked of cigarette smoke, but she imagined it covered up other, more unpleasant odors. The drapes were already drawn tight so she went into the bathroom and turned on the light. She watched as a roach darted across the floor, disappearing behind the toilet. A steady drip, drip, drip brought her attention to the sink, the drain lined with rust.

"How is it?" Dani asked as she looked over her shoulder.

"I'm going to vote that we skip showers."

"That bad, huh?"

She left the door cracked, just enough to cast a little light into the room. "I'm going to stage the other room. Be right back."

But Dani followed her, leaning against the adjoining doorjamb as she watched her stuff pillows under the covers, shaping them as if two people were sleeping. Then she took the locket and placed it on the nightstand beside the bed.

"We'll leave the lights on in here for an hour or so. If he's going to try to get in, I would guess it'd be well after midnight." Then she shook her head. "This is a crazy plan, Dani. Unless he's desperate to get his hands on you, I can't believe he'd try something with me in the room." She shrugged. "Of course I was in the room the other night. It didn't take much to get me out of the way."

"Quit blaming yourself," Dani said. "We were…distracted, for one thing. And we were surrounded by cops. We felt safe. Besides, it happened so fast, I don't think I even had time to scream."

"Yeah, you did."

Dani smiled. "I did? All I remember is him hitting you and you falling. When I woke up, I was in the car."

Harper stared at her. "I'm sorry, Dani. I should have—"

Dani held her hand up. "Stop. You act like you let him in and stood by while he took me." She pointed to her cheek. "You have a battle scar to prove otherwise."

Harper nodded. "You're right. I was distracted." She held her gaze. "I'm still distracted."

Dani's smile was…it was sweet. "Well, then I guess that makes two of us."

Harper laughed lightly. "And that's not a good thing. Come on. Let's go next door. Maybe you can find you a cooking show to watch."

* * *

The cooking show couldn't hold her interest. There were too many other things vying for her attention. Like the bed bugs that she imagined were hopping all over her, and the stale cigarette smell that was stifling...and the roach she'd seen slinking across the carpet—the worn, dirty, stained-with-God-knows-what carpet. Most likely it was the anticipation of the clown finding them tonight. Anticipation? No. More like expectation. She didn't know what sixth sense told her that he was close, but she could practically *feel* him. The hair on the back of her neck was standing on end. Harper felt it too, she knew. Harper was pacing. Harper would stop and listen, alert to every noise from the parking lot. Loud voices from outside brought them both to their feet once, her heart thudding nervously until Harper shook her head, indicating it wasn't their guy.

They'd turned the lights off in the adjoining room—the room where the locket was—at eleven. Now as midnight approached, she knew she'd have to turn the TV off, plunging the room into darkness. The yellowish, dim light from the bathroom was barely enough for them to see by.

"We need to be alert. We can't assume that he doesn't know we have two rooms," Harper said quietly, barely louder than a whisper.

Dani nodded. Harper had already given her a gun. She held it in her lap, wondering if she could actually use it if she had to...wondering if she could really pull the trigger.

Harper pointed at the TV. "It's time."

It took a few seconds for her eyes to adjust to the darkness. She blinked several times, trying to focus on Harper, who was still pacing slowly, back and forth, pausing to listen every so often. Dani let out a heavy breath. It was going to be a long night.

CHAPTER FORTY-SEVEN

Harper felt the stress of the day—the week—begin to settle on her shoulders. She was tired enough, sleepy enough, to contemplate lying on the bed. Still, she continued to stand. She rolled her shoulders several times, then resumed her pacing. They had turned the light off in the bathroom too, leaving the room in pitch darkness. She'd finally opened the drapes a little to let in some light from the parking lot. Dani was in the chair; she'd put a towel down to sit on. She'd fallen asleep a couple of times, only to jerk awake again as if from some bad dream. Harper had almost told her to relax, to sleep if she wanted, but she didn't want them to let their guard down. Not tonight.

He was coming tonight. He was arrogant enough to think that he could pull it off. And why not? He'd managed to snatch Dani without much resistance before and that was with four cops surrounding her. Yeah, she'd let her guard down. She'd been distracted. But not tonight.

She could feel it. The air was charged, her senses were alert...she was ready. But how would he do it? Would he silently

creep inside? She had no doubt that he could unlock the door, chain and all. It would probably be child's play to him after he'd managed the deadbolts at the safe house. Or would he do it loudly? Would he kick the flimsy door in with a loud crash? Would he hope to catch them sound asleep, too startled to put up a fight?

No. She imagined him slithering in, quiet as a snake ready to strike. He wanted Dani, not her. He would come with a knife, she guessed. He would kill her quickly. Get her out of the way. Dani would be screaming, but he'd silence her somehow. And he'd take her away before any of the other few guests even stepped out of their rooms, wondering what the commotion was about. Or maybe they wouldn't even bother, not wanting to get involved, thinking it was only a domestic spat. Yes, that's probably what would happen.

He'd have Dani then. No. He'd have Danielle Stevens. What would he do with her? Would he rape her? No doubt. Would he keep her for a few days? Or would he fear getting caught? Would he take what he wanted from her—whatever it was—then kill her? Would he do it quickly? Or would it be slow...torture?

Like Jan had endured. A quick image flashed through her mind...the mass of bloody, sticky hair, the broken fingers, the knife wounds on her arms, her legs, the slash across her cheek... the dull, cold eyes. Only it wasn't Jan. The hair was blond. The eyes, blue.

She clenched her fists into tight balls. No. Not again. It would *not* happen again. She turned slowly, seeing Dani watching her. She relaxed her hands, then took a deep breath, letting it out slowly before going to her. She stood behind the chair, resting her hands on Dani's shoulders.

"It's going to be okay," she whispered.

* * *

She heard the quietest sound...almost no sound at all...yet it was. She glanced over at Harper, who held a finger to her lips.

Harper's head was tilted, her gaze fixed on the adjoining doors. The door on their side was opened, leaving only the small, thin door from the other room between them...and their stalker.

There...she heard it again. Her heart was pounding, the loud beats deafening. She gripped the gun tighter, but her palms were damp with nervousness. Harper took a step toward the door, which she'd left slightly ajar once she'd killed the bathroom light. Harper held her weapon at her side as she stood there quietly, listening. She slowly turned her head toward Dani, motioning for her to stay back. Dani nodded, acknowledging her request. She was nearly paralyzed with fear as it was...she had no intention of moving.

She literally jumped in her tracks, however, seconds later when Harper slammed open the door, banging it against the wall as she burst into the other room. Dani stood on the threshold of the two rooms, her eyes wide as Harper struggled with a man...his white clown face glowing eerily in the dark room. He threw Harper against the wall, then tackled her to the ground. Dani held her gun up, but her hands were shaking so badly, she couldn't even attempt to fire it. Harper rolled them over, only to have him kick her off again. It was then that Dani saw the knife he held. Without thinking, she ran forward, ripping the old lamp off the table and hitting him with it.

He staggered only a moment, but it was long enough for Harper to scramble out of his grasp. The clown turned toward Dani, his face an odd mixture of anger and hatred, yet conceit nearly oozed from his eyes as he stared at her, a smile—an evil smile—forming. It lasted only seconds, yet it felt like minutes. Then Harper threw herself at him, knocking him back once again. The knife fell from his grasp as they rolled on the floor, then he raised his arm, his fist connecting squarely with Harper's face. Dani could almost hear the bones breaking as Harper collapsed.

He stood, picking up the knife as he turned toward her. It was in slow motion that he took a step closer.

"Gotcha again, little girl."

She raised her arms, the gun clasped between her trembling hands. She was so scared, she couldn't take a breath, couldn't think. She couldn't move.

"Oh, Danielle. You're not going to shoot me. We have unfinished business, you and I."

He was only ten feet from her. Now seven, six. Five. Her hands were shaking wildly, the gun swinging back and forth as her finger tightened on the trigger. Could she pull it?

The gunshot was louder than she expected. Time seemed to stand still as he faltered, his eyes wide with disbelief. He took another step toward her, his white-gloved hand reaching for her, trying to grab her. Then he fell to his knees, teetering there before falling forward, landing with a final thud on the dirty carpet, the knife falling harmlessly from his grasp.

Harper was standing there, her gun still pointing at his prone figure. It was only then that Dani realized that she hadn't been the one who had pulled the trigger after all. Her hands were shaking so badly now, the gun nearly fell to the floor. Then Harper was there, taking the gun, pulling her close, whispering words that Dani never heard. She clutched at Harper's shirt, burying her head against her, her entire body trembling, shaking uncontrollably.

It was over.

It was finally over.

CHAPTER FORTY-EIGHT

Harper winced as the paramedic put a bandage over the cut on her cheek. "Not so damn hard."

Emergency lights flashed from every direction, and the parking lot was filled with police cars. Dani had been whisked away by the FBI. As expected, they'd swooped in before the blood had even dried. They'd apparently tracked down Dani Strauss, as she thought they would. What she wasn't expecting, though, was to see Reid and Lieutenant Mize materialize out of the crowd.

She stood, waving the paramedic away as Reid came toward her.

"You okay?"

"Yeah." She looked past him. "Where's Dani?"

He motioned behind him. "FBI. Giving a statement."

She nodded. "What the hell are you doing here?"

"The FBI tracked you. Mize brought me along. We got here about an hour ago. We were at the local PD, briefing them when the call came in." He smiled. "They haven't seen this much

activity in Claude in years, if ever. Half the town is probably gathered here."

She looked back toward the motel. "Have they brought him out yet?"

"No. They're still working the scene. No ID on him, they said."

Reid stepped aside as Mize approached. Harper could tell by the look on his face that she was in more than just a little trouble.

"Well, you've taken insubordination to a whole new level."

"Yes, sir."

"You've also given new meaning to the term 'rogue cop,' Detective Jeremiah."

She nodded. "Yes, sir."

"But we'll discuss all of that in my office." He leaned closer. "I'm glad you got the bastard, Harper, but you're looking at a suspension. You know that, right?"

"Yes."

"But he killed a cop," Reid said, coming to her defense.

"Yeah. And it very well could have been two cops and a damn actress if things hadn't worked out. We'll talk in my office."

"Yes, sir."

He turned to walk away, then stopped. "Good job, Harper."

Reid nudged her shoulder. "So? You really okay?"

"Do I look okay?"

"You're going to have a nice black eye there, it looks like. You did pretty good with him, though. He was a big man."

"Yeah, he picked me up like I was one of his damn dolls."

She turned around, hearing her name being called. She saw Dani in the crowd of cops, looking for her. She raised her hand and waved, trying to catch her attention. Dani saw her and hurried over. Harper saw her hesitate, and she wondered if Dani was fighting an urge to hug her, hold her, make contact. Dani only briefly nodded at Reid before turning her full attention to Harper.

"Are you okay? Anything broken?"

"Just my pride," Harper said with a smile.

"Are you sure? I thought—"

"I'm fine."

Dani held her gaze for a long moment, then properly acknowledged Reid. "Detective Springer, you sure got here fast."

"Yeah, as I was telling Harper, we were hot on your trail."

"The FBI grill you?" Harper asked Dani.

"Yes." Then she smiled. "They were actually pretty nice. They're going to try to keep my name out of it." Dani turned to Reid. "Do they know who the guy is? The FBI wouldn't tell me much."

"Not yet, no. They found his car. There's like four dolls in there and a bunch of clown shit. Oh, and yeah, an LAPD detective's shield."

"Even though I was certain it was him, it's nice to have that confirmed," Dani said. "At least I won't be looking over my shoulder from now on."

Reid turned to her. "They're running his prints to see if he might really be LAPD and was just using a fake name. His shield looks authentic."

"He certainly seemed authentic to me," Dani interjected. "Nothing raised a red flag at all."

"It would make sense then that he knew police procedures," Reid said. "I guess you're probably ready to get the hell out of Texas, huh?"

Dani flicked her gaze to her, meeting her eyes for a quick moment. "It's been an adventure, that's for sure."

Reid nudged her arm. "Mize is coming over again," he said quietly.

Lieutenant Mize stepped into their little circle, his eyes on Dani.

"Ms. Stevens, I trust you're okay. I know it's been a hell of a week."

Dani nodded. "Harper took the brunt of it. I'm fine. A little shook up, but physically fine."

"Well, on behalf of the Dallas Police Department, I must extend my apologies for the actions of my detective." He

cleared his throat. "Detective Jeremiah was acting without authority and against orders. If you wish to file a formal complaint—"

"Seriously? She just saved my life."

He leaned closer, his voice quiet. "I'm aware of the circumstances. I'm simply required to make you aware of your... options." He straightened. "So I take it we won't be hearing from your attorney?"

Dani shook her head. "No. I...I have no complaints regarding Detective Jeremiah's actions."

"Very well." He cleared his throat again. "You must be exhausted." He tossed a quick glance over at her. "You, too, Harper. It's going to be a while before we clear out of here. Reid...find a nice motel for us, if you can. We're only thirty minutes from Amarillo. Get rooms for all four of us. We'll head back to Dallas about noon or so." He looked at his watch. "Been a while since I've worked around the clock. Let's say we'll head back about one. I would imagine I'll be here another couple of hours."

"Yes, sir. How will you get to Amarillo?"

"I'm sure these FBI fellows will be heading that way. I'll get there." He turned his attention to Dani. "Again, Ms. Stevens, I'm grateful that you're okay. I know you gave a statement to the FBI. I suspect that will be sufficient for our report as well. We won't detain you any longer than necessary."

"Thank you, Lieutenant."

He nodded, then touched Reid's shoulder as he turned to leave. "Text me the motel info."

"Yes, sir."

CHAPTER FORTY-NINE

"Is this place okay?"

The adobe siding and signature red roof of the La Quinta Inn was a far cry from the dingy motel they'd checked into eight hours earlier. A cobblestone driveway led them to a covered area by the double doors. Dani looked in at the brightly lit lobby. It hadn't hit her yet that they were no longer on the run, that there was no longer a creepy clown chasing them.

"Perfect," she said.

"I'm sure they have nicer ones in town," he offered.

"Reid, this is fine," Harper said. "We just need a place to get cleaned up and rest for a few hours."

Harper was sitting in the backseat, having offered the front to her. It had been a fairly quiet drive to Amarillo with Reid trying to make conversation occasionally. Thankfully, it wasn't much more than half an hour before they hit the lights of the city. The motel had been easy to find.

If the desk clerk thought it odd for them to be checking in at four thirty in the morning, she didn't show it. There was, however, one awkward moment.

"If it's okay with you," Dani said to Harper, "I'd rather share a room. I'm still a little...shook up," she said honestly. "No need to get four." She held Harper's gaze. "Unless..."

Before Harper could answer, Reid said, "You're perfectly safe here. Mize said—"

"It's fine with me," Harper said. "Just three rooms."

Reid looked between them, frowning slightly, but he finally shrugged. "Okay, whatever you say."

The room was nice, spacious, and, most importantly, very clean. She would have rather had a room with a king bed, but she didn't know how they would have explained that to Reid. She didn't realize how tired she was until Harper closed the door and let out her own weary sigh.

"Why don't you shower first," she offered.

"No, you go ahead. I've got to rummage through my bag and see if I have anything that's clean."

Dani stared at her for a moment. Things seemed...well, different between them. Maybe she'd been presumptuous—or selfish—when she'd requested to share a room. Now that the threat was over...now that they were going to say goodbye... was there any need? Was it necessary to spend these last six or seven hours together? In bed?

God...she wasn't ready to say goodbye.

"Dani?"

She blinked, not realizing that she was still staring. "Yes. I'll shower."

As she stood under the steady stream of warm water, she felt some of her stress dissipate. Stress associated with the stalker, that is. Another kind of stress seemed to settle upon her, though. She would be leaving. Going back to her lonely, public life. She imagined Shelly had been trying to reach her, and honestly, she hadn't given her assistant a thought in days. In fact, she hadn't really given her *life* much thought either. No matter how much she wanted to pretend otherwise, she was Danielle Stevens, not Dani Strauss. She had responsibilities. She had commitments to honor. And for a few days, all of that had been swept aside. She'd simply been Dani Strauss...a woman. And really, the past

week was almost like a dream—chased by a stalker, protected by a beautiful woman...a woman who had become her lover.

How long had it been since she'd called someone her lover? Had she ever? She and Traci had been fumbling teenagers. And Tara? They'd had a secret affair for a year, an affair that was physical, never emotional. It had been enough. It had been enough to keep her sanity...barely. But it wasn't enough for Tara. Or perhaps it was too much. After Tara's death, she hadn't sought out anyone else. She hadn't dared. But then she'd gotten "discovered," her life had changed, and she'd found it easy to play the part. She'd been pretending her whole life anyway. Pretending to be someone she wasn't. She had resigned herself to the fact that she would never have anyone—a lover—in her life. She would continue to play the part, continue to pretend. Until it choked the very life out of her.

She was at that point, wasn't she? Isn't that why she'd vowed this would be her last movie? Wasn't that why she wanted to disappear, fade away?

But fade away to what? To where? Was she ready to be Dani Strauss, lesbian? Was she ready to quit hiding who she was? Was she ready to go back home? See her parents? Her sister?

Was she ready for all of that?

Was she ready to say goodbye to Harper?

She turned the water off and reached for a towel, wondering what was going through Harper's mind. She seemed a little distant, withdrawn. She'd been under stress this week too, Dani reminded herself. The Raggedy Ann dolls had brought back horrible memories for her. Add to that, Harper must be feeling some guilt for having slept with Dani. Did she view it as cheating on her dead lover?

She stared at herself in the mirror. And here she was, hoping to have one more night with Harper. One more night where she could be Dani Strauss, lesbian. One more night where things would seem...natural. No pretense. No games. Just two regular people...making love.

Would Harper give her that? One more time...would Harper give her that?

* * *

Harper came out of the bathroom, surprised to find Dani awake, the lights still on. The covers were pulled to her waist, and she was propped against pillows, her hands folded together in her lap. They hadn't talked about anything, and Harper wasn't sure what to do. Should she assume Dani wanted her to share her bed? Wasn't that the reason Dani hadn't wanted her own room in the first place? But still, she hesitated.

Dani, however, did not.

"Come to bed."

Harper held her gaze. "I guess we should probably... probably talk."

Dani shook her head. "Probably not. I don't want to talk, Harper. Not now."

If Harper went to her, what did that say? Before...it was an emotional need—and physical, yes—that Dani had. Wasn't it? Her too. But now? The threat was over. The...the *situation* was over. They could relax. There was no need to offer each other emotional support. There was no need to hold each other... to kiss, to touch...to make love. If Harper went to her, there would be no excuse for it, no justification. They would make love because they wanted to. If she did that...if Harper went to her, then she feared Jan would be gone for good. Is that what she wanted? Did she want Jan to stop lurking around, stop haunting her nights...and her days? If she went to Dani, was she consciously pushing Jan away?

Dani was waiting, as if sensing the war going on inside her. Dani, not Danielle Stevens. No, she'd never been Danielle to her. Just Dani, a beautiful woman who harbored a secret she didn't dare tell anyone...except Harper. A woman with her own demons, her own fears. A woman who just wanted to be... normal. And Harper could give her normal.

Harper could give her that.

She walked over to the door and turned out the light. The lamp beside the bed wasn't obtrusive. It cast a soft glow

around Dani—a halo. Harper stood beside the bed, then pulled her shirt off and tossed it down. Dani folded the covers back, inviting Harper in beside her. This time, Harper didn't hesitate. It was with sure hands that she removed Dani's shirt, tossing it aside without care. Their mouths met in an almost quiet kiss—gentle—lips moving slowly, deliciously so. A soft hand touched her breast, and Harper sucked in her breath as Dani's thumb circled her nipple.

"Lay back," Dani whispered. "Let me make love to you."

Harper's muddled brain tried to protest. *No!* It was Dani who needed *her*, not the other way around. *Wasn't it?* But she had no willpower to stop Dani as soft hands removed the underwear she'd slipped on only moments earlier. The feeble attempt she made to take control, to roll them over, was met with firm resistance as Dani settled her weight on top of her. A warm, wet mouth covered her breast, a tongue stroked her nipple, and Harper closed her eyes, resigning herself to give whatever Dani wanted...whatever she needed.

It didn't take long for her to know Dani's intent as she kissed her way down Harper's body, a persistent mouth nibbling on her skin, eliciting moans that Harper couldn't contain. Knowing hands spread her thighs, and Harper felt a chill run up and down her heated body. She wanted to tell Dani to hurry. But no. Not hurry. Take her time. Take all night, if she wanted.

* * *

Dani's hips rose up when Harper entered her. Her arms were wrapped around Harper's head, holding her at her breast. She could feel how wet she was, could feel Harper's wetness, too, as it coated her thigh. She groaned as Harper's fingers plunged inside, her hips rolling against Dani's as she sunk deeper, filling her.

Tiny gasps—moans—filled the room as their bodies slapped together, a little harder now, a little faster. Dani kept pace, her breathing labored, her hands finally releasing Harper's head, only to clutch at the sheets when Harper moved to her other nipple, her tongue swirling around it almost frantically.

"God...*Harper*," she whispered.

She was exhausted. They both were. Yet they couldn't seem to stop. Not after the second time. Not even after the third. They hadn't spoken...not with words, anyway. Dani didn't need words. This was their goodbye. She knew it. Harper knew it. They were saying goodbye with their hands, their lips...their mouths.

And it would never be enough.

CHAPTER FIFTY

Harper had taken two days. Mize had told her it would take that long to sort everything out. She had taken two days. Dani hadn't even taken one. Despite her offer to drive her there, Dani had opted for a cab ride to the airport. It all seemed a little dreamlike now…now that it was over with.

Their last kiss had been bittersweet. They were just inside Harper's front door. The taxi had already honked twice. Harper hadn't known what to say. Dani, too, seemed at a loss for words. Yet when she walked away, she turned back, their eyes holding.

"I'm going to miss you. You made me feel alive, Scout. I'm going to miss that."

Harper had just nodded, unable to repeat the words—even though they were true. Dani had made *her* feel alive too. But she didn't say them. She wasn't even able to say the one word she dreaded the most.

Goodbye.

She had closed the door before the cab had pulled away… closed the door on Dani leaving. That didn't make it any less

real though. She had leaned against the door, her eyes shut. Surprisingly, it wasn't Dani's image she saw. It was Jan's. Jan... back in the day. Smiling. Laughing. Flirting. Back in the day when they were younger, happier. Back when they'd first met and things were simple, before being a detective had consumed most of her time. Before the murders. Before Jan's death. Jan was smiling. Jan was waving.

Jan was fading away.

Tears had run down her cheeks. Jan was saying goodbye.

Dani had said goodbye.

Once again...Harper was all alone. Old wounds became new again. Even Jan's ghost wasn't there to keep her company. She had pushed off from the door and shuffled into her bedroom, collapsing on the bed.

* * *

"Today's the day, huh?"

She didn't remember showering, but she was sure she had. She didn't remember eating, but there were dirty dishes in the sink. She didn't remember driving to work this morning, but obviously she had. Here she sat.

She nodded, taking the cup of coffee that Reid offered.

"You look like shit," he said bluntly. "And I'm not even talking about your black eye. Does it hurt?"

She touched her cheek lightly. The swelling had gone down some, and the bandage on the small cut had been removed the next day. The black eye, however, covered half of her cheek.

"No," she lied. At least it wasn't broken. For that, she could be thankful.

Instead of sitting at his desk, he pulled a chair closer to hers. "So? You talk to her?"

She raised her eyebrows.

"Since she left. She call or anything?"

"No. Should she?"

"Well, I mean, you two got kinda close while she was here."

"She was scared. I was the only one she trusted."

It was his turn to raise his eyebrows. "Is that all it was?"

"What are you insinuating?"

"I'm saying that it looked like maybe you were a little closer than just that. But Harper...Danielle Stevens. I mean, I hope you didn't do anything stupid."

"Stupid?"

"Like, you know, try something."

She smiled. "With Danielle Stevens? Right."

"Yeah, I know. But admit it. You had a little crush, didn't you? I mean, you spent a lot of time together."

"You jealous?"

He laughed. "Yeah."

She took a sip of the coffee, grimacing at the lack of sugar. "So they find out who the clown guy was?"

"Not that I've heard. He wasn't LAPD though. Fake badge. Lot of reporters hanging around yesterday. Not sure if the FBI was able to keep Danielle's name out of it after all."

She nodded. "Didn't think they could."

"What do you think your suspension will be? A month?"

"Or two. I wouldn't be shocked if it was six."

"That totally sucks. You were right all along. There's no way they would have caught the guy if Danielle was taken out of the equation."

"And you were right. It could have ended very badly. Then what? If Dani had been injured...or worse, can you imagine the publicity this would be getting? Publicity. Lawsuits." She shoved the coffee away. "Doesn't matter. It's over now. We move on."

"Yeah. Back to normal."

Normal? What was normal? She turned away from Reid, letting out a deep breath. What was normal? She didn't even know anymore. Feeling this miserable? Was that normal? Yeah. For her...miserable was normal. She'd had a reprieve...for a week or so, she'd had a reprieve. Now? Back to normal. Only this normal seemed way worse than before. How was that even possible?

"Harper? My office."

She nodded at Lieutenant Mize's command. She pushed away from her desk with a quick glance at Reid. Her phone was

in her pocket, and she heard the quiet ding of a text message. She ignored it…for a few steps. As she stood at Mize's door, she pulled the phone from her pocket.

"I miss you, Scout. A lot. Do you miss me?"

Harper felt her heart jump into her throat, felt it try to choke the breath from her. With a click of a button, the text disappeared and she shoved her phone back into her pocket.

"Harper, come in. Sit down."

She moved into one of his visitors' chairs, sitting down with a sigh. Dani missed her. A lot. Did she miss Dani?

Yeah…a lot.

"Do we need to go over the particulars?"

Harper looked at Lieutenant Mize. Particulars? "I don't think so."

"It worked out, Detective. You got the bad guy. A cop killer. A stalker, a rapist…a cop killer." He shook his head. "You were damn lucky."

She said nothing. She didn't feel so lucky.

I miss you. A lot.

"I had to talk like hell to get your suspension down to a few months."

She shrugged. "Why? You don't even like me much."

He frowned. "Why do you say that?"

"Your wife. You take it out on me."

His brows drew together as if he was about to protest. Then he relaxed and nodded. "I suppose I do. But this suspension has nothing to do with that. You were blatantly insubordinate. You went dark. Unauthorized. With a civilian. And not just any civilian. A damn famous actress, for God's sake." Mize slammed his fist on the desk. "I got my ass chewed for that, Harper. If anything had happened to her, we'd probably both be looking for new jobs."

I miss you. Do you miss me?

"Do you have anything to say? Do you want to meet with your rep? You want to appeal? This isn't set in stone. You have options, Harper."

Do you miss me?

Yeah…I miss you. A lot.

She stood up. "I don't think I'm going to be suspended, Lieutenant."

"I know you feel like you did the right thing, Harper. In hindsight, yeah, it probably was. But it was unorthodox, for one thing. You broke every damn rule in the book. You've got to be accountable."

"No."

"No?"

She pulled her weapon from the holster at her waist and laid it on his desk. She did the same with her shield.

"There's no need to suspend me. I'm resigning."

His eyes widened in disbelief? "*What?* Harper, if this is some ploy to reduce your suspension, it's not going to work. I talked them into two months. I think that's fair. They're not going to give a rat's ass if you threaten to resign."

"I quit. I've had enough."

"Are you serious?" He walked around his desk and stood in front of her. "You can't just quit, Harper."

"Why not?"

"You're a damn good cop, that's why. We need good cops."

She met his gaze. "You ever call Tucson? Pull my file?"

He shook his head. "Never had the need to. Why?"

"It might explain a few things. If you're interested." She shrugged. "Doesn't matter." She took a step away. "I need a break, Lieutenant. More than two months."

He stared at her. "You're really serious."

"I am."

He walked back around his desk, standing behind his chair. "Harper, I'm not going to accept your resignation. You take the two months. You see how you feel. Then we'll talk."

"Lieutenant—"

"Two months. Give me two months."

She stared at him and him at her…neither blinking. She finally nodded. "Okay."

"Good. Take a break. Relax. I'll see you in a couple of months."

She got up to leave, then paused. "The guy...do we know who he was?"

"Yeah. He was a damn FBI agent who got dismissed a couple of years ago. Not sure why he was fixated on Danielle Stevens, though. I guess we won't ever know." He shook his head. "It's one of their guys, so they're not divulging much."

She nodded. She had known he was a professional of some sort, but she never would have guessed an agent. No wonder he seemed to always be one step ahead of them.

Reid was waiting for her when she walked out and he barely let the door close to Mize's office before he was on her.

"Well? What did he say? How long? How long?"

"Two months."

He smiled and nodded. "That's good, though, right?"

She clapped his shoulder affectionately. "You free tonight?"

"Free? Yeah, sure. You want to get together?"

"I thought maybe I'd swing by. Crack that bottle of Crown you've been saving."

He grinned. "Hell, yeah. I'll spring for a pizza or something."

"Great. See you tonight."

Harper took the stairs down, pausing at the landing between the first and second floors. She pulled her phone out, staring at the text again. What did it mean? What did she *want* it to mean?

"Oh, Christ, Harper, get a grip." She leaned against the wall, taking several deep breaths. What did she want it to mean? She was afraid to even go there. They'd spent one week together. One freaking week.

I miss her.

CHAPTER FIFTY-ONE

Dani's hand involuntarily went to her neck, but the locket wasn't there. She didn't realize how often she'd fidgeted with it. No wonder it was worn smooth.

"So what shall I tell her?"

She turned, staring blankly at Shelly. "I'm sorry. What?"

"You've been a million miles away ever since you got back. I said Pamela has been fielding questions from some of the tabloids. There are rumors swirling that you were seen at some dump of a motel in Claude, Texas—wherever that is—and that there was some police event or something. Do you want to respond?"

How could she respond? Did she really think her name could be kept out of it? "No. What else?"

Shelly looked at her notes. "The *People* interview. She's rescheduled it for when you're actually filming in Dallas. Three months. They'll do it the second week of filming."

"Fine."

"I've also got a list of properties, like you requested. I can set up appointments whenever you're ready."

Did she still want to move? Now that the stalker was…was gone, was there any need to move? Especially since she'd be going on location in a few months. And after that…well, she was going *somewhere*. She just didn't know where.

"You can cancel that, Shelly. I'll stay here."

"But what about the stalker? You think he gave up since you've been gone?"

"We'll see how it goes," she said evasively. "What else?"

Shelly set her iPad aside. "Are you okay? You've been…well, more indifferent than usual," she said with a quick smile. "Like I said, a million miles away."

Yes, she was. Because—in a weak moment—she'd sent that damn text to Harper and she'd gotten no reply. She should have just let it go. She knew that. But…she missed her. A lot. Apparently Harper wasn't feeling the same.

Was she surprised? No, not really. Harper was still living with Jan's ghost. She imagined that once she'd left, Harper's guilt had returned in full force. And Harper would deal with it alone.

"I am a million miles away. Sorry." She walked over to where her purse was and took out the locket. "I'm going to have cut this short, Shelly. I've got an appointment with a jeweler."

"It broke again? I can take it, if you'd like."

"No. I'd rather do it." She folded the locket protectively in her palm. "Thank you, though."

"Should I come by tomorrow?"

Dani shook her head. "There's no need. I'm having lunch with Pamela on Friday. Why don't you join us?"

"Okay. She already mentioned it to me. She said you had initiated it. That's rare for you."

Dani smiled. "I have some things to discuss with you both."

Shelly seemed surprised by that statement, but she didn't question it. "Okay. See you then."

When she was finally left alone again, she plopped down on the sofa with a sigh. She was in a funk, and she couldn't seem to pull herself out of it. She had no interest whatsoever in what Shelly or Pamela had lined up for her. It would be a miracle if she could make it through the filming without throwing her

hands up and running away. The only glimmer of hope she held onto was that maybe...just maybe she'd run into Harper while she was there. But that was still months away. In the meantime, she would most likely turn into a crazy, eccentric recluse that Pamela and Shelly wouldn't know how to deal with. Of course, once she broke the news to them that she was leaving—leaving LA, leaving the business—they might not care.

Then what would she have? No one. Absolutely no one. She had distanced herself from everyone in this town, so much so that being called aloof was now a compliment. It beat the other words she'd heard: snooty and unapproachable. Unapproachable? Yes. But snooty? No, not in the least. On set, she was as friendly as anyone, with cast and crew alike. She was Danielle Stevens, star of the show. But when the camera was off, she retreated, back into her own private world...a world where she let no one enter.

Not until she met Harper Jeremiah.

CHAPTER FIFTY-TWO

Harper didn't know what she was going to say to Reid. She couldn't very well tell him about Dani…about how close they'd really gotten. She couldn't tell him that they were lovers. She wouldn't infringe on Dani's privacy like that. Still, it would be nice to talk to someone about what she was feeling. Reid probably wasn't the best one to pick for a heart-to-heart, but as far as friends went, he was the closest she had.

She paused before knocking. Was she really considering going to LA? She shook her head. Dani was probably…well, since she hadn't answered her text—she'd been afraid to type the words—Dani probably was kicking herself for sending it in the first place. She'd been afraid to reply to Dani. Afraid of what she might say.

She took a deep breath, then knocked several times. Reid opened the door almost immediately.

"You came."

She raised an eyebrow. "I thought we had a date."

"Yeah, but that didn't mean you were actually going to show up. Come on in. Pizza will be here in about thirty minutes."

The bottle of Crown sat on the counter with two glasses already beside it. She smiled at him and nodded when he asked if she was ready.

"On the rocks?"

"Yeah."

"Oh, hey…did you know that Danielle's last name is really Strauss, not Stevens?" he asked as he dropped a couple of cubes of ice into the glasses.

"FBI tell you that?"

"Yeah. That's how they tracked you. You already knew, huh?"

"We used that name to rent the car."

He handed her a glass. "I'd offer to do a toast or something, but that seems wrong considering you're going to be suspended for a couple of months."

"Yeah…about that. I…" But she stopped. Lieutenant Mize had said to give him two months. And maybe she *would* change her mind. What else was she going to do? Become a security guard at a bank or something?

"What?"

"I'm thinking about getting away."

"Like a vacation?"

"I'm thinking about…going to LA."

He laughed. "Oh, yeah…you got a crush."

She actually blushed. "We're friends, that's all."

"So you got that close that you can go visit? Danielle Stevens? Wow…now I'm really jealous."

"You were around her enough, Reid. She's just a regular person. She's not a character you see in the movies."

"How would you know? You didn't even know who she was."

She touched his glass with hers. "But I know now," she said with a grin.

He sighed wistfully. "She's so damn pretty. I mean, I've seen Danielle Stevens without makeup on and she's still gorgeous."

And I've seen her completely naked, she thought. He had no idea how beautiful she truly was. But it wasn't just her physical beauty. That may have been what attracted her, but that wasn't what drew her to Dani. Underneath it all, Dani was a young woman from a small town, still living in small-town fear of her

aging parents. She was alone and vulnerable, yet still strong. Through this whole ordeal, Dani had only broken down one time. And that one time had tugged at her heart. But it wasn't just that, either. Dani could read her. Dani could look into her eyes and know what she was thinking...feeling. Dani could sense her guilt...or her lack of it. Dani knew about Jan. Harper hadn't been able to tell anyone about Jan yet Dani...she'd told Dani after knowing her one day. She'd told Dani everything.

"I miss her." The sound of her own voice startled her. She hadn't meant to say the words out loud. She smiled apologetically. "I mean...she was around 24/7. I kinda miss her."

Reid grinned. "You kinda have a crush on her."

"Yeah, so I do," she admitted.

"That's okay. I do too. And let me tell you, I have a *much* better chance with her than you do," he said with a laugh. "Although picturing you and Danielle Stevens together..." He wiggled his eyebrows. "That's kinda hot."

Harper slugged him on the shoulder. "Do *not* picture me naked!"

He laughed as he rubbed his shoulder. "Not so much you I'm picturing naked, Harper."

A loud knock on the door signaled pizza, and Harper let out a grateful sigh, ending *that* conversation.

Instead of using the table, they took the pizza into the living room and relaxed on his sofa. Reid put the TV on but muted the sound.

"Let me tell you," he said, waving his pizza at her. "I think Mize was really upset about the suspension. I know you think he doesn't like you, but I think it bothered him."

She put her piece of pizza down, picking up her drink instead. "I quit, Reid."

He stopped in mid-chew, staring at her with wide eyes. "*What?*"

"I resigned. He wouldn't accept it. He told me to take the two months to think about it."

He dropped his pizza. "Why the hell would you resign? Just because you got suspended? Come on, Harper. You had to have

known that was coming. You took off with her, wouldn't even tell me where you were going."

"It's not because of the suspension." She took a deep breath. "Remember me telling you about the serial killer in Tucson?"

"Yeah. The Raggedy Ann doll freaked you out."

"He killed eight women." She swallowed. "The last victim... her name was Jan. She was my...my partner. My wife."

"Oh, Jesus, Harper...I'm sorry."

Harper shook her head. "I'm just telling you this because... because I can't do this anymore, Reid. Dani—Danielle—she became important to me. I needed to protect her. I didn't protect Jan...I *had* to protect Dani." She met his gaze. "Do you understand? If I'd failed—again—it would have killed me."

He nodded. "That's why, that night in the car, you were so emotional."

"Yes."

"I'm sorry," he said again. "But you got that guy in Tucson, right?"

"No. He never surfaced. Never killed again."

His eyes widened. "Oh, man. You don't think this guy..."

"No. When the first Raggedy Ann doll showed up, I'll admit, the thought crossed my mind. Things were too different, though. My guy would wait for the victims to return home. He raped, tortured, killed...left the doll. We had no suspects." She blew out her breath. "And I had no closure."

"Wow. Makes sense why this case became so personal to you, Harper. You should have told me."

"What I did was wrong. Dani could have gotten killed. I think this guy was so angry, so mad that he had her and she got away, that he let his guard down. Or else he was so arrogant he thought he'd never get caught. But that night, he came in with a knife. I don't think he intended to abduct her. I think he was mad. I think he was over the whole stalking thing...I think he just wanted her dead. I think he was through playing games. He wanted it over with as much as we did."

"How could he not have known you'd be waiting?"

"I was a cop, but I was a woman. I guess he thought we'd be trembling in fear of him. That's how I picture him, anyway. An

egotistical man playing cat and mouse with two inferior women. It may have even insulted him that they were relying on me—a woman—to protect Dani."

"Maybe you should go into profiling. You seem to have this guy pegged."

She picked up her pizza again, knowing it was cold. "I think I'm...I'm tired, Reid. I always wanted to be a cop—a detective. Always. But now...I think I'm done."

"What are you going to do?"

"I have no idea."

"Well, I think you should do what Mize said...take the two months to think about it."

"I will."

Then he smiled. "So you're really going to LA to see Danielle Stevens?"

She drank the last of her drink. "No. I'm going to see Dani Strauss."

CHAPTER FIFTY-THREE

Dani stood at the window, staring out at her neighbor's pool. From this vantage point, she could only see a portion of it, but the blue water rippled invitingly. She fingered the locket at her neck, so glad to have it back. Mr. Chandler had called her the very next day after she'd dropped it off, and she'd gone immediately to pick it up. The locket was her lifeline to...to what? Her grandmother? To her innocence? She had felt naked without it. Naked...lost, adrift. Detached.

Lonely.

Alone.

Sadly, now that she had the locket back, back where it belonged, those feelings hadn't changed much. She had stopped hoping Harper might call. Or text. Something. Harper had been so blatantly absent that Dani wondered if she would even see her when she returned to Dallas.

She'd heard from the FBI once, not much more than a courtesy call, really. She thought she might hear from Harper, if

nothing else, to let her know about her suspension. After all, it was her fault that she was getting suspended.

Was that it? Was Harper angry? Did she blame Dani?

No. She hadn't seemed upset about the looming suspension. It was expected and she had merely shrugged it off.

Then why hadn't she called? Why hadn't she replied to her text?

"Because obviously she doesn't miss you."

She pounded her thigh with her fist. She had to get over this. She had turned into nothing but a walking zombie. Even Shelly had stopped coming by. That, of course, had less to do with her mood and more to do with her announcement to her and Pamela that after the filming she would be "taking a break." It was more than a break, of course, but she hadn't told them that. She thought it would cause much less of a stir than to say she was quitting.

Right now, her plan was to head to Tennessee as soon as she was finished in Dallas. Head back home and see her family. Try to reconnect with them. After that, she'd decide what she was going to do. She had money. That wasn't an issue. She had done nothing extravagant at all and had invested practically every penny she'd made. She could go anywhere, do anything.

She only needed to pick a place. She would eventually make friends. And maybe, one day, she'd meet someone…someone special. Someone who she could share her life with. She touched the locket at her neck. Yes. Someone special.

She closed her eyes for a moment, seeing Harper's face. Not the picture of Harper, the photo that she'd stared at for countless hours, no. The image she had of Harper was the real thing. Sometimes serious, sometimes smiling…but those eyes never seemed to change—those dark, trusting eyes.

Those eyes that she couldn't wait to see again. Those eyes that she feared she would never see again. Those eyes that—

The doorbell chimed through the house, startling her. Shelly usually called before she came over. Pamela had been known to pop over unannounced though. She sighed. She wasn't in the

mood for Pamela. Pamela said she was making a mistake—a *big* mistake—by taking a break.

"The fire is hot right now, Danielle. You're almost thirty. It goes downhill from there. There'll be someone younger and prettier to take your place. There's no time for a break."

Dani had replied with a smile. "I'm happy for them to take my place."

She took a deep breath before opening the door. She wasn't in the mood for Pamela, but she could handle Pamela. However, when she opened the door, it wasn't Pamela standing there.

Her heart stopped. Her breath left her. She held on to the door for support.

"I miss you too. A lot."

Dani stood there…blinking stupidly at Harper before finally finding her voice. "I've been…*God*…miserable, Harper."

Harper stepped forward, and Dani nearly fell into her arms. She held her tightly, soaking in her strength, breathing in her familiar scent…feeling her loneliness fade away as Harper's arms held her tightly. It never once occurred to her that she was outside of her house, in view of anyone who might be lurking, in view of any neighbor who might be home. And she didn't care.

"I missed you so much, Harper."

"Me too. Everything was…empty." Harper pulled back, meeting her eyes. "I didn't want to do empty again."

"Oh, sweetheart…no." Dani leaned closer, kissing her gently. "Not empty. Not anymore."

When they pulled apart, Harper gave her an apologetic smile. "I'm sorry I didn't call. I didn't know what to say. And the more days that passed…well, I was afraid that—"

"You're here now." She raised her eyebrows. "Can you stay? With me? For a while?"

"If you want."

"I want. How long is your suspension?"

"Two months."

Dani smiled. "That's *all*?" She took her hand and pulled her inside. "I think you got off easy, Scout."

She didn't bother with pleasantries. She didn't mind her manners. She simply led Harper back to her bedroom. They needed to talk, yes. But not now. All she wanted right now was to reacquaint with Harper...her body, her lips, her mouth. She, too, wanted to chase the emptiness away. She wanted to forget about the long, lonely days she'd spent since leaving Dallas.

Harper was here. Now. Finally.

CHAPTER FIFTY-FOUR

Harper stood next to Dani, her eyes feasting on the trees… red and brown, red and yellow, red and orange, barely a hint of green left on this brisk October day. She looked out in awe as the mountain was bathed in a kaleidoscope of brilliant fall colors.

"So these are the Smoky Mountains, huh?"

"Isn't it beautiful? I didn't realize how much I'd missed it." Dani took her hand and tugged her down the trail to the overlook. "This was always a favorite stop when we went to my uncle's place." She leaned her shoulder against Harper's. "You like?"

"I love." She turned to Dani, meeting her eyes. "A lot."

Dani smiled sweetly, then leaned closer and quickly kissed her. "I love you too." Then she grinned. "And quit worrying."

"I can't help it. They're going to hate me."

"My parents are not going to hate you. Everybody likes you. The director loved you. You got a speaking part. And you looked great in a uniform."

Harper smirked. "I had two words."

"And you did them beautifully."

Harper laughed, then let her smile fade. "Are you sure you're not going to miss it? I mean, you were really good. A natural. I liked all of your movies."

"Thank you. But no. I'm not going to miss it. Not one bit. I'm looking forward to our life. No more Danielle Stevens."

"Okay. I guess that's good. Because, you know, this bodyguard stuff is kinda hard work."

Dani laughed and linked arms with her as they made their way back to the car. "Hard work, huh? Were the perks not good enough for you?"

"Oh, they were good. Very, very good, in fact."

"I thought so." Dani leaned closer. "What about you? You going to miss being a detective?"

"Not one bit. I'm kinda looking forward to going back to Tucson, seeing the family again."

"And I'm looking forward to meeting them. I just hope they don't...I mean, they loved Jan. They might not accept me."

"They'll accept you. You're not Jan. You're not replacing Jan." Harper paused. "You're Dani. I love you for who you are. They will too."

"I hope so. I wish I could say the same about my parents."

"You told me not to worry."

"I know. That doesn't mean *I'm* not worried."

"Tell you what, if it doesn't go well...if they're mean and nasty to us...then we'll just rent a cabin somewhere out here in the mountains and enjoy these fall colors that you love so much. How's that?"

"Deal." Dani's smile faltered a little. "I really hope that's not the case, though. It's important to me that they get to know the real me. They don't have to like me—or even you—but I want them to *know* me. I want to be a part of their life again."

"Then tell them that."

Dani paused at the car, looking back out over the mountains. "It's good to be home." She looked at Harper. "Thank you. I wouldn't have the courage to come back here without you."

"Home...to me...is wherever you are."

Dani held her gaze, a soft, gentle smile on her face. "Oh, Scout...I love you so much."

Harper smiled as she opened the car door for Dani. She got a warm, sweet feeling whenever Dani called her Scout. She closed the door, then stood, taking one last look at the colors. She took a deep breath. They were less than an hour from Dani's childhood home, an hour away from meeting her parents. An hour away from officially starting their life together. An hour away from telling someone about their relationship. They hadn't even told Reid.

Would telling someone make it real? She tilted her head thoughtfully, gazing out across the mountain. No. It was already real. Jan—while she'd always have a place in her heart—had faded away. Her ghost didn't visit any longer. At first, she hadn't known whether to be sad or relieved. Now? Now it was a part of her past and she was ready for her future, whatever that might bring. And that began with meeting Dani's parents.

It would be okay, though. She had a feeling. A good feeling.

She walked around the car, seeing Dani watching her through the glass. Their eyes held.

Yes...she had a good feeling. She hoped it lasted forever.

This time...she hoped it lasted forever.